Ann Hazelwood

For the **LOVE** *of* **QUILTS**

C&T PUBLISHING

Executive Book Editor: Julie Schroeder
Copy Editor: Hannah Alton
Graphic Design: Lynda Smith
Cover Design: Michael Buckingham

Published by C&T Publishing, Inc., P.O. Box 1456, Lafayette, CA 94549

Library of Congress Cataloging-in-Publication Data
Names: Hazelwood, Ann Watkins, author.
Title: For the love of quilts / Ann Hazelwood.
Description: Paducah, Kentucky : American Quilter's Society, [2018] | Series:
  Wine country quilts series ; book 1
Identifiers: LCCN 2018031989 (print) | LCCN 2018035124 (ebook) | ISBN
  9781683395225 (ebook) | ISBN 9781683391159 (pbk.)
Subjects: LCSH: Quilting--Fiction.
Classification: LCC PS3608.A98846 (ebook) | LCC PS3608.A98846 F65 2018
  (print) | DDC 813/.6--dc23
LC record available at https://lccn.loc.gov/2018031989

POD Edition

Dedication and Thanks

For the Love of Quilts

This book is dedicated to all of the quilt lovers out there. One doesn't have to be a quiltmaker to enjoy the history and beauty of quilts. There are consumers, serious collectors, teachers, appraisers, and business owners who share their appreciation every day. I happen to be all of these things. Thank you for whatever way you choose to love quilts.

My personal thanks also goes to my husband, Keith, my sons, Joel and Jason, and my extended family, who support my writing and love of quilts. They make it a pleasant journey.

Last but not least, I want to acknowledge a special shop that is called For The Love Of Quilts. They truly appreciate what a special industry this is. Please visit them at 115 N. Elizabeth St. in Lima, Ohio. Contact them at 419-228-9801 or www.theloveofquilts.com

Mariner's Compass block

Chapter 1

"This view is unbelievable!" Holly said after another bite of her chicken salad sandwich.

"I know!" I said with a sigh. "I can't imagine being able to look at this every day. Wine Country Gardens has always been my favorite place to go out here. Chris and Bill, the owners, live in a wonderful house on this hill, and their addition now allows them to host weddings and events. I get plants, flowers, and lunch all in one stop. I usually eat here and then drive into Augusta to see Carrie Mae's shop."

"I know that's where you usually get your quilts," Holly acknowledged. "I've come to some of the wineries out here, but I don't think I ever went into any shops."

"You'll love Carrie Mae," I said. "She loves quilts as much as I do, and she's been collecting incredible antiques for many years. She's quite an icon out here, since she's had her business for over forty years. She's quite a character and wears a cute little bun on the top of her head. Sometimes she attaches a flower to it." I had to smile. "She lives above that shop of hers, by the way. I've learned so much from her about antiques as well as quilts. She lights up when I walk in the door."

"Well, of course," Holly said with a chuckle. "She sees dollar signs, I'm sure. When are you going to decide if you have enough quilts? How many do you think you have?"

"I've never counted them and have no plans to ever stop buying them," I replied. "Quilts are my lifeline. I'd rather cut my food bill or cut my electricity before I stop shopping for quilts."

Holly looked shocked. "Well, I shouldn't get on your case, Lily," she admitted. "You have been so gracious about lending me your quilts when I have to lecture or teach quilting. I've learned some things from you as well."

"Hey, it helps me justify having a whole room full of quilts," I joked. "They are my babies."

Holly laughed and shook her head. "Do you ever buy a new quilt?" she asked as she drank her iced tea.

"I've bought new baby quilts now and then for others, but as you know, I'm a sucker for the old, bold, and beautiful! I love the patina of old fabric as well as antiques. There is a story behind every one. If only quilts could talk." I paused. "You know, we should probably go soon."

"Well, I hate to bring this up again, but have you been looking for a job?" Holly asked hesitantly.

"Not really," I answered casually. "I certainly don't want another editing job. Leaving Dexter Publishing was the best thing that's ever happened to me. I was dying on the vine reading other people's words."

"I'm sure, but you're going to have to make money at some point," Holly warned. "That little nest egg of yours isn't going to last forever. I'm just sayin'!"

"I know, I know. Thanks for reminding me," I said, suddenly feeling uncomfortable. "It's time to make a change. I just haven't decided what it will be. Since we're being so blunt with one another, you should be making a change as well. How long are you going to put up with Monster Moe? I don't know how you stand it!" Monster Moe was my nickname for Maurice, Holly's abusive husband.

"Maybe the two of us should run away together," Holly suggested humorously.

"I can say this much," I snickered. "I would rather be as poor as a church mouse than live another moment with that husband of yours."

"I can block him out," Holly retorted with a more serious voice. "I have a nice roof over my head and an active charge card." Holly waved her card to the waitress coming our way.

"He's already said he wants you dead," I reminded her. "That has to be so scary for you."

"Oh, he says a lot of things. I'm his slave. He's not going to get rid of me. I just stay out of the house as much as I can, as you know."

"Do you know how sad that sounds?" I questioned. "You have this beautiful house and can't even have your friends over. It's your house too, remember. He didn't waste any time getting his name on some of your money before you were even married! He's got such control over you that you knock yourself out to get dinner on the table for him at the same precise time nearly every single day. He doesn't deserve that."

"Don't spoil my day, Lily," Holly requested, her voice tinged with sadness. "I know all those things, but it's not as easy as you think. I'm having more health issues, and what if

I couldn't get insurance in the future?"

"That's a bunch of baloney," I said, raising my voice. "Okay, time to go. Let me go say goodbye to Chris and we'll be on our way."

"Yes, please!" Holly replied.

Chapter 2

We left in Holly's new SUV and drove down the road to Augusta. We passed the Yellow Farmhouse Vineyard & Winery on the corner, and Holly commented about how adorable it was.

"We can come back this way, if you want to stop," I suggested. "The folks there are so nice, and I love their wine."

When we turned the corner that took us into the heart of Augusta, I felt like I was entering a village all its own. Shops opened and closed in short periods of time, except Carrie Mae's Uptown Store. The sizable shop seemed to be a staple that kept the little town together.

"Look across the street, Lily." Holly pointed. "That restaurant is called The Silly Goose. How cute is that?"

"Yes, it's fairly new. I've only eaten there one time, but it was very good."

"Do you think Carrie Mae is open? There's all the stuff on her sidewalk, but I don't see one car."

"Well, she lives upstairs, but I don't recall her being closed on any given day."

"Good, the door's open," Holly said as we walked inside.

"Well, if it isn't Miss Lily," Carrie Mae greeted me with a big smile. "How have you been?"

"Fine, just fine," I said, giving her a hug. "I brought my good friend with me today."

"Well, any friend of my Miss Lily's is a friend of mine," she said, putting her arm around Holly.

"I think I'm seeing some quilts here I haven't seen before," I said, heading towards the hanging quilts.

"Yes," Carrie Mae said as she joined me. "A gentleman from Tennessee came through last week asking terrible prices for them, so I had to talk like a Dutch uncle to get him to come down. There's a red-and-white one that I knew I had to save for you. Have you seen this pattern before?"

She opened up a large four-block design that had red-and-white Flying Geese pieces going through the blocks. It was rare indeed, and very striking.

"No, this is awesome!" I said, taking it out of her hands. "It's rare to see so much white in a red-and-white quilt."

"It is terrific, but I wonder if you have anything in blue and white?" Holly asked Carrie Mae.

"Why, this indigo-and-white Delectable Mountains quilt over here is in pristine condition," Carrie Mae bragged. "It says on the ticket that it's from Pennsylvania."

"Oh my goodness," Holly gasped. "I don't have this pattern."

"Why don't you girls talk and look around while I let my little doggie out?" Carrie Mae suggested. "I'll be right back."

"Sure, take your time," I said as we pulled more quilts off hangers.

When she left the room, I knew the red-and-white quilt

had to come home with me. I needed a quilt fix. Holly was a bit hesitant about the high price on the blue-and-white quilt. She had all the money in the world, but when it came to certain things, she was as tight as a drum. She kept picking the quilt up and putting it down again.

"This place is huge! She has a basement too! I've never seen so much stuff. I'm going to go down and look."

"Carrie Mae has been collecting for a long time."

When Carrie Mae came back down, she offered to knock off fifty dollars from each of the quilts. I told her I would have bought it without the discount.

"What about any new doll quilts?" I asked as I looked around.

Carrie Mae scratched her head. "There's a cutie pie in that doll bed over there," she said. "It's in good condition for a doll quilt. You would know if it's genuine. I can't get high prices for the little quilts like some dealers do."

It was a perfectly-pieced tiny Grandmother's Flower Garden. The binding looked original to the quilt.

"The man I bought it from sold me mostly glassware," Carrie Mae revealed. "I don't think he knew what he had with this little quilt."

"I'll take this as well," I said, handing it to her. "I wonder what Holly is finding downstairs?" I went downstairs and saw that Holly was holding a Wedgwood vase in her hands.

"I'm going to get this if she can give me a little discount," Holly revealed. "I'm not paying that much for the quilt. I'd rather have this instead."

I shrugged my shoulders.

Forty-five minutes later, Holly was anxious about getting home in time for the monster's dinner. I had two quilts and Holly had bought her vase, so we were pretty happy. We tried to get into a couple of other shops, but they were locked. Unpredictable hours were a pet peeve of mine. You would think every penny would be helpful to these unique businesses. You can always tell the serious business owners by their hours.

Chapter 3

As we headed home in the late afternoon, it made me sad to leave the rolling hills. One beautiful scene after another caught our attention.

"I don't want to go back to the city,' I complained. "My neighborhood is unique, but I crave the open green spaces and fresh air. The Hill is all about smelling red spaghetti sauce."

Holly doubled over in laughter. "You're serious about this, aren't you?" she asked.

I nodded.

"What about leaving Bertie? You're like family to her. It would devastate her if you left."

"Bertie is eighty years old," I stated. "She's been a great landlord, but she can't decide my future. She knows all my comings and goings, which drives me crazy at times. All she has to think about is her cat, Sugar."

"Oh, yeah, how is Sugar?"

"She's getting old, too, but she's beautiful and very spoiled. Sugar is like the child Bertie never had."

"Does Bertie still read a lot like she used to?" Holly asked.

"Yes, and her mind is as sharp as can be. You name it and she can talk about it. Thank goodness for that, because she loves to talk!"

Holly dropped me off at my apartment, located on The Hill in St. Louis. The Hill had an Italian history like no other. It was known nationwide for its Italian residents, restaurants, and bakeries and the tiny houses that lined the streets. I loved walking the neighborhood, where many were still speaking Italian. It was great to get fresh bread and the best cannoli whenever I wanted. I took the apartment years ago, even though it was on the second floor. It was close to Dexter Publishing, so it became home, and I never left.

Like always, Bertie heard me return as I approached my staircase.

"Did you have a nice day, sweetie?" she immediately asked. "I see you've done a little shopping."

"Yes. Holly and I went to the wine country and had lunch. Of course, we had to do some shopping."

"Oh, more quilts?" Bertie asked, staring at my bags.

"Sure, I'll show you," I said as I entered her apartment.

"Come here, Sugar," she called as she picked up her furry white cat. "You can't get your fur on Lily's nice quilts."

As I showed her the quilts, I knew it gave her joy. She knew my collection was growing and didn't scold me in the least.

"Will you have a cup of tea?" she asked when I put the quilts away.

"No, thanks," I responded. "I have things to do, and I'm pretty exhausted. You should take a walk, Bertie. It would do you good. It's still daylight and nice out. Spring has sprung, and Harry's jonquils are in full bloom." Harry was a neighbor who admired her in his own cranky way.

"I know, I know." She nodded. "He came by around noon to brag. That guy needs a life."

I had to chuckle. Sometimes I felt they both needed one. "He's smitten with you, Bertie," I teased. "I'll bet he'd love to marry you!"

She threw up her hands in disgust. "Lily, wash your mouth," she scolded. "He's a lonely old geezer for sure, but I don't have time for him!"

"I've seen the two of you together, and I think there's a spark or two," I continued to tease.

"He's got bad knees, a bad hip, and a little touch of dementia, if you ask me," Bertie said, shaking her head.

I laughed. "See you later. Holler if you need anything," I said, puffing up the stairs.

I took the quilts to my quilt room. Yes, I had an entire bedroom converted into shelving for my quilt collection. Red and white dominated the colors. My new quilt was well-received as I situated it next to a friend. Every quilt had a friend that complemented the other. I hadn't thought of it that way until a quilt shop owner once said to me that she didn't put a bolt of fabric on the shelf unless it was next to a complementary friend. I also had a special shelf where all my doll and crib quilts were folded by size. I'd decided long ago that my passion for red-and-white quilts came from my own doll quilt, which was a red-and-white Four-Patch. I wondered what had happened to my very first quilt.

Chapter 4

After I had a shower, I was about to enter the quilts into the computer when my cell phone rang. It was my sister Lynn.

"Where have you been?" she asked with concern. "I tried texting you and got no response."

"I was just with Holly having lunch out in the wine country," I explained. "I guess I didn't catch it."

"I'm jealous! Does this mean you have another new quilt?"

I had to chuckle. "How did you know? Actually, I have two new purchases!"

"I can't keep up with you," Lynn confessed. "The reason I'm calling is that I have a show coming up at the Kilmore Gallery this weekend. I want you to be sure to come to the reception."

"Cool! You know I wouldn't miss it, so just text me the information. I promise to pay attention."

"Why don't you bring a date? I could use live bodies, as well as potential customers."

"I think you have the wrong number," I joked. "Did you have anyone in mind in case I really do give that some thought?"

"No, but you could always bring Alex. He looks good at events like this."

I chuckled. "You know we're like brother and sister, so don't go calling it a date."

"Do what you can, please. Have you heard from Loretta or Laurie?"

"Nothing. It's probably my turn to respond. I'll email everyone about my new quilts."

"Oh, yeah, that'll be big news," she joked. "Carl is waiting on me; I have to go. Love you!"

"Love you, too!" I echoed.

Lynn was one of my three sisters. I am the youngest. Loretta, the oldest, lives in Green Bay, Wisconsin. She's a nurse and is married to Bill, who is a schoolteacher. Loretta was the only one of us to have a child. Her daughter is Sarah, a darling girl in her early twenties that we all spoil and adore. She may be the lucky one to end up with all my quilts one day.

Laurie is the second-oldest and is the free spirit of the family. She lives in Fish Creek, Wisconsin, which is about an hour from Loretta. Fish Creek is a tourist town in Door County where Laurie can sell all of her trinkets, as we call them. Her shop, located in the center of town, is aptly named Trinkets. She sells jewelry, beads, chimes, potions, yard ornaments, and essential oils. She lives with the spirits and always has a new cure for something. Laurie has been divorced for a long time. Her husband left her for another woman, but Laurie didn't seem to care. She has long hair, sometimes worn in braids, with shades of gray creeping in. She is still a happy hippie in her own world.

Lynn lives not far from me in a wonderful contemporary house. Her husband, Carl, is a very busy attorney who lets Lynn do her thing in the arts. Her watercolors are amazing, as is her studio. Carl's past medical history is the reason they have no children. They both seem extraordinarily happy.

As diverse as we are, we are very close. Our parents were good, God-fearing people who adored their children. They'd had one son, but my mother miscarried. She told us she'd named him Lewis. She wanted us all to have names that started with the letter L. Her name was Laverne. I wasn't privy to as much of her life as to the lives of my older sisters. While we were growing up, birthdays were a big deal, so we continue to celebrate them together when we can.

We were all creative in some way. Lynn painted very well. Loretta made quilts, and Laurie created her crazy world. I was creative with words, and had always hoped to write my own book one day. My freedom now was an opportunity to make something happen with something I enjoyed. I loved Missouri and its diversity, so I knew I would never leave to be closer to Laurie and Loretta.

Chapter 5

I woke up the next morning to fresh air coming in my window. Noise from trash collectors and beeping horns told me the rest of the world was in action. As soon as I had my coffee, I wanted to get groceries and then go by Rosie's Antique Shop, which was a couple of blocks down from me. Rosie's tiny shop carried a multitude of things and was in the middle of many of the neighborhood's Italian bakeries and restaurants. I thought I'd see if Lynn wanted to have lunch. I decided it could be a pretty stress-free day if I stuck to my game plan.

I fixed coffee and then checked my emails. A group sister email had been sent from Laurie. She reminded us that our Aunt Mary had celebrated a birthday recently and that Laurie had sent a card from all of us. Laurie was considerate and sensitive in that way. She mentioned that all the shops in Fish Creek that had closed for the winter months were now open.

I took a moment to respond to her. I thanked her for sending the card and then told her about my new quilts.

Other folks talked about their kids and job; I talked about my quilts. I knew she would roll her eyes at my silly passion. Off I went, and Bertie was on the front porch to greet me. "Do you need anything from the store?" I asked as I continued walking.

"Wait, wait, yes," she said, out of breath. "I want some more of that organic honey you brought me once before. Sugar loves it when I give her a drop or two."

"Bertie, I'm not sure you should be giving her that. It may not be good for her."

"Oh, it's just sweets for my sweetie. No harm done. When will you be back?"

"I don't know. Lynn and I are going to meet up for lunch. You have a good day!"

"Oh, tell her I said hello. The last time I saw Lynn, she wanted to know all about Walter and if I had seen him lately. Tell her he's been quiet."

I chuckled. Walter was the ghost that Bertie was convinced she lived with. When Laurie was visiting a few years ago, she told Bertie there was a male ghost in her apartment. Laurie always claimed to have that special spiritual gift, which most of us ignored. Bertie was convinced the ghost was Walter, the previous owner who had died in the house. I just always told Bertie that as long as he was good to her, there was nothing wrong with it. When Bertie misplaced things around the house, she always blamed it on Walter.

Lynn and I had agreed to meet at a popular restaurant called Rigazzi's. They had the very best pizza on The Hill, as far as I was concerned.

I was running a little late, but when I arrived, there was Lynn with one of the restaurant's fishbowls of beer.

"What are you thinking?" I asked her, grinning. "It's not even cocktail hour."

"It is somewhere! I have to have beer with pizza. That's just the way it is. Go ahead and get one for yourself!"

"No, no. I think I'll have iced tea," I countered.

"Carl will be late from a dinner meeting, so I can go home and take a nap if I feel like it."

"You're a bad influence, sister," I teased.

"Speaking of sisters," Lynn began. "We need to discuss going to Fish Creek for Laurie's birthday. We can celebrate yours as well, since they're both in June."

"That's fine by me! I'm a free woman now, you know."

"Yes, and that's not normal. If you think I'm going to pay your way to Fish Creek, think again. Any leads?"

I laughed. "I'm not looking for leads, and I can pay my way to Laurie's, not to worry. I'm not going behind a desk ever again! I'll eat cereal and tuna the rest of my life before I do that."

Lynn laughed and shook her head in disbelief. "Did you ask Alex or anyone to come to the reception with you?"

"No, but I'll do it for you. However, I'm perfectly comfortable coming alone."

After we'd devoured most of the large pizza, Lynn said she had to run. I wrapped up the leftovers and followed her out the door, then headed to Rosie's. When I entered Rosie's shop, she was putting out some darling toothpick holders for a lady to examine.

"Hey, Lily Girl," she said. "It's about time you stopped by. I've been missin' you. I've been savin' a right nice quilt to show you."

"Oh, Rosie, how sweet!" I responded. "You finish up with

this nice lady first. Those holders are so pretty."

"I can't decide which ones to buy," the lady confessed.
"They're all pretty, so I'll take them all!" Rosie lit up with joy.

"So when will you be selling the shop?" the lady asked Rosie.

I couldn't believe what I had just heard.

"Well, my ad will go in tomorrow's paper, so who knows
how long it'll take to sell this place. I want to sell everything
lock, stock, and barrel, not piece by piece."

"I understand," the woman said. "Thanks for the
discount. I'll try to be back again before you leave. Good luck
to you!"

Chapter 6

When the woman shut the door, I stared at Rosie.

"I can't believe what I just heard. You're selling?"

Rosie nodded with her head down. "I was going to tell you the next time I saw you," she confessed. "I can't continue. I'm spending more time at the doctor's office than I am here. It's just getting to be too much for me. The antique market is down, and I'll never live long enough to see it turn around."

"Well, there's no doubt you deserve to retire," I said consolingly. "I'm selfish, I guess. How long have I been coming here?"

Rosie laughed. "I remember the first time you came in the door," she reminisced. "You were focused on one thing, and that was quilts. I think the first one you bought from me was called Lady of the Lake. It was so pristine. I was going to keep it for myself until I saw the look in your eyes. It had your name on it."

I laughed. "I was so happy with it, and of course the Irish Chain you gave me on my birthday. What dealer gives their customer a quilt?"

"You deserved it."

"I feel so badly that you have to let this all go."

"Don't worry. I'm not going anywhere soon. Who would want a buy a shop full of things nobody wants? I know shops that have been for sale for years. Now, let's forget about that, shall we? I put back a dandy quilt you will love. It's in the back room. You look around some."

That wasn't hard to do. Rosie always had new things that she referred to as "smalls." She said people liked buying small things and that she could make just as much money with smalls as she could with furniture.

She was taking such a long time. I was about to go find her when she returned.

"Rosie, what took so long?"

"Oh, darn it, anyway!" she complained. "I can't find it. I've had so many things go missing lately. I'm so sorry, Lily. I'm sure it's here somewhere. I'll give you a call when I find it."

"No problem. I love coming here. I just hate to hear your news."

"It's time, it's time," were her last words as I went out the door.

Off I went around the corner to grab a few groceries. I hardly ever cooked, because there was too much good food readily available in the neighborhood. The delicatessens were to die for and made up a lot of my diet.

When I got home, I opened a bottle of red wine I'd bought from Wine Country Gardens and nibbled on some garlic bread. The red wine was called The Other and was one of my favorites. No one had ever explained the name to me.

I went out onto my little porch balcony, which overlooked

the street. It was big enough for a few wicker chairs and a table. The breeze felt good as I put my feet up on the matching footstool. The streets were always busier around the dinner hour. The wonderful aromas from the restaurants would sometimes drift my way. I kept thinking about Rosie and her decision. I couldn't imagine what it must be like to give up something you have been doing for so many years. I hoped her missing items were just misplaced and not stolen. My cell phone rang just as I was about to go back inside. It was my buddy, Alex. "How's the world treating you?" I asked Alex.

"Well, a robbery down the street isn't a good thing," he confessed, sounding anxious.

"Really?"

"That's the word. It was the tavern that's closed a lot. I can't think of the name right now. The word is that the incident is drug related. I hate to see this end of town get hammered with news like that. They have no clues, from what I hear."

"Aren't you scared?"

"Honey, I wouldn't have what they're looking for," he quipped.

I then decided to tell him about Lynn's reception at the Kilmore Gallery and asked if he'd be interested in going.

"Sure, sounds great!

"You want to just meet up there?" I asked.

"I'll pick you up."

Alex lived in a neighborhood referred to as the Central West End. It was a trendy, artsy area that had its ups and downs with crime. Many folks want to live there to enjoy the outdoor venues and culture. I was he suggested we meet there. I didn't want folks to think we were a couple.

Alex and I had met at work. He left before I did to pursue freelance writing and was doing quite well. He always wanted to write a novel, but I didn't think he'd ever settle down long enough to accomplish such a feat.

I also felt I had a novel in me. I was a better storyteller than Alex. I could write about my passion for quilts, but it would be a struggle to concentrate on any other subject. Just like with my future plans, I hoped it would fall into place. It was getting chilly, so I went inside and called it a night. I crawled under the few quilts that my mother had made. She'd died when I was a teenager, so her quilts were a means of keeping her with me.

Chapter 7

I woke up to the sound of dogs barking. That meant that Bertie was out with Sugar. I rolled out of bed and reluctantly started the day.

I checked my email, and there was my sisters' group message. They had decided that a trip to Fish Creek was definitely going to happen. Loretta got cute by noting that I may have a new job by then and might not be able to go. They just couldn't resist an opportunity to remind me that I needed a job.

I sat down with my coffee and responded by telling them I was certain to go with them. I agreed they could celebrate my birthday as well. Growing up, Laurie and I shared many of our birthdays together, which sometimes meant getting the same birthday gift. We were never jealous and laughed about agreeing to cut our birthday cake in half to please everyone.

After I got dressed, I paid bills and photographed my new quilts to put on the computer. I liked keeping track of where and when I purchased them, as well as what I paid.

I sat right in the middle of my quilt room and started to pray. Where was I going with my love of quilts? Was I simply a hoarder in denial? Could I possibly sell one? They were like my children in that I could tell where each of them had came from, and likely the story behind them. They each had a name and timeline of their personal history. My big question was how I could connect my future with my passion. Since I liked to write, would anyone care to read about my quilt journey? Alex was a good amateur photographer who could take photos for publications. Suddenly, a knock on the door startled me.

"I hate to bother you, honey," Bertie interrupted. "I made some soup and thought you'd like some. You do so many nice things for me." She looked at me oddly. "Are you okay, honey?"

"Oh, sure," I responded quickly. "I was just doing some thinking and planning in my quilt room."

"You're not happy, are you?" she asked softly. "I can tell!"

I smiled. "Actually Bertie, I've never been happier," I said. "I'm excited about making changes in my life. The hard part is deciding what the changes will be and when to make them."

"You don't mean like moving elsewhere, do you?" Bertie asked, suddenly looking worried.

"Yes, a move may be in order.'" I nodded. "It may be to Fish Creek to join Laurie, or across town."

"Oh my heavens," Bertie sighed. "I won't hear of such an idea."

"Not right away! I'll be here for a little while. Thanks for the soup." I knew I sent Bertie down the stairs while she felt filled with worry. It was good that I'd started preparing her for my absence, which I knew would eventually happen. I needed to take a walk to continue my thinking. I looked at Bertie's soup and decided it may not be edible. That was not unusual. She could come up with some strange concoctions. I grabbed a jacket and ran down the stairs before Bertie could get my attention. I passed Harry's house and saw him sitting on the porch. I waved and kept walking before he could engage me in conversation. I knew my walk was taking me towards Rosie's shop. I stopped at Tony's coffee shop and got a coffee to go. For the life of me, I couldn't pronounce the real Italian name of his place, but Tony was the owner.

Then, there it was. There was a plain and noticeable sign in Rosie's window advertising that her shop was officially for sale.

"Good morning, Lily Girl!" she greeted me cheerfully.

"Good morning!" I responded enthusiastically. "I just thought I'd stop by and see if you found the quilt you were anxious to show me."

"No, I'm sorry to say. I even asked Melanie to help me look for it. Yesterday, I lost a lovely gold locket that I was intending to show to a young man. Melanie thinks I sold it, but my memory isn't that bad. It was here. I guess I should get a camera, but I've never had any problem with shoplifting in all these years."

"I always heard that if a shoplifter is successful once, he'll be back again," I shared.

She nodded in agreement. "The thing about your quilt is that customers don't go into my back room. Only Melanie can go back there. That's where I had your quilt."

"Tell me about Melanie. She's only been here a couple of times when I've been here."

"She's a dear. She loves antiques and came in here on a regular basis. One day, she asked if she could work here. She caught me at the right moment when I needed some help. She agreed to work as needed, which many folks can't do."

"So when she works, you're usually gone?" I asked.

She nodded. "Yes, usually when I have my doctor's appointments. Now, the other day, she did stay while we washed some glassware."

We were interrupted when a man came in and bluntly asked how much Rosie was asking for her shop.

"Only the contents, mister," she replied. "The building doesn't belong to me."

"How much is all this, then?" he pressed, giving the store a quick glance.

"If you're a serious buyer, we can discuss the details at the proper time," Rosie eloquently answered.

"Okay, thanks," he said with an insolent tone. "Good luck!" Out the door he went.

Rosie and I burst into laughter.

"I guess I'll get a lot of that before it's all said and done," Rosie admitted.

"It has to be the right situation, Rosie. I encouraged her. Don't rush into anything."

"You mean like you and your plans?" We both chuckled again.

Chapter 8

I could tell the man's visit bothered Rosie. I stayed a while to ask questions about this and that to get her mind off of things.

"I need someone like you to take this business off my hands," she said. "You live right here and are so knowledgeable about most things. I think it should be a sign for you."

"Oh, no, I couldn't possibly get involved in your sale," I argued. "I want real change, and I'm certain it will mean getting out of this neighborhood. Please don't take offense. I'm flattered you think I could handle a business like this, especially the financial part of it."

"You are very capable, my dear," Rosie insisted. "You are an honest, levelheaded woman that customers could trust."

"Thanks, Rosie. I'll do whatever I can to help you find a buyer. Your sign just went up, so things could take a while."

I said goodbye and continued on my walk. It made me want to walk in Klondike Park in the wine country. The open spaces and views could be so energizing. Perhaps in the morning I could set out early and then have lunch somewhere.

I stopped in front of St. Ambrose Church, which was quite an icon in the neighborhood. The statue of an Italian immigrant family, made by St. Louis artist Rudolph Torrini, represented those who came here from Lombardy and Sicily in the 19th century, which generated the growth of the Catholic Church in the region. This large church also dominated a lot of the neighborhood's social life. I loved local history.

I sat down on a bench nearby to rest and check emails on my phone. It also gave me time to think about Rosie's situation. I sure didn't want to fall into the trap she'd suggested, despite how much I wanted to help her. A car honked to get my attention.

"Can you tell me where to find Elizabeth Avenue? I'm looking for the boyhood homes of Joe Garagiola and Yogi Berra."

I nodded and smiled. The driver was awfully handsome. "You're a baseball fan, are you?" I asked as I got up from the bench.

"I am; how about you?" he asked in a friendly voice.

"Only if it's the St. Louis Cardinals," I joked.

"Is there any other team?" he responded. "Are you waiting for a ride or something?"

I chuckled. "No. I'm on a walk and just stopped to rest and look at my emails," I explained.

"It's a good spot! Look, I don't typically stop and ask women if they want a ride, but since you did me a favor, it's the least I can do."

"No, thanks," I responded.

I then proceeded to give him instructions to Elizabeth

Avenue. He listened intently, and I got a closer look at his face. He looked to be about my age. He was nice enough and handsome enough, but not trustworthy enough for me to accept a ride. However, I could easily go for a man like that, but trusting the opposite sex wasn't my strong point. I liked hanging out with Lynn, Holly, and Alex, but it wasn't going to lead to a special someone. Lynn always told me I wasn't meeting anyone because I didn't have my antenna up. We parted ways by exchanging friendly smiles and quick waves. On my way home, I picked up a spicy Polish hot dog from a corner vendor. It was tasty, and a lot more appetizing than the soup Bertie gave me.

"Hey, missy!" Harry hollered from his front porch when I walked by. "Was Bertie out today?"

"I don't know," I said. "Why don't you go find out for yourself?"

"Oh, she'll just complain and give me grief," he said. "If it's not one thing, it's another."

"She made soup, so you may want to stop by," I teased.

He waved me on.

Somehow, I knew he'd be on his way shortly. What a pair they made!

When I got home, I checked emails again. My sisters' group email was active regarding our trip to Fish Creek. Laurie had booked a condo for us near her shop. It was at the entrance to the famous Peninsula State Park, a place we all loved. Shopping was great in that area as well. I loved the large antique mall that usually carried a lot of antique quilts. The trip was sounding really exciting and like something to look forward to.

Chapter 9

I didn't want to embarrass my sister at her fancy reception, so I dressed in all black with bright, colorful jewelry to have a more artsy look. I had to admit that I looked good, with a fresh haircut that had a swing when I turned my head. I convinced myself I didn't look like a nerdy editor or a hoarder of quilts!

Alex was right on time and looked pretty dapper. He was always a sharp dresser, and his choice of a wild-colored shirt was perfect for the occasion. Alex gave me a whistle of approval when I twirled around.

"What a colorful pair we are!" I bragged. "Lynn will be thrilled."

"I stopped to get her a bouquet," Alex said.

"Aren't you thoughtful? Why didn't I think of that?"

When we arrived, the gallery was already filled with Lynn's admirers. The champagne fountain was flowing, and Lynn was greeting guests as quickly as she could. When she saw Alex and me, she dropped everything to greet us. "You guys look great, and you brought flowers!" Lynn said graciously as she accepted them. "Lily, you look so sexy with that haircut!"

I blushed and hoped no one had heard her.

"I already adore her, as you know," Alex teased. "I can't wait to see your latest work, Lynn."

Alex took off when he saw a friend of his, and Lynn excused herself to say hello to another artist she knew. I took a glass of champagne from the waiter passing by and began to look at my sister's work. I was intrigued by a large watercolor floral design that would have taken up a whole wall in my little apartment. How did she do it, and where did she get all that talent?

"It's pretty magnificent, don't you think?" said a voice near me. I turned around to a familiar face, but couldn't place where I recognized him from.

"Yes, it's my favorite, I believe," I stated, as I tried to remember.

"As I told you before, I don't normally ask women if they need a ride, but I may have second thoughts again, seeing you here tonight," the man teased.

"Oh, you're the baseball fan looking for directions!" I finally recalled. "You looked familiar."

"I have to say, you hang out at really cool places," he joked. I blushed.

"Lynn is my sister. I proudly boasted. "Do you know her?"

"Why, yes, very well," he answered quickly. "She's your sister?" I nodded. "I've known Carl and Lynn for a long time. Carl and I went to law school together. I love Lynn's work and have a bit of it in my office."

"That's wonderful," I said as I awkwardly stared at him.

"So, did you find the houses on Elizabeth Avenue that you were looking for?"

"I did, thanks to you!" he said flirtatiously.

"Where do you live?"

"St. Charles."

"Oh, what a lovely historic town," I commented.

"That it is." He nodded. "I'm sorry, but we never exchanged names."

"I'm Lily Rosenthal," I said, reaching for his already-extended hand.

"Marcus Rennels, but Lynn and Carl know me as Marc," he said.

"Nice to meet you," I said, continuing to smile.

"Are you going to buy this gorgeous piece, or do I have to?" Marcus teased.

"I certainly can't afford it. It will need a lot of space around it, don't you think?"

"I couldn't agree more," he replied.

"Hello, Marc," Lynn said, joining us. "I see you've met my sister."

"Actually, we informally met before," he noted, looking straight into my eyes. "So, Lynn, has this wonderful piece been spoken for?"

Lynn shook her head in astonishment. "Of course not. It will likely live here for a while," she replied modestly.

"Well, I'd like to purchase it."

"Really?" she asked in shock.

"You can thank me for that, Lynn," I joked. "He knew I loved it and was about to buy it, so he saved the day. It's really gorgeous, Lynn!"

"This is surreal!" Lynn gasped. "Follow me, Mr. Rennels."

It was an amazing encounter. I couldn't wait to tell Alex all about it. I found him munching on shrimp and stuffed mushrooms, engaged in conversation with an older woman.

"Lily, meet Elsie Langford," he said. "Elsie, this is my good friend, Lily Rosenthal."

"Nice to meet you, Elsie," I replied.

"I'm writing her bio for *Spirit* magazine," Alex explained.

"I can't wait to read it," I said.

"There you two are," Lynn interrupted. "I thought you had left. Lily, can I talk to you for a second before you leave?"

"Excuse me," I said as I followed Lynn over to the bar. "What's going on?" I asked when we got there.

"You do know that Marc Rennels is single, don't you?"

I shook my head and snickered. "I only know he loves baseball and your paintings," I joked.

"Well, he thinks you're quite catchy and wants to take you out sometime," Lynn said with excitement.

"Catchy? What does that mean?"

Lynn heaved a big sigh. "It means you've captured his attention and he wants to get to know you better. Get with it, sister!"

I had to chuckle at seeing her so serious. "Well, whatever!" I replied. "I doubt if I'm his type, but I'm sure glad you made that sale. Now stop trying to find me a man! I can find my own."

"It appears as if you already have!" Lynn teased. "By the way, you look really great tonight. I really appreciate your coming, and please give this guy a chance if he calls, okay?"

"Okay, okay, I'll be nice."

Alex and I said goodbye, and off we went. We headed to a corner bar, where we stuck out like a sore thumb. We started talking about the evening, and Alex's humor had us in stitches in a very short time.

"Are you going to go out with the big spender?" Alex asked teasingly. "Did you see the price tag on that baby?"

I nodded. "I think he bought it to show off," I decided. "He knew I loved it."

We finished the evening with a pizza and arrived home around midnight.

Chapter 10

I woke up early, as I was anxious to go to Klondike Park, which was just three miles from Augusta. I'd barely had a glimpse of the place before, so I got online before I left to get a sense of the 250-acre park.

The article I found said the park was the jewel of St. Charles County. It used to be a quarry that mined silica needed for the glass factory across the river. The large, impressive building in the park used to be a B&B, but is now used as a conference center. The article went on to say the park had four miles of natural and paved trails, which was awesome. I went on to read about their cabins and places to pitch a tent, but without running water or restrooms other than in the conference center, that wasn't going to happen.

An interesting side note in the article was about the mountain goat which appeared frequently to hikers. He had a repulsive smell that would warn folks when he was around. Finally, after enough complaints, he was captured and sent him to a nearby farm. I found it all so fascinating.

I dressed in layers to start out into the cool morning. I

loved my morning walks. When I was younger, I was an avid runner. I planned to walk at least an hour before leaving to have lunch. Bertie was still asleep as I quietly went down the stairs. It was a beautiful day, and I was happy to get in my SUV and drive away.

Driving out to wine country was an escape to fresh air. Once I got through the morning highway traffic, I entered the scenic countryside with a big smile on my face. I pulled into the conference center parking lot when I arrived and entered the building. As I was pulling some brochures from the rack, a uniformed woman approached me, asking if she could help.

"I just came out here to walk for a while this morning," I explained.

"Sure. The walking trails are marked on the map, and if you want to venture up the hill behind us, there's a rest stop with a beautiful view along the way."

"Is that where the goat was usually spotted?" I asked with a smile.

She grinned and nodded. "Yes, but you don't have to worry about running into him anymore," she assured me. "It's a beautiful day, so enjoy!"

I got a bottle of water out of the car and walked along the trail, wondering whether to climb the hill. Something told me it would be safer to do with another person. I thought of Alex and how he would love doing this. Along the way, I noticed that the rock, sand, and cliff were pure white. I got out my phone and took a few pictures. The views while walking were impressive. I felt I was somewhere far away from home. After a while, my appetite was mounting. I was ready for lunch, so I turned around and followed the same path back to my car.

I got in my car and headed to Augusta. I was disappointed to see The Silly Goose wasn't open for lunch, but then I saw a sign a block down for Kate's Coffee. Perhaps they would have something besides sweet rolls to satisfy my hunger. I was delighted to find a cute little house with a charming patio garden behind it. A group of girls were giggling with delight and eating food that looked like lunch.

I went inside to order and a friendly man behind the counter asked if I had been there before. I explained how I'd frequented the area but hadn't known about a coffee shop. I then asked who Kate was. He smiled and said he'd named the place after his mother. The menu had plenty to choose from, but trying one of his offerings of quiche and salad was perfect for me. It was so interesting to watch the sampling of customers. Most seemed to be new customers like me. Feeling satisfied and ready for the next activity of the day, I walked over to Carrie Mae's shop.

"Well, Miss Lily, I didn't think I'd see you again so soon," Carrie Mae greeted me.

"You can't keep me away," I said with a big grin. "I spent the morning walking at Klondike Park. I also discovered Kate's Coffee around the corner. What a wonderful place!"

"Oh, indeed," she agreed. "They are so nice to deliver when I request it. Say, Lily, while you're here, I could use your expertise on some antique fabric I acquired recently. Let's go downstairs to look at it."

We walked down the stairway crowded with antiques. Carrie Mae pulled out a large old suitcase and put it on the table for us to look inside. When she opened it up, I couldn't believe my eyes.

"When you said old fabric, you really meant old," I said with a gasp.

She snickered at my comment. "Yes, mostly chintz that was likely furnishing fabric," she divulged. "I'm sure most of it goes back to the mid-1800s, but I wanted your opinion. Perhaps you could give me an idea of what to charge for this."

Chapter 11

I tried to help Carrie Mae as much as I could. She had a new stack of feed sacks for me to look at as well. They were of no interest to me, but I knew the red-and-white ones were hard to find and had more value. Hours had passed, and suddenly it was five o'clock, when Carrie Mae normally closed the shop.

"It was a pretty quiet day here for you," I pointed out. "Is it always that way during the week?"

"It depends. I wish we had tourists and folks like you coming in more often. You know, Lily, you ought to think about moving out this way, since you like it so much."

"I know you must think I'm lost, but I want to make sure my next move is the right one."

"Sure, I understand. There are always plenty of empty buildings out here. We need more retail for all the guests that stay at our many B&Bs."

"Is rent pretty cheap?"

"Well, yes, but you get what you pay for. So many buildings need to be restored, but those who have done so never seem to regret it."

"All good to know, but I need to get on home. I'll be caught in the rush hour traffic for sure."

"Someday, we need to share dinner together. I still like to cook once in a while. We'll eat off of china and have some good wine."

"It sounds great, but I don't like driving on these roads after dark."

"Not to worry. I have plenty of spare rooms upstairs where you can stay the night in."

"Thanks, but I'd better get going," I said as I moved closer to the door. I drove home very happy and managed to get through the traffic until I got closer to my neighborhood. I suddenly felt misplaced and knew this couldn't be my home for much longer. Bertie was sitting on the porch, but I managed to keep going, telling her I needed to make a phone call.

I went out on the porch to check my emails and phone messages. The first email was from Holly, complaining again about Monster Moe. She needed friendship quilts for a lecture she was giving. I knew just the quilt that she could borrow. The second email was from the sister group. Loretta told us that Sarah was engaged. She seemed to be excited, so I was sure she'd be sharing wedding plans soon. Now that was exciting news! The third email was from Alex, wanting to borrow a quilt for a photo. He hoped I would return the call. I had one phone message from Marcus Rennels. It was brief and to the point, and he suggested we have a drink together. That I would think about! I couldn't help but think his interest in me was because I was Lynn's sister, however.

I was suddenly distracted by loud sirens from police

cars and fire trucks. There was no doubt something had happened close by in the neighborhood. Folks were starting to gather outdoors to see what was happening. I knew Bertie would be right on it. Sure enough, my doorbell rang, and there stood Bertie.

"What do you suppose happened?" she asked frantically. "I don't see smoke anywhere."

"I have no idea, but don't worry, we'll hear soon enough. Maybe Harry will learn something. You know they make such a fuss over the least little call these days."

"Harry was by earlier. I'm sure nothing happened to that old man. He'd be nothing to fuss over."

"Bertie, shame on you! You know you would be devastated if anything happened to him.

She shook her head and waved her hands, going out the door.

Chapter 12

I didn't think much more about the sirens the rest of the evening, but first thing in the morning, Bertie was at my door as soon as she heard my footsteps.

"Lily, did you hear? Can you believe what happened? Did you turn on the TV this morning? It's just awful!" She looked like she'd seen a ghost.

"Bertie, slow down. Tell me what happened."

She took a deep breath. "Rosie was shot and robbed."

"What?" I asked, unsure I'd heard her correctly.

"Someone shot her in the back, Lily. In the back." She was in tears.

"No, no," I said, running to the TV to turn it on. "Are you sure? Who told you?"

"Everyone. It's all over the neighborhood."

"She's really dead?" I said, feeling faint.

"They say it looks like they only took money. God bless her soul. I hope she didn't know what hit her. That whole block is roped off with yellow tape."

"I can't believe it. Rosie never hurt a soul. Why would

they think to rob her for money?"

"I'm telling you, this neighborhood is going to pot. We try to look out for each other, and then someone comes in and does a terrible thing like this. She didn't have a chance."

"I'm going to get dressed and find out more. Did they say on the TV if they had a suspect?"

"I think they interviewed someone who said they heard gunshots. It must have taken place after Rosie closed the shop at five."

"Okay, Bertie, thanks for telling me, but you go talk to Harry and see if he knows anything more. Rosie had a young girl working there that may know something."

Reluctantly, Bertie left my apartment.

I dressed, skipped any coffee, and flew out the door. I passed a few policemen who were going door to door, asking folks if they'd seen anything.

When I got to Rosie's block, I saw that Bertie was right. I couldn't get near her building. Some folks were gathered around, talking about it all. The bakery next door was closed, which meant the search was serious and wouldn't be over anytime soon. It appeared there was nothing I could do until I heard more. I wanted to cry. Rosie's life didn't have to end this way. My phone rang in my pocket. It was Lynn.

"I can't believe it, Lily. Is it as they say on TV?"

"I'm afraid so. I'm standing near her shop right now, and it's all roped off. I'm still in shock myself."

"She was such a treasure, and had been there for so long. I hate this kind of violence in this close-knit neighborhood."

Nothing Lynn could say could comfort me. I picked up some coffee at Tony's coffee shop and walked back home. Bertie and Harry were sitting on the porch in silence.

"Hear anything?" Harry asked.

I shook my head, then quietly walked past them and went upstairs. I went straight to my quilt room and pulled out the red-and-white Irish Chain quilt that Rosie had given me. Rosie didn't carry many quilts, but when she got in this red-and-white one, she knew I had recently had a birthday and that the quilt had my name on it. When I tried to pay her for it, she had refused. She said I had spent enough money with her through the years and that it was time she did something nice for me. That was the way Rosie was. I couldn't help but wonder what kind of quilt she'd been saving for me in the back room. I held the Irish Chain quilt close to me in hopes that she was watching. "I'm so sorry, Rosie," I whispered aloud. "God bless you."

A hard knock at the door startled me. I put the quilt down and went to answer. It was one of the policemen I had seen going door to door. He introduced himself and said he just had a few questions. I invited him in and told him about my relationship with Rosie.

"So tell me, when was the last time you saw her?" he asked, ready to write down my reply.

I told him all about my last visit and that she'd had something in the back room for me, but couldn't find it. I added that she mentioned she'd had many things missing lately. "She'd recently hired a young girl by the name of Melanie. Be sure to talk to her. Rosie said she and Melanie were the only ones to go into the back room. Rosie was not absentminded. She had someone shoplifting from her."

"I see," he said with some hesitation. "Did you know she had her shop for sale?"

"Yes, she told me. I was there when she first put the sign

up. A man came in and inquired about the price. When she put him off, he left in a huff."

"Can you describe him?"

"Not really. He was a middle-aged man with a receding hairline. I couldn't even tell you what he was wearing."

"Well, thanks a lot," he said, walking towards the door. "Here's my card in case you think of anything. You've been very helpful."

"Please don't give up. We have got to find whoever did this."

He nodded and went out the door. It made me feel somewhat better that the police were taking this very seriously. I could only imagine how they were trying to reassure the business owners and residents that they would be safe.

Chapter 13

The next day, Holly came to see my Red Cross signature quilt. When she arrived that afternoon, she was really down in the dumps. It didn't help when I told her about Rosie. She had been to her shop with me once before, but didn't connect the dots when her murder came out in the news.

"I wish I had a family contact for Rosie," I shared. "I haven't seen any notice of her funeral or even a memorial service."

"That's odd. What do you think will happen to her things?"

"Good question. She has a nephew she mentioned, and an employee named Melanie." I noticed Holly wasn't listening. "Okay, so what did the monster do now?"

She shook her head in disgust. "I almost wish he would physically abuse me and get it over with," she admitted. "His yelling at me is horrid and I can't escape it. I can't always leave the house when he has one of those spells."

"I've told you to start recording those outbursts. You have got to stand up to him."

"He'd kill me if he found out I was doing something like that. I'll admit it. I'm truly afraid of him."

"I know, and I'm not insensitive to that. I hope you lock your bedroom door at night."

"It doesn't matter, to be honest. If he wants me to do something or wants to explode, he does it right outside the door until I open it."

"The police need to hear this, and you should get a restraining order before he really does kill you. The mere fact that he says he wants you dead is a huge warning, friend."

She nodded.

"I'm glad you gave me those letters describing his abuse, in case something happens to you. Do you know how hard it is to listen to all of this and watch you do nothing?"

"I know, I know. Look, I'd better get going. This quilt will be perfect. I'll get it back to you soon."

"I'll be going back to Augusta soon. They have some events coming up, if you want to go."

"I'd love to if I can," she said humbly.

"Remember, I'm going away with Lynn to Fish Creek for Laurie's birthday. We usually share our birthday celebrations."

"Oh, I'm jealous. I've always wanted to go there. Is Lynn driving?"

"Yes. I'm hoping they can help me come to some decision about my next move."

"Please don't move to Fish Creek, Lily. I don't know what I'd do without you."

"I hear you, but it is an option. Oh, my cell is ringing. I'll be right back, okay?" I went to the kitchen, where I'd left my phone, and saw that it was Marcus.

"It's Marcus, the baseball guy, as you've referred to me,"

he greeted me. "I've called you before. Did you see my call?"

"Yes. Sorry, I've been kind of busy."

"I'm calling to see if you would go to the baseball game with me tomorrow."

"Baseball game? Are the Cardinals playing tomorrow?"

"Yes, at one o'clock. Are you available?"

"Sure! It's been a while since I've been to a game."

"Great, I'll pick you up at noon," he said happily. "We'll have lunch at the ballpark, if that's okay."

"Love those hot dogs," I said before hanging up. I had to suppose that Lynn had told him where I lived. I walked into the living room, where Holly was still waiting.

"I have a date tomorrow!" I announced.

"Really? Who's the lucky guy?"

"Marcus Rennels," I stated. "Lynn calls him Marc. I met him when he asked me for directions as I was out walking one day. I then ran into him at Lynn's reception. Turns out they are friends, and he bought a painting of hers that night."

"Cool. What does he do for a living?"

I told her what little I knew from Lynn, but again, she wasn't listening.

"I'm so jealous," she said sadly.

"Jealous?"

"Yes, that's so awesome. But I'm stuck with a monster in my house of horrors."

Chapter 14

The next morning, I got up early for a walk, which I hoped would take me past Rosie's shop. I hoped that by now, they would have posted funeral information for the neighborhood folks.

The yellow police tape was gone, but the sign indicating that the shop was for sale was still in the window. The inside of the shop was completely dark when I peered in. *How sad,* I thought.

I went into the bakery next door to see if they had any updates.

"My wife said she asked Rosie's nephew, who was moving some furniture yesterday, and he just said she was cremated and didn't want a funeral," Tony said, shaking his head. "It doesn't seem right. She knew so many folks, especially around here."

"Then the nephew inherited the business?"

"We really don't know," he said. "Everybody has been asking about it."

"What do you know about that girl Melanie who was

working there?" I had to ask.

"I don't know a Melanie, but I did see a young girl helping Rosie's nephew," he replied. "We weren't around the night it happened. I told the police that."

"Any word on her killer?"

He shook his head.

"Well, if you hear anything, would you give me a call?"

"Why, sure," he said. "You're Lily, right? I know you always come in here."

Bertie was on the front porch when I returned. I told her what I had learned about Rosie being cremated.

"I hope it was Rosie's idea and not someone else's," I added. I told her I had to shower and get dressed to go out. She would get the idea when Marc showed up, and then she'd have plenty to gossip about.

Marc was on time and wore a Cardinals jacket. He looked just as handsome as I remembered. I had on a red blazer with my best jeans. It was the best that I could do. I hadn't had a real date in so long that I wasn't sure what I needed to look like! To my delight, Bertie wasn't on the front porch when we left. Marc was driving the Mercedes. As soon as we drove off, Marc asked if I knew anything about the robbery down the street from me.

"I have so many questions about it all, Marc, but today's about baseball, right?"

He laughed and nodded.

Our seats at the ballpark were amazing. They were in the bottom section behind home plate, which offered any kind of refreshment as part of the ticket. Marc said he'd shared the tickets with another law partner. In the end, Marc showed off his baseball knowledge while I just enjoyed all the amenities.

The Cardinals were playing the Dodgers. They barely pulled off a win in the ninth inning, so Marc was completely happy. It was just as much fun watching him as watching the game.

We stopped for a drink at a sports bar downtown until most of the traffic had cleared. I had to admit, we were both having a good time. He was very easy to talk to and had a great sense of humor.

"I love coming to the ballpark!" I admitted. "This was a rare treat for me. And I needed this as well, Marc. Thanks for asking me to go. It made me forget about my job situation and everything else."

"Lynn said you're looking for a job."

"I hate to disagree, but I'm really not," I answered. "I want to make a big change in my life, which may involve moving, so getting a job is not my focus." I could tell my answer surprised him.

Chapter 15

Marc's inquiries led to one question: was I considering a move to Wisconsin since I was meeting up with my sisters? I had no answer for him.

When he brought me home, Bertie and Harry were walking on the sidewalk. Their looks were priceless as they tried to figure out who my date might be. I had told Marc ahead of time about my neighbors, so he was quite amused.

Thankfully, Marc announced he had to be on his way and couldn't come inside my apartment. He wanted to know if we could meet up again, and I responded that it would be fun.

I got a quick peck on the lips as he said goodbye. It was nice, and nothing I felt uncomfortable with. *Who could want more?* I asked myself.

I was about to crawl under my covers for the evening when Lynn called on my cell phone.

"How did it go?" she boldly asked.

"How did you know we went out?"

"He asked me first if I thought you would go. I also told

him where you live."

"We had a really good time. Perhaps the Cardinals' win helped," I joked.

"Will you go out again?"

"We'll see," I said, leaving her hanging.

We continued the rest of the conversation by talking about our trip to Fish Creek. Lynn had made reservations at the White Gull Inn for our birthday dinner. I knew that would be a costly affair, but we deserved it. Laurie had arranged for us to stay at Evergreen Hill Condos, which were down the street at the entrance to Peninsula State Park. She thought we'd like walking among all our activities.

Lynn had suggested that Loretta bring her daughter, but she'd objected, saying the trip wouldn't be the same for her. We both were challenged on what to give Laurie for her birthday. She had such different tastes than the rest of us. We both hung up with excitement for our trip.

My night was full of sleep as rain poured down my roof. As I lay in bed the next morning, I knew my plans to go to wine country would have to be delayed. I had many domestic things to do that I had been ignoring, plus the packing for our trip.

After I got my coffee, I turned on the news to see if there was any update on Rosie's murder. There were so many more deaths, in it seemed to have gotten lost. How can the authorities possibly follow up on so many crimes?

I was still in my robe when Bertie's familiar knock came to my door. I guessed she'd heard my footsteps when I got out of bed.

"Good morning, honey," she greeted me. "That was quite a storm last night, wasn't it?"

I nodded. "I somehow mostly slept through it."

"Say, will you be going out today?"

"I hadn't planned on it with this weather. Why?"

"It's Harry. I'm concerned about him. I heard an ambulance go down the block last night. He's not answering his phone, but then he never does, come to think of it."

"Oh, Bertie, you worry too much. I'm sure he's fine. I think if you sit on the porch today, someone will say they've seen him," I suggested.

"Maybe so. He's an ornery soul, so you may be right."

I closed the door and shook my head. As much as I thought of Bertie, I would move away from her in a flash, if I had a place to go.

As I began my housework, I kept going into my quilt room. It was like a magnet to me. My walls, filled with folded quilts, were like walls and walls of fabric for the quiltmaker. The room was dominated by red and white, since that was the majority of my quilt collection. Red was so powerful and strong. I'd learned that my favorite red was referred to as Turkey red, because the dye-fast color was developed in the country of Turkey. That dye was never made in the United States. In the mid-1800s, red was most frequently partnered with green. The undependable green dye took on the name "fugitive green" because the color would go from dark green to blue-green before turning to yellow and then white. The frustration for quiltmakers encouraged them to leave out the green and make only red-and-white quilts. That trend peaked between 1880 and 1930. I loved the graphic patterns it created.

There were many patterns, like Irish Chain and Drunkard's Path, but I had expanded my collection to include more intricate patterns like Mariner's Compass and New York Beauty. I avoided quilts that contained a lighter red referred to as Congo red. Because I kept good records, it was easy for me to know whether I had already purchased a pattern. There were variations to patterns, which I allowed.

My quilt room had no windows, so I didn't have to worry about direct lighting. I had one quilt on the wall, but shelving took up most of the space. I kept a large worktable in the center of the room with a light overhead to examine the quilts as they arrived. I moved them around and refolded them as often as I could. I loved handling them. They were my family.

Chapter 16

In the late afternoon, Lynn called to see if I wanted to come to a Memorial Day picnic at her house. I had a feeling Marc would be there, so I didn't want to commit. I knew I didn't want a relationship, so I didn't want to encourage anything.

"Could you bring that wonderful salad of yours?" Lynn begged. "I could really use it, and it's so delicious."

"How many people are you having?"

"There may be as many as twenty-five, but we'll see."

"Is Marc coming?"

She paused. "He said he had another commitment, so you're safe, if that's what you're worried about. By the way, Laurie called last night, and she is so excited about our visit. She wanted to know if I had any suggestions on what to give you for your birthday."

"Did you tell her I could always use another red-and-white quilt?" She chuckled. "Actually, I was thinking of giving her some kind of quilt. How do you think she would respond to that?"

"As long as it's not traditional, she'd love it, but it would be a very generous gift on your part."

At the end of the day, the rain finally stopped. I couldn't believe I had managed to be homebound for the day. I had veggie soup cooking in the crock-pot to make the day seem homey and inviting. I also had leftover bread from the bakery, so I was all set for dinner. Bertie was likely smelling the fruits of my endeavor all the way downstairs.

I was ready to relax on my porch. The smell of rain was so refreshing. Tomorrow the neighborhood would be bursting with Veteran pride, which included a parade. I had hopes for a beautiful day for the parade as well as for Lynn's outdoor picnic.

Neighbors ventured out of their houses during cocktail hour to discuss the news of the day. I could only wish they had news about Rosie's murder.

I chose to eat my dinner on the porch, and before I knew it, darkness came overhead and I dozed off into the night.

When I awoke at four a.m., the neighborhood was dark. and asleep. I went to bed hoping I could reconnect with the dream I'd been having. I didn't wake up again until nine, which was late for me.

I took my coffee to the porch to see the early activity of the day. Red, white, and blue were the colors of the Memorial Day festivities. I went inside to make the wine vinegar salad that had mandarin oranges, blue cheese, bacon bits, and roasted almonds. It looked good. I was starting to get excited about joining folks for some fun.

When I left the apartment, I was prepared to tell Bertie of my whereabouts, but she wasn't there.

Cars were everywhere in Lynn's neighborhood. There

had to be more than twenty-five folks, I decided. I recognized very few people, but Carl was the first to greet me.

"Oh, Lily, we are so glad you decided to join us," he said. "Lynn is in the kitchen, and I know she'll be happy to accept that salad of yours."

"You must be Lynn's sister," commented a very attractive woman wearing a low-cut sundress. "You look just like her. I'm Kate, by the way. I work at Carl's law firm."

"It's nice to meet you. I'm Lily, and Lynn is waiting for this salad."

When Lynn saw me, she seemed elated.

"I don't think there will be enough of this salad for all these people, but here goes!"

"Thanks so much, sis," Lynn said, giving me a hug. "I'm so glad you came. We'll have plenty of food, I think. I decided to have some things catered. Get yourself a drink and have some fun."

"I will, but do you need me to help with something?"

"Not a thing. I'll bet there's someone in the crowd who likes quilts," she teased.

"That was unnecessary, Lynn," I quipped.

"I'm just sayin'," she chuckled.

Chapter 17

I wandered over to the bar, where there was a young man happy to pour me the drink of my choice. There were two empty stools, so I perched myself on one of them rather than work the room to find someone to talk to. The man and I made small talk as he prepared drinks for others. I kept hoping the food would be out soon so that I could eat and leave. Why wasn't I a social butterfly like Lynn and Laurie? Loretta and I were more subdued, like our mother.

I had to acknowledge one thing about Carl and Lynn: they were friends with quite a diverse set of folks, which I enjoyed seeing. I assumed many were from Lynn's art world from the way they were dressed.

As I looked across the room, I couldn't help but notice how the woman in the sexy sundress had Carl's undivided attention. Was Carl so nice and accommodating that he didn't realize how bad it looked? I hoped Lynn wouldn't notice. What was it about cleavage that got men so excited?

"Well, look who's here," a familiar voice said from behind me.

"Oh, Marc! Lynn said you wouldn't be coming." I responded nervously.

"Well, she was correct," he said with a nod. "I finished early and decided to come anyway. Is this seat taken?"

"Ugh, no; please!" I quickly responded.

"You don't look very happy to see me," he teased after he received his drink.

"I'm just surprised to see you, that's all," I covered.

We then heard the dinner bell ring, as well as a welcome call from Carl to come and help ourselves. The long food table was loaded with goodies.

"Oh, good. I'm famished," I said to Marc. "How about you?"

"I am! Let's get in line," he said, being the first to get up from the stool.

So there I went, joining a man like he was my date. Lynn spotted us immediately and came over to gush over Marc's surprise arrival. I wanted to give her one of my mean sister stares, but she wouldn't look at me. Each of the sisters knew that certain look.

Marc and I engaged in small talk about the Cardinals game that day. Another couple joined us, and Marc introduced me as his good friend.

My nerves had me eating more than I should have. I had to admit my salad tasted wonderful. When I passed on going to the dessert table, I announced to Marc I would be leaving soon.

"Why so soon?" he asked seriously. "I thought we could go for a drink somewhere."

"I'm sorry, but I almost didn't come because I have some things I need to do," I explained rather dramatically. "Lynn begged me to bring my salad, so I couldn't say no."

"Was that your salad with the mandarin oranges?" he asked in surprise. I nodded and grinned. "I love it!" I blushed. "I could have made a whole meal out of it."

"Thanks, Marc. Enjoy the party," I encouraged him. "Oh, keep an eye on Carl. I think he's overdoing his hospitality with the hot chick over there. You could be a nice distraction for him."

Marc looked Carl's direction and gave a serious nod to me. "I will," he said as we parted ways.

I went over to say goodbye to Lynn, but she was talking to so many folks, I wasn't sure she heard me.

I was glad to get back home to my little apartment. Bertie was sitting on the front porch, and she said I'd missed a great parade. She then mentioned that I'd had a male visitor in a suit, but he didn't leave a name.

"He didn't leave even a card?" I asked with interest. She shook her head.

I went upstairs with wonder. Could he have had anything to do with Rosie?

It was not an easy night to get to sleep. The neighborhood was still noisy, and I was uneasy about Marc trying to get to know me better. Was he doing it because I was Lynn's sister?

Chapter 18

I was up very early the next morning with the early sunshine on the season. I was making my bed when my doorbell rang. It couldn't have been Bertie, because she always knocked.

"Are you Lily Rosenthal?" the mailman asked as soon as I opened the door. "I have this certified letter for you to sign."

"Oh, sure," I obliged.

Out the door he went, and I quickly glanced at whom the letter was from. It was listed as George L. Willis, Attorney at Law. This looked scary. Was someone suing me? I quickly tore it open to read the message.

The first paragraph stated that Mr. Willis was representing the estate of Rosalind L. Langford. This had to mean Rosie. It stated that the inventory of her said address would be for sale, and that Rosalind L. Langford requested that Lily Rosenthal have the first right of refusal on the purchase. I had to read it again before I understood what it meant.

The letter went on to say that the inventory was for sale at the recently-appraised value, which included a list of items, but did not include the building, fixtures, or its name. It then said that I had two weeks to decide before the inventory would be offered to other interested parties.

I sat down at the kitchen table to read the entire letter once again. Why me? I thought I'd made it clear to her that I wasn't interested. When did she decide this?

I wanted to call Mr. Willis and tell him I had no interest whatsoever, but something told me to hold off for a bit. Without knowing much, it seemed like the asking price was very reasonable. Rosie did complain about the antique market being terrible. She said no one wanted those old things anymore.

Who could even advise me on such a matter if I did actually become interested? There was only one person I could think of, and that was Carrie Mae. She would know if the appraisal was fair, and perhaps why on earth Rosie would offer such a thing to me.

I called her at once. Her shop didn't open until ten, but perhaps she would answer from upstairs.

"Good morning," she finally answered.

"Carrie Mae, it's me, Lily," I began. "Will you be in the shop today?"

"Why, sure, honey. I'm not going anywhere."

"I need some advice from you. I'll be there before lunch, if I leave soon."

"That's fine. Be careful!"

I put on jeans and a plaid shirt before putting the lawyer's letter in my purse.

I ran down the stairs and hopped into my SUV, hoping

I would have enough gas for the round trip. My adrenaline was pumping and I didn't know why. Purchasing Rosie's inventory sounded exciting, but operating a business in the neighborhood did not. I couldn't let that happen.

I was hitting rush hour traffic on the highway, but once I got to Weldon Springs, it went smoother. I passed Wine Country Gardens in hopes that I could stop on the way home.

A call from Lynn was coming in, but I ignored it until I got to Augusta. Hopefully it wasn't an emergency.

When I finally arrived, I parked right in front of Carrie Mae's Uptown Store. She had already put extra merchandise out front to start her day. I eyed a Victorian quilt stand that I thought about purchasing. You couldn't have too many of those.

I called Lynn before going inside. When she answered, she was out of breath.

"Where were you?" I asked with concern.

"Downstairs getting some paint. Thanks for getting back to me."

"What's going on?"

"Well, I didn't get to say goodbye to you at the barbeque, and I wondered if you and Marc got together afterwards."

"Oh, for heaven's sake, Lynn, let it go," I advised. "I actually was a little perturbed when he showed up after saying he wouldn't be there."

"What is it about him that you don't like, Lily?"

"Nothing! He's a great catch for someone. I'm focused on other things right now."

"Like what?" she asked with sarcasm.

"Look, I'm at Carrie Mae's in Augusta right now. Is

that all you called about?"

"I guess."

"Well, thanks for looking out for me," I said before hanging up. She ought to be more concerned about that attractive woman hitting on her husband at the gathering, but I thought I'd best not tell her about that.

Chapter 19

"Hey, Miss Lily," Carrie Mae greeted me with a big grin. "You always brighten my day. How can I help you?"

"Is anyone else in the building?"

"Heavens no, honey. I'll be lucky to have five people in on a Monday."

"I guess it's easier for you since you live upstairs."

"Yes, it gives me a lot of options. I love it."

"Do you remember me telling you about a little antique shop in my neighborhood having a robbery? It was called Rosie's, and she was murdered."

"Oh my, yes. Saw it on the news, too. Did they catch the killer?"

"No, but did I tell you that her business was for sale?"

"Maybe you did, but I forgot," she said, sitting down on the stool behind her counter.

"She had just put a "For Sale' sign in her window when that happened. Rosie thought I should buy the place since I liked it so much. She did what she could to try to get me a job, I think."

"Oh, I see."

"Well, I told her I needed a change in my life, but not in the same neighborhood." Carrie Mae nodded in agreement. "So anyway, I got this registered letter from her estate attorney in the mail this morning. Read this." I handed her the letter.

She read it very carefully and then shook her head in disbelief.

"What do you make of that?"

"Well, Miss Lily, you'll have to answer that one," she said with a chuckle. "It seems like the appraisal value is very reasonable, without seeing the itemized list, of course. Do you think family may have taken out some of the merchandise?"

"I have no idea."

"If you purchased the inventory, what would you do with it?"

"I don't know, and why would Rosie want me to have it?"

"It's a slap in the face to the family, I would think," Carrie Mae noted. "There must be a reason she didn't want them to have it."

"I thought that, too. Do you think I can trust the appraiser?"

"Well, when you see the itemized list, you'll have a better idea. I would want to talk to the appraiser in person."

"That's good advice."

"So you're actually thinking about it?"

"Perhaps."

"Well, you need to ask a lot of questions, because they're going to want to rent that space."

"Yeah, you're right."

"To spend that kind of money, you're going to have to

sell the inventory to get a return on your investment. How do you feel about being tied down to a business?"

"It depends. There've been times I've envied you and Rosie, doing what you love. Rosie said retail gets in your system." Carrie Mae smiled and nodded in agreement. "When I think of being in the quilt business, I think I have a feel for it. I love old things for some reason. Both you and Rosie have been complaining about how down the antique market has been, so that isn't very encouraging."

"Yes, but my dear, the market goes up and down. I've lived long enough to see both. There has to be a willing buyer and a willing seller in this business. Timing is everything, and I have to say it's a buyer's market right now, which is good for you."

"That's true."

"You know, success in anything you do is doing what you love. Going to a job that is different every day is better than going to a cookie cutter job like so many folks have."

"You're right. I can't do that again." I thought of my boring desk job.

"You have quite an investment in your quilt collection. What plans do you have for it?"

"My intent has always been to improve it as I buy."

"How do you feel about selling some of the quilts?"

"I could," I said, nodding. "I have some I need to move, and my tastes have changed a bit."

"Well, quilts fit in nicely with other antiques, you know. You could open a shop that carries both."

"Don't get me wrong, I couldn't possibly sell my red-and-white quilt collection."

Carrie Mae laughed. "I can't sell some of my precious

things either. That's okay. You should see what I have upstairs for my own enjoyment."

"Oh, that makes me feel better. I can only imagine." We both laughed.

"Sometime, I'll show you!"

Chapter 20

Carrie Mae called Kate's Coffee Shopand ordered us a couple of roast beef sandwiches for lunch, which she said were very delicious.

"Thanks, I ran out this morning without any breakfast. I'm starved."

"Lily, I want you to take every bit of your two weeks to think about this purchase. This is a big step and investment. I tell ya what; when you arrange a meeting with the appraiser, I'll meet you there and give you my opinion."

"Would you?"

"I don't drive much anymore, but I'll see if my daughter, Susie, can bring me."

"That would be great."

"So will you put everything in storage, if you should buy it?"

"Yes, I suppose."

"You can't sell anything in storage, and I would try to avoid a second move if I were you."

"Oh, it's all crazy, isn't it? I guess I have no business even thinking about any of this."

"You just received the letter, so at least see the inventory before you make a definite decision."

"Okay, I will."

Randal, the owner of the coffee shop, arrived with our sandwiches. He stayed to chat for a while as I complimented him on his shop.

"Carrie Mae, I am so pleased you bought that ungodly yellow house behind you on Chestnut Street," Randal noted. "It really needs some work. It's been vacant way too long."

"Well, like you said, it sat there long enough."

"What do you plan to do with it?"

"The first thing is getting a new roof so I can use the place for storage," Carrie Mae shared.

"Oh dear, I'd better get back," Randal said, looking at his watch. "Enjoy your lunch, ladies!"

We both went to the back room, which was once a kitchen, years ago.

"So where's this house Randal was asking you about?"

"Down the hill," she said, pointing. "You can see a bit of it out the back window because it's bright yellow."

"You must have a lot of help, Carrie Mae," I observed. "I don't know how you do everything."

"I do have good help, especially with moving furniture when I have to. There are plenty of folks around here who can always use a little extra cash."

Customers were starting to come in, so we moved out front to finish our sandwiches. I thanked her for lunch and gave her a big hug for her good advice. I promised I'd keep her posted on my appraiser appointment.

As I drove home, I noticed how the Queen Anne's lace

flowers were starting to open. That meant it was almost time for my June birthday. I needed to concentrate on the birthday trip to Fish Creek. It would be the right time to discuss my possible purchase with my sisters. If I knew them, I was sure there would be three different opinions.

I drove past Rosie's when I got to the neighborhood. I wished I could just go visit her like I used to. I couldn't help but feel that the option to buy her things was a sign for my future. God had a plan for me, and I needed to be listening.

Chapter 21

I made an appointment with the appraiser for the day before Lynn and I would leave for Fish Creek. I called Carrie Mae and told her I'd appreciate her help if she could get away. She said she wouldn't know until she knew Susie's schedule.

I had most of my things packed for the trip, but I still hadn't decided which quilt to give Laurie for her birthday. She loved birds, but the only quilt I had with birds was priceless and was given to me by a dear quilter friend. I had to decide soon.

As I packed, I tried to remember that it was a bit cooler up north than what Missouri was experiencing. When I finished, I finally returned Alex's phone call. I caught him at a good time, so I told him about my opportunity to buy Rosie's inventory.

"Are you out of your mind?"

"I'm meeting with the appraiser tomorrow. Carrie Mae is joining me to give her advice."

"Wow, sounds like a done deal to me," he surmised. "I guess I'll have to help you pack, right?"

"Okay, sounds good. I'll remember that," I said sarcastically.

"And where do you think you'll be going with it, or are you going to rent the same place?"

"I don't know, but I can't stay here in this neighborhood. I can decide more when I see how many boxes will be. She mostly carried smalls, ya know. Before I forget, would you come to Klondike Park to hike with me sometime?"

He laughed. "Where's this coming from?"

"Well, it's out in Augusta and I thought it would be good to have someone with me."

"Is that the park that was a quarry?"

"Yes."

"Sure, sounds cool. Let me know. Back to your purchase; how long will they give you to move everything out?"

"I just don't know. Don't get too excited. This may not happen."

"Yeah, right. My gut tells me otherwise."

"Don't judge me, mister," I joked.

"Have you heard from Mr. Big Spender lately?"

"I take it you mean Marcus. No, I think he's given up on me, which is just fine. I think Lynn and Carl are pushing this."

"Playing hard to get, huh? That's what women do!" I chuckled. "Hey, any word out there on Rosie's killer?"

"None. There are so many killings on TV every night, I don't know how they keep them all straight. Since the killer only stole her money, I keep wondering if Rosie had a secret place where she kept her cash. She wasn't the type to keep a lot in the drawer, I don't think. He may have been hacked off when he didn't find much and shot her in a rage."

"Unsettling. I can't wait to hear what they find out."

When I finally got to bed, all my doubts and fears came to life. I prayed that God would give me guidance on making a good decision. I also wanted Rosie's killer caught. That was a big request that I would have to leave in God's hands.

The next morning, I decided to take a walk in the neighborhood, pick up some coffee, and go peek in Rosie's window.

I said hello to Bertie, who didn't have a clue what I was up to. I listened a bit to her aches and pains before I asked if she needed anything. She waved me on as she sat on the porch looking for Harry.

When I went by Rosie's window, I noticed some things were rearranged. i'd ask the appraiser about that.

I was surprised to see there was still a "For Sale" sign in the window. Perhaps no one else was waiting in line to buy the business like I'd thought. I was sure money was the bottom line for the heirs.

I went back home to shower and change for my one o'clock appointment. I checked on Carrie Mae, and she said Susie was able to bring her. That relaxed my nerves quite a bit.

Lynn called as I was getting dressed to verify the time she'd be picking me up for our trip. I didn't tell her about my appointment. I decided I would tell her on our way to Fish Creek. Hopefully my sisters would be helpful in this matter.

Chapter 22

Mrs. Carter, the appraiser, was already inside the shop when I arrived at twelve forty-five. The door was unlocked, so I went on in.

"Lily Rosenthal?" she greeted me in a pleasant tone. "I'm Gladys Carter."

"Thank you for meeting me here," I said.

"Of course," she replied. "Here is the itemized list of the inventory. The family has taken some of the furniture, so this is what was left. You look around, and if you have any questions, I'll be in the back room."

"Thanks. I'll be having an antiques dealer join me for some advice. I hope you don't mind."

"Of course not. What shop are they from?"

"The Uptown Store in downtown Augusta, owned by Carrie Mae Wilson."

"Oh, I know it well. It's been there a long time. I'm going to lock this door so customers won't be trying to come in."

I began looking at all the incredible antiques. Minutes later, Carrie Mae and Susie knocked at the door. I was relieved.

"I'm so glad you're here," I said, giving Carrie Mae a hug.

"Have you met Susie?" Carrie Mae asked.

"Nice to meet you, Lily. My mom talks about you often." I grinned. Susie looked just like her mother.

I showed them the list, and we each took an aisle to examine. I saw many things I had never paid attention to before. Curiosity got the best of me, so I went to the back room to ask a few questions.

"The last time I was here, Rosie said she had a special quilt put back for me," I explained. "She went to get it and it wasn't there. At that time, she said she was experiencing some shoplifting. Did you find any kind of quilt back here?"

Mrs. Carter thought before she spoke. "No, I can't say I did," she said cautiously.

"Do you think Melanie, her helper, may have removed some merchandise?"

"I've never met a Melanie. I've just dealt with Mr. Willis, the attorney handling the estate. He's the one who told me the family had taken some of the furniture."

"I see," I said, feeling disappointed.

When I returned to Carrie Mae, she was examining the jewelry. She gave me a thumbs up of approval. I went to look at the five quilts that were listed. They were utilitarian and had little value. Textiles were not Rosie's strong point.

Susie was looking at some antique dolls and a toy sewing machine. We all remained silent for a good hour. I made a few notes and asked Carrie Mae if she had any questions.

Mrs. Carter came out from the back room and introduced herself to Carrie Mae. She told her how much she enjoyed her shop.

"So if you make this purchase, will you be taking it to Augusta?" Mrs. Carter asked. I was shocked and didn't know what to say.

"I don't know," I responded. "I plan to take advantage of my two weeks to think about it. I have to go out of town tomorrow. I'm sure I'll have an answer when I return."

"Is this building for rent if she decides to stay here?" Carrie Mae asked Mrs. Carter.

"Yes, but I don't know what the rent will be," she replied.

"There's some lawn furniture behind the building," Carrie Mae noted. "I didn't see it on the list. Can Lily have that?"

"Sure. It has little value and may have been put out for trash pickup," Mrs. Carter casually explained. "You are welcome to it."

We all left the building together and exchanged farewells.

"Do you want to go to Tony's and have a coffee to discuss this?" I asked Carrie Mae and Susie.

They agreed, and I was on pins and needles to hear what they thought.

"So I want your honest opinion," I told Carrie Mae when our coffee was served.

"Okay, you asked," she answered firmly. "If you don't want to buy it, I will. In other words, if you purchase this and don't want to go into business, you can sell it all to me. Her values were very low, especially on the jewelry."

"Really?" I responded in shock.

"She's got a good five hundred dollars' worth of lawn furniture out back, I'll have you know. Those items are hot right now."

"I only know about dolls," Susie began. "I collect them, and I can tell you the values on them are very low. I don't think she knew anything about antique dolls."

"Well, neither do I," I said with a laugh. "Thank goodness you guys were here to help me."

"Now, honey, I'm not saying you need to start a business or anything like that, but if I take it off your hands, you will make a profit. There's still plenty of room to mark things up. She had some pieces I haven't seen in a long time."

"You don't have to do that for me," I said.

"Well, you have a lot to think about on that trip of yours," Carrie Mae replied. "I'm sure you will decide wisely. Whether you buy it or I do, we can store it in the yellow house."

"Thanks, everyone," I said with total gratitude. "I want to do the right thing for me and Rosie."

Chapter 23

I came home with my head spinning. How adventurous should I be? Carrie Mae's offer was beyond helpful.

Lynn would be here shortly to pick me up. I had to decide how much I wanted to tell her, because she'd be advising me for sure, since I was the youngest in the family.

I went downstairs to give Bertie my travel information in case of emergency.

"Honey, I don't know what I'll do without you," she teased.

"You'll love being in charge. Now don't let anyone look at my mail, you hear? I'll only be gone a few days. Has Harry said if there's been any news about Rosie's killer?"

"No."

"Oh dear, here's Lynn. I have to get my bag and go now." I gave her robust body a big hug.

I ran upstairs to get my humongous suitcase and locked the door.

"Good heavens, Lily," Lynn exclaimed when she saw my suitcase.

"I love this suitcase because number one, it's red, and number two, it's huge and holds a lot of quilts. So is Carl okay with you leaving?" I asked as we went on our way.

"Oh, sure. He's a busy man, as you well know. I'm sure he's glad I'm gone." Somehow that didn't sound like Lynn.

"So when do you get time to spend together?" I asked seriously. She shrugged her shoulders.

"Good question. With him becoming a partner, it's rare. I'm pretty busy myself, you know."

"I guess it's a good thing I'm not married," I joked.

"Speaking of, Marc said he's getting the message that you're not interested in him."

"Yes and no. The last thing I want to do right now is get in a relationship when I don't know where I'll be living. But he's a great guy. We had a good time at the ballgame."

"You can chew gum and date at the same time, you know," she teased.

"Okay, because you and I are the closest in the family, I'm going to share something with you about my circumstances right now. I hope to get feedback from all of you, and I hope it's all positive."

"Okay, so let me be your sounding board. I'll bet I can then predict what the others will say." We chuckled.

I began with Rosie's suggestion that I buy her shop, but I really got Lynn's attention when I told her about getting the letter from the estate attorney. To her credit, she stayed quiet until we got to the part about meeting up with the appraiser. She had many questions.

She pulled over to get some gas, and that's when I told her about Carrie Mae's offer to store my inventory in an empty house she'd just purchased. I added that she was willing to purchase the inventory if I changed my mind.

"Unbelievable!" Lynn finally said. "What kind of friend does that?"

"It's a good business deal for her in many ways."

"Did you give her an answer?" I shook my head. "Can you afford this?"

"Yes, barely. It's a buyer's market right now. Carrie Mae admitted all of the values were really low on the appraisal."

We grabbed some fast food and got on our way. I was pleased with how Lynn had received my information.

When we got closer to Green Bay, I wondered why Loretta didn't just let us pick her up.

"She wanted her own transportation," Lynn recalled. "She wanted to leave on her own if she had to. By the way, that whole family happens to be big Packers fans. Have you noticed all the license plates around here?"

"Oh yes, it's their lifeline." We laughed. "Now, I want to be the one to tell Loretta and Laurie," I warned Lynn.

"Mum's the word, but the sooner you do it, the better. I'm anxious to hear their responses. I really think you may be on to something here, Lily. Good luck making the right decision."

"Thanks, Lynn. I was counting on you. If you were against any of this, I'm not sure I could do it."

Chapter 24

After driving through precious villages like Egg Harbor and Sturgeon Bay, we arrived at Fish Creek, which was nestled in a charming valley down the hill. We got a text from Loretta saying that she would meet us at Evergreen Condos around eight. The condos were hidden among the trees, but aligned with the main street of Fish Creek, so they had convenient access to everything.

Lynn and I shared the large bedroom with two beds, and Loretta had the upstairs bedroom to herself. Loretta's room had a good-sized living room and a kitchen overlooking the pool.

We called Laurie and agreed we'd have a casual meal at the Cookery restaurant down the street. It was known for its white fish chowder and mile-high pies. Laurie met us there with totally excited. She was sporting a different hairdo with a streak of red. She was looking more and more like my dad.

"I can't believe you're here!" she gushed when we sat down in a large booth together. "There's so much to do with such little time."

We were famished, so we indulged ourselves. After we finished dinner, we also purchased bakery items and a Cherry pie to have for breakfast over the next couple of days.

When we got back to the condo, Loretta greeted us. She had gained some weight, but looked happy. I loved hearing her talk because she sounded like our mother.

Laurie didn't leave us to go to her home until midnight. We all agreed to say goodnight and that we would meet up at Laurie's shop at ten the next morning.

It was so invigorating to be in a different environment. I could hardly sleep from all the excitement.

After breakfast, the three of us walked to Laurie's shop. We passed other enticing shops I knew I had to visit before I went home.

There was no question that Laurie's shop was the most colorful and appealing one on the street. Her small front yard was packed with glass gourd ornaments, chimes, and trinkets. Inside were mostly small, unusual gift items and her essential oils. I knew I'd have to purchase some things for Holly and Bertie. Laurie was talking a mile a minute, describing everything she had. She had prepared small gift bags of samples for us, which was so thoughtful.

Laurie had arranged for a friend to watch her shop so she could go exploring with us. Lynn and I were mostly focused on clothing at some of the boutiques, while Loretta was into home decorating.

We arranged to meet for coffee down the street at three to plan the rest of our day. I forgot how much fun it was to meander through wonderful shops. Before we knew it, it was time to meet.

We talked, giggled, and bragged about our purchases. I'd found a new black top to wear to that night's dinner. Lynn had purchased one just like it in a different color. Loretta found a mirror for her bathroom, which totally pleased her.

Loretta and Lynn were tired, so they walked back to the condo while I went on to the Hide Side Store to buy something for Alex. It was an impressive shop on the corner that carried everything made out of leather you can imagine. I found a perfect little leather satchel for him to carry a camera in or whatever.

Holly called while I was on my way back to the condo. I could tell she had been crying.

"What happened?' I asked, knowing it would not be good.

"Maurice cancelled my trip to California to see my sister," she revealed. "When I came home from the grocery store, he was so angry because I had left a messy kitchen. I should have known it was too good to be true when he said I could go see her."

"Holly, you don't need his permission to go see your sister. Don't let him do this to you. Make a new reservation."

"It's his credit card, Lily," she complained.

"Okay, I'll loan you the money. Don't let him keep you from your only living family member. Stand up to him, girlfriend."

"Easier said than done. It's just easier to let him have his way. He'll be decent for a little while when he knows he's won."

"I can't stand to hear this, Holly," I said, with anger. "It's your choice. Did you tell your sister?"

"No. She'll be furious with me, just like you are. I'm sorry to call you on your trip, but I didn't know who else to talk to."

"Anytime. Go have a stiff drink and then go knock him down."

"Funny. I will have a drink. When I become an alcoholic, you'll know why."

"You have a choice there, too. Go run up his charge card. That will have a nicer result." She finally laughed.

Chapter 25

I didn't tell the girls about my call from Holly. My sisters were all independent women that would never have tolerated a life like hers.

Everyone looked divine when we got in Lynn's SUV to drive to dinner. The White Gull Inn was the finest restaurant around. They had such history and amazingly good food. If you could afford it, they had elegant rooms for rent in the building next door. Laurie said that on certain nights they had fish boils, but she didn't think that would be our cup of tea.

The elegant charm of the table settings and live harp music playing in the background said we had chosen the right place. We could hear ourselves talk in conversation, which wasn't always possible with some restaurants.

We chose to have their lobster bisque, but the list of fresh seafood entrees was too difficult to choose from. Lynn was our wine connoisseur and wisely chose our wine. From the very first sip, the party began.

We'd finally gotten through the many courses when the waiter brought out a large chocolate birthday cake that said

"Happy Birthday, Lily and Laurie." It reminded me of the many birthdays I'd shared with Laurie growing up. The waiter then announced our birthdays to the two dining rooms, and they all sang that dreaded song we hated to hear. Many toasts were made, and we were getting sillier as time went on.

"Remember, there will be gifts waiting at the condo," Loretta announced.

"I'm spending the night on your couch, because I don't want to miss a thing," Laurie insisted. We all cheered.

When we got to the condo, Laurie insisted I be the first to open my gift. She said it was from the three of them and that I'd better like it. They all laughed.

Through the tissue, I could see the colors red and white. It was a stunning red-and-white sampler of six-inch appliquéd and pieced blocks. I had never seen such an intricate piece like this in a two-color combination. Some woman had to have been insane to have made it. I gasped.

"There are no words!" I exclaimed. "Where on earth did you get this, and how in the world could you all ever afford it?" They looked at one another, and then Lynn broke into tears.

"It's the quilt Rosie was saving for you," she said, choked up. I was stunned into silence. "I stopped there one day, and she said I should tell you she found the quilt. She apologized for the hefty price, but she was going to tell you to make payments, because you'd have to have it. She knew it was rare. When I heard the news about her death, I was so glad I had made the purchase."

"Oh my God!" I gasped, breaking into tears. "I told myself that someone stole it from her. This is unbelievable! Thank you all so much. I'm sorry it was so expensive. I will treasure this forever, you guys!"

"It was meant to be," voiced Loretta. They all were i tears and each gove me a hug.

"Okay, is there anything for me?" Laurie asked to break the emotion.

"Sure, here is mine," I said, handing her a gift bag. She opened it in two seconds.

"A bird quilt!" she exclaimed. "I didn't know there was such a thing. It is beautiful! How could you stand to give this up? It's red and white!"

"You're family, and I figure you might leave this for me in your will," I teased. They all laughed.

Loretta gave Laurie a bathrobe and slippers with red cardinals on them, and Lynn gave her a small bird painting she had done.

"I think this may be the time to share with all of you what has been going on in my life," I began. They suddenly were still and quiet for the first time all evening. "You may forget everything when you wake up tomorrow, but here goes."

They listened intently without interruption. I think some of my words were slurred. Loretta was the most sober of all of us, so I knew I'd get a response from her when I finished.

"Please don't give me advice tonight, but in the morning, after you all have slept on it, let me know your opinions." I could tell, however, that their faces didn't show any objection.

They each agreed, which surprised me.

"Well, then, are there any more secrets my sisters are keeping?" teased Loretta.

All of a sudden, Lynn started crying. Before she could talk, she was sobbing. We all sobered up very quickly. What was this about?

Chapter 26

"My husband is cheating on me," Lynn said between sobs.

"Carl?" Loretta asked loudly. Lynn nodded, and we were stunned.

"No way," Laurie countered. "You must be mistaken."

I was speechless, but a flashback of Carl flirting with that gal Kate jumped into my mind.

"Lily, did you know?" Loretta asked in panic. I shook my head. "Lynn, please calm down and tell us why you think that's the case."

Lynn sniffled, blew her nose, and tried to talk as we waited.

"He isn't denying it," she said finally.

"What?" Laurie screeched. "What man does that? Who is it?"

"Let her talk," instructed Loretta.

"I tried to ignore the usual signs at first, like him coming home smelling like perfume, him working late hours, and his defensive behavior, instead of feeling sorry for myself."

"Carl adores you!" Laurie stated. "I just don't believe it."

"Oh, he said he loves me, but that he's not going to offer any excuses," she replied. "He said I either trust him or I don't."

"Well, that's a bunch of crap," Laurie furiously stated. "Do you think it's somebody at work?"

"I don't know what to think, but I said it had to stop immediately," Lynn stated firmly. "He was never like this. Something is different."

I came over to the couch and put my arm around her. She held her head down in shame.

"Lynn, you are going to get through this, with or without Carl." I said. "If he's sorry at all for upsetting you, he'll change. I doubt he wants to lose you."

"I think he's really angry with me for accusing him," Lynn said. "Isn't that crazy?"

"Well, sure; if he's having a good time, he wouldn't want it to end," Loretta said. "You are an attractive, talented, and intelligent woman who doesn't deserve to be treated like that."

"Oh, guys, I didn't mean to spoil our party," Lynn said tearfully. "I guess the wine made me tell you." We all looked at each other in sadness.

"Hey, we're here for you, sis," Laurie reminded her as she raised her wine glass.

"Thanks," Lynn said, taking a deep breath. "Please don't say anything to him right now until I work this out."

I knew better than to tell her about that Kate I met at her picinic. I'd bet money she was the culprit in this affair.

It was two a.m. before Laurie pulled out her blanket and pillow for the couch. We were all exhausted from all the wine and emotion we had shared. Lynn and I went to our room, and she fell fast asleep. I'd been hoping to get to sleep before her, since she snored something terrible. Now, I felt sorry for her and was glad she could sleep.

Late the next morning, Loretta was the first one up to make coffee. We shared some bagels and discussed our plans for the day. The large antique mall was our main destination, and then we'd meet up for dinner at the popular pizza place across the street called the Red Tomato. It was owned by a friend of Laurie's, who'd invited us to come.

No one brought up their opinion about me purchasing Rosie's antiques, which I took s a good sign.

Once we got to the mall just outside of Fish Creek, we went our separate ways, looking for the things we were interested in. I saw many quilts, but my common sense said I needed to watch my spending in case I needed it for my big purchase. I did weaken when I found a precious doll quilt from the 1860s in scrappy madder prints.

We arrived early at the cute pizzeria. We were exhausted, but not too exhausted to have more wine.

"Okay, sisters, is the jury still out on what I should do regarding Rosie's antiques?" I asked boldly. They looked at each other.

"We know it's perfect for you," Loretta said first. "All those in favor of Lily going for it, say aye."

Everyone raised their wine glasses and said "aye" as loudly as they could.

"Seriously? Does this mean now I have to do this?" I joked. They laughed and nodded.

"Yes, indeed," Lynn exclaimed with a big smile. "You can do this, sister!"

Chapter 27

We had a much more somber night when we returned from dinner. Lynn was dreading going home to Carl, especially since we didn't encourage her to stay with him. Loretta was nervous about planning Sarah's wedding because her in-laws were causing trouble. I seemed to be the only one to have something to look forward to when I got home. I would call Carrie Mae before responding to the lawyer with my firm answer. I felt good now that I had my siblings' approval. I couldn't seem to let go of the red-and-white quilt that originated at Rosie's Somehow it was meant to be.

"Lynn mentioned you have a man named Marcus that has been pursuing you," Loretta said. "How come that secret didn't come out last night?"

"Because it isn't one," I responded. "He thinks the world of Carl and Lynn, so he likes that connection."

"Oh, now, Lily," Lynn argued. "He likes you a lot. He's a good catch and may not always be available."

"Right now, it's a catch I don't need," I stated. "Right

now, I have to decide what to do with all my new old stuff."

"The way I see it," Laurie said, "you have two choices. You can sell it all at a profit to Carrie Mae or open your own shop. By the way, you'd better not sell that quilt we just gave you."

I shook my head. "I'll love it forever!" I said, giving the nearby quilt a gentle pat.

"I think Lily will know what she wants to do when she signs the check," claimed Lynn. "By the way, I offered my help to pack everything. Anyone else available?"

"Oh, I wish I could," voiced Laurie.

"Don't worry," I said, smiling. "Alex and Holly have offered. I'm so happy I have your support," I said with sincerity. "You seem to know I need a change. Holly and Alex were worried that I would decide to move here."

"Now that would be cool!" Laurie joyfully responded. "I could easily help you find a place to rent."

"Now wait a minute, you all," Lynn protested. "She's not moving away from me, and that's the end of that!"

"I'm hoping Carrie Mae will help me find something in Augusta, where my things will be stored. I love those little winery towns. Things keep pointing in that direction."

"Sounds like a good plan," voiced Loretta.

"It's not a done deal, so all options are on the table."

"We just want you to be happy," Laurie said.

By eleven, we all fell into our beds. We all had a long day ahead and wanted to get up early.

Lynn fell asleep very fast, and I just lay there with my eyes open. I knew that on the way home, I'd have to tell her about my suspicions of that Kate I'd met at her picnic. Maybe she already suspected her. I was so disappointed in Carl. I truly loved the guy, and Lynn was such a complement to him. She'd noted that he didn't try to call her once on the trip, which really hurt her feelings.

Between Monster Moe and Carl, why in the world would I want to bring a man into my life?

I made myself think about Rosie's antiques waiting for me. Was my mind already made up? Would Carrie Mae confirming I could use her storage space help me make my decision? Was I really comfortable spending my life's savings? Would I be thankful in the end that Rosie guided me to do this, or would I end up regretting every moment of the experience?

Chapter 28

The four of us shared feelings of sadness as we all prepared to say goodbye. Loretta was the first to leave and said that next time our get-together would include Sarah. We told her to keep us posted about the wedding plans.

Laurie was in tears, but so eternally grateful that we'd made the trip. She seemed to be especially concerned about Lynn and what she was facing. I felt the same and was glad I would be there for her.

Lynn and I thanked Laurie for everything and for how well-planned our days together had been. When she left, Lynn and I looked at each other, embraced, and got in the car to go home.

We were silent for most of the first hour. I think we were recapping our great moments together as a family.

"I worry Carl may have moved out while I was gone," Lynn expressed.

"Surely not!" I replied in disbelief. "Maybe the two of you should go to counseling."

"He had a pretty negative reaction when I suggested it."

"This is a pretty bizarre question, but do you think he wants to be caught or accused?"

"It's not bizarre. I've thought of that myself. He's so defensive that it seems phony."

"You're supposed to say you're sorry, is what he's wanting. I've learned a lot from my friend Holly's husband."

"I'm so sorry she's still putting up with him."

"I am, too. Holly is smart, attractive, and quite funny. Abused women have many excuses to justify staying with their men. It never gets better, only worse."

"I won't let Carl humiliate me," Lynn stated firmly. "If he doesn't want to fight to save our marriage, I don't want him."

I thought carefully about my next question. "Do you know a Kate that Carl works with? She was at your picnic."

"Oh, sure." She nodded.

"You were pretty distracted that evening, but didn't you see the two of them flirting with each other?"

She thought for a moment. "They were having a good time, but they have work in common, so I didn't think anything about it."

"Sister, what I witnessed was more than water cooler talk. When I left, I told Marc to go break them up before Carl got in hot water."

"Really? Are you suggesting he may be having an affair with her?"

"If you decide to play detective, I would start with her."

"I'm so stupid and naïve," she admitted, shaking her head.

"No, you are a sweet person who trusts her husband," I said consolingly.

"Thanks for filling me in, Lily. I'm glad you didn't bring

that up with the others this weekend."

"I'd prepare for battle. He's not going to admit anything, so keep that in mind."

It was seven o'clock when Lynn dropped me off. I was sure Bertie was wondering where I'd been. Luckily, she wasn't on the porch, and I went on upstairs.

I couldn't wait to unpack my birthday quilt and introduce it to the others in the quilt room. I opened it up on the large table and noticed a label for the first time. There was a piece of muslin safety-pinned to the corner of the quilt. It read, "Happy Birthday, Lily, from Loretta, Laurie, Lynn, and Rosie." It was so touching that Rosie was a part of all of this.

"Thank you, Rosie," I whispered as I hugged the quilt. My cell phone rang, and it was Alex.

"Did you just get home?" he asked.

"Yes, just a few minutes ago. How was your weekend?"

"Uneventful without you, sister," he noted. "I want to hear about your trip in the great state of Wisconsin. I'll bet there was a lot of wine flowing and good Wisconsin cheese."

"You're right about that," I assured him.

I then began to describe the chain of events in Fish Creek. When I told him about Lynn's confession, he was furious. I knew how fond he was of Carl and Lynn.

"Does she suspect someone in particular?"

"She has a clue."

"It's sounding pretty juicy. I want to hear more."

"Not tonight you won't. I'm dead tired."

"Tomorrow is actually your birthday, which is why I'm calling. I'd like to take you out for dinner or fix it myself, if you have the time."

"That's very sweet, Alex, but I've been celebrating quite

enough."

"I'll grill some steaks and open a bottle of my best wine," he suggested with excitement. "We'll sit on the porch and watch all the weirdos and criminals drive through the neighborhood. It's better than a movie."

"Okay, I'm in. Can you throw some of your great pasta on the menu? I love it so."

"You've got it."

"Thanks. Signing off!"

Chapter 29

I woke up another year older. This was not helpful in planning my future. I felt as if the clock was ticking on how I would measure my success.

My cell phone rang, and it was Loretta wishing me a happy birthday. She then quickly changed the subject to ask how Lynn was doing.

"She's a big girl, and I'm here for her," I reported. "I want them to keep their marriage if it's at all possible."

"I agree. What do you have planned for tonight?"

"Alex is cooking for me. He's a great cook, so I'm looking forward to it."

"Great. I'll let you go, then."

We'd only just hung up when Lynn called to wish me the same. She was glad I had plans with Alex.

"How was Mr. Carl when you returned?"

"Well, it's puzzling. He's acting as if nothing happened. I think he thinks I'll drop the topic."

"That figures. I'd still have a little visit with Miss Kate if I were you. Tell her that since the two of them are such good friends, you want her opinion on whether Carl is cheating on you."

"Great idea. You're something, Lily!"

"And while you're at it, take note of the smell of her perfume and compare it to what you smelled on Carl."

"Yes, sister!" she replied before we hung up.

I went into the kitchen and pulled a chocolate muffin out of the freezer. I needed a special treat today, I told myself.

My doorbell rang, catching me by surprise. Bertie always knocked. Who could it be?

"Lily Rosenthal?" the gentleman at the door asked, holding a bouquet of red and white flowers.

"Yes."

"These are for you."

I gladly accepted the arrangement of beautiful flowers, which were mostly red roses.

"Oh my, Thank you!"

A card was clearly placed on top for me to see. It read, "Happy birthday from Marc and the Cardinals." Oh my goodness. He was certainly a determined guy. I couldn't remember when I'd last received flowers. I took the arrangement to my quilt room, where the large empty table was happy to receive them. All the red and white together was awesome!

Laurie was the next to call. She was her usual perky self and quickly asked about Lynn.

"She needs support from all of us," I encouraged her. "Carl is pretending that her accusations never happened."

"That creep! I hope Lynn is smart enough to know how he's going to play this game."

"She is. I'm on it, too. Thanks again, Laurie, for such a

great visit. I really love my quilt."

I was so lucky to have all this attention on my special day. I hadn't heard from Holly, which was odd because we always took each other to dinner on our birthdays. She was probably still upset about not being able to visit her sister.

As I'd anticipated, Bertie's familiar knock came at my door. When I opened it up, Bertie was standing there with a birthday cake in her hands.

"Oh, Bertie, how did you know?" I asked as I accepted the cake.

"Honey, I could never forget your birthday. Now, I have to apologize for not baking it myself. I've been a little under the weather, so I had Harry pick one up."

"Oh, it's chocolate, so it should be divine! Thank you so much. I'll slice a piece for you and Harry. I'm going to Alex's for dinner tonight, so I'll share the rest with him."

"That's nice. Did you get those flowers from that handsome young man that's come here?"

"Bertie, how did you know I received flowers?"

She grinned. "Toodle-oo, honey. Enjoy your day," she said, leaving with a chuckle.

As I closed the door, I was very happy to have a cake from a bakery instead of one made by Bertie. The last time she baked for me, she'd gotten the sugar and salt mixed up!

Chapter 30

Alex's place smelled divine when I arrived. His street was lined with Victorian homes that were restored or in the process. Alex's building had been converted into a two-family apartment. He had the luxury of having most of the place to himself, since his landlord traveled most of the time. He took advantage of the large wraparound porch and beautifully landscaped backyard patio.

Alex and I always had so much to talk about. When I reported about my day so far, he suggested I give Holly a call to see if she was all right.

"I suppose I should," I said with a nod.

"Call her while I brew us some coffee for that scrumptious cake you brought. I made us some cupcakes, but those can wait."

I tried to call Holly, but it went straight to her answering machine.

"Do you know that she doesn't turn her cell phone on because she doesn't want her husband to contact her?"

"What?" Alex asked in disbelief.

"It makes it impossible for me to reach her sometimes. How do you help someone like that?"

"It's like any addictive abuse. My friend, Jack, is an alcoholic and I can't help him, either, until he realizes himself that he needs help."

"Oh, this cake is so delicious," I interrupted.

"Happy birthday, Lily Girl!" Alex cheered.

"Oh, Alex, Rosie always called me Lily Girl," I sadly noted.

"Oh, I'm sorry. Hey, let's take our coffee to the porch. This is the time of night that things really get interesting on this street."

Alex and I were a lot alike. We had the same sense of humor, which was great. He got tired of his friends trying to fix him up, just as I did. He was perfectly happy with his life.

When I got ready to leave, he surprised me with a pertinent question.

"Isn't your two weeks about up for getting back to Rosie's attorney?"

I gave a sigh. "Yes, I'm going to call tomorrow and accept their asking price."

"Terrific! What took you so long to tell me? You go, girl! Let me know when we can start packing."

"I will. I'm so glad you approve. Thanks for dinner. It was just the way I wanted to spend my birthday."

We hugged each other and he watched me drive off.

When I got to my neighborhood, it was so very peaceful. I quietly made it into my little apartment with a smile on my face. Tomorrow would be the day of commitment. Carrie Mae had given me options, which really helped. I somehow knew that if I took one step at a time, my answers would come. It was a good way to end my happy birthday.

When I awoke, I was breathing heavily from a very disturbing dream. Perhaps it had evolved from my indecision regarding my future. I'd dreamt I was lost and was asking directions. When someone asked where I was going, I couldn't tell them.

I got up in frustration with a slight headache. It was only four a.m., but I went out onto the porch to regain my senses. I dozed off on the couch until five, when the trash hauler made a loud noise. I was now ready for coffee. I took my coffee mug and checked my emails.

I saw a happy birthday email from Holly, but she didn't mention the dinner. What was going on with her? I always prayed that God would show her a way out of her situation, but perhaps she wasn't listening.

I showered and dressed, planning to make my big phone call around nine.

Chapter 31

At nine o'clock sharp, I picked up the phone and called Mr. Willis. I was surprised that he was the one answering the phone.

"It's good to hear from you, Ms. Rosenthal," he greeted me. "How are you today?"

"I'm good, and I have an answer for you regarding Rosie's inventory," I stated. "I wish to exercise my option to purchase."

"Very good," he responded.

"I have some questions regarding how much time I have."

"Sure. The way the agreement reads, as soon as you provide your approved financial statement, you can start removing the merchandise. If I recall, you won't be renting this building, so you'll have thirty days to evacuate."

"Oh, that's very good," I said in relieved. "I'll be cashing my savings in various capacities, so it won't take long to pull together."

"Excellent. Just let me know when you're ready so we can

arrange for you to sign on the dotted line. Congratulations. I look forward to hearing from you."

I hung up feeling I had taken the first step. I didn't really know who I should tell. I decided to send a group email to my sisters so they could all know at once. It would be a brief "stay-tuned" message.

Within minutes, Lynn called and was happy about my decision.

"I could really use your help to pack," I reminded her.

"No problem. Just tell me when. I am so happy for you."

"How are things with Carl?"

"He continues to pretend nothing is wrong."

"And how is that working for you?"

"Not well."

When we hung up, I called Carrie Mae.

"I was hoping I'd hear from you today," she said.

"All I need to do is take my check and sign the papers," I stated. "I can't believe I'm doing this!"

"It's wonderful, honey. I'll get that Chestnut house all cleaned up so it's ready to store things. The furnace is relatively new, so we can keep the temperature regulated. The new roof is finished."

"That all sounds good. I don't know how I can ever thank you."

"I'm sure we can work out a trade or two on some of that fantastic stuff you just purchased." I chuckled.

When I hung up, I weakened and called Holly. The phone rang and rang. Finally, she picked up the phone.

"Hello," she whispered.

"Holly, are you okay?"

"Yeah, why?"

"You didn't call to have dinner on my birthday." There was silence as if she hadn't heard me.

"I have to go," she whispered. "I'll get back to you."

I well knew from prior conversations that Monster Moe had come back into the room. What was she going through right now? Despite Moe's desire to keep me away, I thought I might stop by her house anyway.

It was almost noon, so my goal was to arrange for my money to be funneled into my account so that I could write Rosie's estate a check. On my way to the bank, I called Alex.

"You didn't change your mind, did you?" he quickly asked. I laughed.

"I'm on my way to the bank, so I thought you'd want to know."

"Awesome! Let's meet for drinks tonight and celebrate."

"Not just yet. Wait until I sign the papers."

"Okay. I'll go ahead and gather boxes and put them in my car."

"Good thinking, and I'll be able to pick some up from Tony and Al's as well."

"Good luck!" Alex said as we hung up.

The visit to the bank went easier than I'd expected. Just like that, money could be moved however I preferred with a stroke of the pen. The bank officer was very interested in my plans and offered to help me get a future loan if I needed it.

With that done, tomorrow I would sign papers and pick up a key. Could this really be happening? I thought of Holly, so I drove to her neighborhood. It was a beautiful area. It was such a shame Holly could never entertain friends in her lovely home.

I desperately knocked on the door, knowing someone

had to hear me. I thought I saw movement through one of the windows. I was shocked when Maurice answered the door.

"Holly is not here, and by the way, you are not welcome here at any time. Please leave the premises."

"What? You have no business telling me that." I yelled.

"This is my house and you need to get off of my property."

"It's Holly's house, too!" I said as he slammed the door in my face.

I wanted to do something really mean, but thought that if Holly were inside the house, he may do something really bad to her.

I drove away wanting to report his behavior to someone. I was probably one of few people who cared enough for Holly to continue the fight. Many didn't know about her abuse.

Chapter 32

When I got out of neighborhood, I pulled over and called her number. I had to leave a message for her to call and hoped that she received it.

I was about to pull into a car wash when my cell rang. I answered quickly, thinking it might be Holly calling back.

"It's Alex," the familiar voice said. "Have you seen the news?"

"No, why?"

"They've arrested a suspect in Rosie's murder case."

"Oh, that's great. I'll turn it on when I get home. What did they say?"

"Evidently it's a young kid that did some odd jobs for her every now and then."

"A kid?"

"Well, he may have been twenty, but he looked pretty young, from what I could tell."

"Was he from the neighborhood?"

"Good question. You'd better ask Bertie or Harry."

"Don't worry, I will."

"Say, by the way, did you get the cash?" he asked, referring to my bank visit.

"I did for one day. Tomorrow, I will owe my soul to the company store." He laughed.

I couldn't wait to hear the evening news. I stared at the TV with a glass of wine, and finally, I saw him. I couldn't say I had seen him before. His bail was quite high, so I didn't think he'd be going anywhere. When the report ended, Bertie was knocking at my door.

"Did you see it? The TV, I mean."

"Yes, do you know him?" She shook her head. "I bet somebody has to recognize him," I commented.

"Harry said he probably wanted drug money and knew she had some cash around," Bertie claimed. "Poor Rosie."

"Oh, Bertie, my cell is ringing in the kitchen. I have to go."

"It's me, Holly," a somber voice said when I picked up the phone.

"How are you?"

"I'm so, so sorry, Lily. I can't believe Maurice talked to you that way."

"You don't need to be sorry. Were you home?"

"Yes. He yelled and screamed about you showing up. He said I was to have nothing to do with you anymore. He claims you will only take advantage of me."

"What is he talking about?"

"I know, I know. He's crazy, Lily."

"I've told you before, there's a hotline you can call, with a lunatic like this."

"Don't you understand? It will only make things worse!"

"You are dead wrong about that. He's going to hurt you

and maybe even kill you, from what you've said. Now I'm on his blacklist."

"He's likely all talk," she protested. "The reason I'm calling is that he's supposed to go out of town for a couple of days, so we can have that birthday dinner. Are you free tomorrow night?"

"Absolutely!"

"How about Zia's at six?"

"I'll be there."

I hung up with such anger for what Moe kept putting Holly through. I hoped he wouldn't chain her to her bed while he was gone. I'd put nothing past him.

Holly and I meeting for dinner on the night I would sign for the inventory was pretty exciting. Hopefully nothing would interfere with our plans.

The rest of the evening was dedicated to making lists of what I would have to do in the next thirty days. I wanted to keep the news of my investment quiet for a while. Everyone would just ask me about "what's next," and I wouldn't have an answer. Somehow, I didn't think I was in charge of whatever was about to happen.

Chapter 33

Mr. Willis told me which lines to sign on, and just like that, I was the owner of Rosie's inventory.

"Congratulations, Ms. Rosenthal," Mr. Willis said, shaking my hand. "I think Rosie would be very pleased to know you took advantage of this offer. Here is your key. The locks will change after your thirty days, so let us know when you're completely out of there."

"I will. Thanks so much."

Off I went, half-scared and half-excited about what may be in my future. I couldn't resist going by Rosie's shop to assess where to start.

When I unlocked the door, I felt as if I wasn't supposed to be there. I turned on some of the lights in the dark, dusty shop and looked around to decide what I may not want to bring with me. I wanted to start cleaning the place, but that would be a waste of time in the packing process. I reminded myself to bring the inventory list so we could mark things off as we packed to make sure everything was accounted for. Tomorrow, I would begin the task of packing with whoever could help me. I locked the door, feeling as if Rosie or someone else were watching.

Bertie greeted me on the porch. I knew this may be the best time to tell her about my purchase.

"So what have you been up to?" she asked as always. "You were up pretty early this morning."

"I took care of some business," I said, smiling.

"Did you get a job?"

"Yes and no," I teased. "I purchased Rosie's inventory from her shop." Her look was priceless.

"You what? You bought her store? How wonderful!"

"No, no, not quite," I said, shaking my head. "I bought her inventory. I'm putting it in storage until I decide what to do with it. Someone else will be renting her spot."

"Now, that doesn't make sense, Lily," Bertie said with a tone of anger in her voice. "Why would you do that?"

"Rosie encouraged me to do so. She knew I wanted a fresh start somewhere. I have some ideas, but I'll likely be moving in the next couple of months."

Her face turned to fear. "To where, for heaven's sake?"

"Well, my things will be stored in Augusta, where I frequently go, so I'll probably end up there."

"You don't mean it," she finally said. "This is your home."

"This is your home," I replied in a kind tone. "I want to do something I enjoy involving my quilts."

I thought she was going to start crying. "I can't believe what I'm hearing," she said in disbelief.

"I'll give you plenty of notice, but right now, I don't know where I'll be going."

Bertie went inside her apartment with disbelief and likely anger. I was grateful that Bertie had never required me to sign a lease.

I called Lynn right away to see if she was available for packing. She was thrilled and said she would be at the shop at ten. Alex was next on my list, expecting my call and willing to help.

"You can only look ahead, honey," Alex encouraged me. "I'll see you tomorrow!"

I felt my news was important enough to call Laurie and Loretta rather than email. I had to leave messages for both of them, but I knew they would be very excited for me.

I was gathering cleaning supplies for the next day when my phone rang.

"Congratulations!" Marc said right away.

"For what?" I innocently asked.

"Lynn just told me about your purchase. I think it's great." Leave it to my gabby sister to tell him right away.

"Thanks, but we'll see where it goes from here."

"How about I take you to dinner tonight to celebrate?" Marc asked with excitement.

"Thanks, but I'm meeting a friend for dinner."

"Another rain check?" he teased. "They're adding up, you know."

"I'm sorry, but there's a lot going on right now. I'll start packing up the place tomorrow."

"Lynn said you're moving it all to Augusta."

Lynn talks too much, I said to myself. "Yes, an antique dealer has an empty house where I can store everything."

"That's convenient. Will you be opening a shop there?"

"I haven't gotten that far. I'll let you know."

He finally got the hint that he was being a bit nosy, so we hung up. How was I supposed to answer those questions?

Did everyone have their own ideas about what I should be doing?

Holly arrived early at the restaurant for dinner. I was so happy to see her. We commented about how much we loved this place. Zia's was probably one of the most popular restaurants on The Hill.

"I'm treating, so let's splurge," Holly chuckled. "It's your birthday, by golly!"

We started with a merlot that Holly chose from the list. She ordered the seafood ravioli and then encouraged me to try pomodori fritti, which was fried tomato slices topped with melted Italian cheese.

We loved Zia's house salad, and for our entrees, Holly ordered the portabella asparagi and I chose mostaccioli al forno, which featured grilled chicken, bacon, broccoli, tomatoes, and mushrooms. It was baked with Italian cheese and breadcrumbs. Everything was rich, heavy, and sinful.

Holly said Moe had called her today several times, which seemed to please her. Who does that? Did she think it was a sign of affection?

"He doesn't know about our dinner, I take it?"

"Heavens, no. I told him I was going to see my niece and we may go out to dinner. Oh, here's my gift. I almost forgot."

She handed me a small, beautifully-wrapped box. Holly had great taste, so I was excited.

I unwrapped a stunning gold bracelet. that fit my skinny wrist which was unusual.

"It's solid gold, Lily," she bragged.

"Holly, you are crazy to spend that kind of money on me. Something tells me that one day you're going to need every penny you can get your hands on."

She dismissed my comment. "While I can do it, I'm going to."

"Thank you so very much. I will treasure this. And I have some good news to share tonight," I boasted.

"What, what?"

When I told her my purchase was definite, she had a look of joy that changed to concern.

"Does that mean you'll be moving?" she asked in fear.

"In time, but not out of state or anything like that," I consoled her. "I just don't know, but I have to make a change."

Chapter 34

Holly and I were stuffed to the max and asked for to-go boxes for our leftovers. When we hugged goodbye, Holly got a serious look on her face.

"Take me with you, please. I'll go anywhere to get away from him."

"Believe me, I'd love to. Someday you'll get the courage to leave him, so we can make that happen." I wondered if she was really serious. "Thanks so much for this amazing dinner."

"My pleasure, girlfriend," she said as I walked away to my car.

I came home wanting to crash in my bed as fast as I could, but after I got into my pajamas, the phone rang. Who could it be at this hour?

"He's home," Holly whispered.

"He got home tonight?" I asked to make certain.

"He said he changed his mind. He asked where I was." I could hardly hear her.

"Oh dear, what did you tell him?"

"I said I went to see my niece. I have to go." She hung up.

That was the end of that. I guessed he was hoping to catch her doing something while he was gone. Wait until he saw the charge from Zia's. We would both be in trouble.

It was such an empty feeling, not be able to help her. So much for her commitment to help me pack tomorrow. It wasn't going to happen with him home. She didn't realize that his frequent phone calls were to track her whereabouts. He seemed to tell her one thing and do another. How could anyone live with someone like that?

I laid there watched the news, hoping to get my mind off of Holly. There were so many murders that it only made me think of Rosie once again. Why were there so many evil people in the world? And I also had Lynn and Carl to worry about.

I finally went to sleep, but awoke very early from tossing and turning all night. I got up and faced the world with a cup of coffee on the porch. The morning's heat and humidity reminded me that summer was alive and well in Missouri.

I left early for the shop despite Lynn and Alex not coming until ten. Bertie wasn't on her porch, which was unusual. I stopped by Tony's to get coffee and a bagel. I wished I could share my news with him, but it was just too premature.

When I walked into the shop, I was reminded that the familiar smell and merchandise were all mine. I took my personal things to the back room, which also had a small kitchenette. They had kept the electricity on, so I had cold bottled water in Rosie's 1950s refrigerator if I needed it.

The first thing I did was post the inventory list for everyone to see so they could mark things off. I went ahead and checked off the five quilts that were going home to my quilt room instead of to storage. I planned to examine each one's condition to see if any needed washing or mending. My favorite in the bunch was a blue scrappy Tumbling Blocks design.

As I opened the back door for fresh air, Lynn walked in the front door. "You might want to keep this door locked unless you want customers today," she cautioned.

"Oh, I forgot. I have to become more businesslike, I suppose."

Lynn nodded with a smile. "My goodness, Lily, you sure don't look businesslike with those holey jeans of yours," she teased.

"You know these are my favorites, so knock it off and get to work."

As Lynn put her purse in the back room, Alex knocked on the door. He had lots of boxes in his hands.

"Just put them in the back room. I'm really glad to see you."

After a small chat between us, I began assigning them areas to pack. Alex was to start on lamps, some of which were attached to the ceiling. I pointed out which one was Tiffany and told him that he had to be extra careful. Lynn spotted the jewelry case, so I let her decide how to pack it.

"Where's Holly?" Lynn asked. "I thought she was going to be here to help."

"She is forbidden to hang out with me," I stated with a sigh.

"You're referring to Monster Moe, I presume?" Lynn asked.

Alex shook his head in disbelief.

"How is your monster, if I may ask?" I said to Lynn.

"Oh, he is trying to be very sweet and considerate these days," she replied.

"Watch your back, Lynn," Alex warned.

I showed Lynn which boxes to pack the jewelry in and told her and Alex about the importance of checking off each item as they packed. I took a few minutes to nose around in Rosie's little office. Seeing her writing on so many things was creepy in some way.

"Lily, look over here," Alex called. "I think this is some of Rosie's blood from the shooting."

We slowly gazed at what appeared to be a splattering of blood on the wooden counter. I froze, picturing the gruesome scene.

"I'm glad you aren't staying here," Alex noted. "You don't know how safe it will be for the next person that occupies this space." I nodded with a sad face.

Finding Rosie's blood put a damper on what could have been a fun day with my best buds. We took a lunch break at Rigazzi's, which was the high point of our day.

"Marc was sure disappointed you didn't go to dinner with him last night," Lynn brought up.

"Good heavens, does he tell you every little move he makes with me?"

She laughed as if she didn't take my criticism seriously. "Don't be so hard on him," she said. "He's just trying to figure you out. I told him to back off a bit and that no one has been able to figure you out!"

Alex roared with laughter. "Good response!" he joked.

Chapter 35

When we got back to the shop after lunch, Holly arrived.

"Hey, girlfriend, I didn't think you could come!" I greeted her.

"Maurice thinks I'm at the grocery store," she explained, with frustration. Alex gave her a strange look. "I felt so bad for deserting you when you need all this help. I can stay for a little while."

"Here, Holly, wrap these in this tissue," Lynn instructed. "We're glad you came, and Lily does need our help."

"I can't believe there's so much stuff," Holly noted. "I've only been here a couple of times. Hey, what's the deal on the old radios? I collect these."

"Well, I'll be happy to sell them to you once I get my sales tax and ID number," I quipped, smiling.

"Okay, it's a deal. Don't sell these to anyone else."

"You will be my first sale, if I ever get that far," I reassured her.

"Well, see, I'm good for something!" Holly joked.

We all knocked off at about five. I wondered what poor

Holly would tell her husband. I couldn't thank everyone enough. Lynn and Alex had taken time off from their work and Holly was risking abuse. I invited them for a drink somewhere, but everyone was tired and wanted to go home. I looked forward to a cold shower myself after all this dust.

When I got out of the car in front of my apartment, I saw Bertie sitting on the porch. As I approached the sidewalk, she went inside. There was no doubt that I was being shunned for my confession.

When I got inside, I sent a group email to my sisters, bragging about the progress and how Lynn came through for me. I knew they would appreciate an update, and I told them I would continue the mission tomorrow by myself. I attached a photo of Lynn surrounded by tissue paper and boxes.

Loretta immediately responded, saying she wished she could be there to help. She ended the email mentioning that Sarah was having second thoughts about getting married. She said she couldn't help but think about all the deposits they had made for the wedding. I guessed the in-laws were making progress with their objections.

I wanted to call Carrie Mae and give her an update, but it was getting late. While I was on the computer, I took the time to google Augusta, Missouri. Google gave me a map showing the different districts, which, for me, was new. Carrie Mae's shop was in the Uptown district, which was appropriate since her shop was named Uptown Store. I was shocked at all the new B&Bs and restaurants. The museum and library were also of interest to me.

Augusta was founded by zLeonard Harold. The town was named in 1855 and incorporated a special charter town. The mostly-German immigrants were attracted to the area because of Gottfried Duden's glowing descriptions.

It was mostly a farming community until the 1870s, when the Missouri River changed its course, leaving Augusta without a boat landing. Instead, they were left with rich, fertile bottom land. The hills were perfect for growing grapes, which spurred much interest. In the 1960s, tourists began to notice. They were more than pleased to check out the romantic wine country.

In 1980, Augusta was recognized as the first US wine district, or Viticulture Area #1. The rolling hills' wine country has been an attraction ever since.

Chapter 36

When I left the apartment the next morning, Bertie was not in sight. I thought for a moment that she might be ill, but decided instead that she was sending me a message about my moving from here.

I stopped by Tony's to get a coffee and bagel.

"Good morning, Lily," Tony greeted me. "A little bird told me that you bought Rosie's shop. If that's true, you know we would all be delighted!"

"I appreciate that, but actually, the shop will be available next month for someone to rent," I revealed. "I did buy her inventory, and may open my own shop one day."

"That's great, but why not here?"

"I haven't decided," I said, trying to put him off. "I'll need this month to get everything packed."

"Well, I'm glad they have someone in custody," Tony noted. "I remember seeing that guy around. I heard they're trying hard to get him to confess and get him convicted."

"He deserves whatever comes to him," I replied. "I'll keep you posted, Tony."

"Thanks, sweetheart," Tony said, giving me a wave goodbye.

I opened the musty, dirty shop and went directly to the back door to let in some fresh air. I'd decided last night that I would start with the stacks and basketfuls of linens Rosie'd had for sale. Her prices were cheap enough, but so many needed love and attention. As I examined each piece, I wondered who might have made them and for what purpose. So much time went into things that were utilitarian. There was a fancy laundry bag with beautiful embroidery and lace. Who would put all that time into this just to use it as a laundry bag? Throughout the shop, large dining room tablecloths and napkins sat without attention. No one wants to wash and iron anymore for any occasion.

I took a break and called Carrie Mae. She said she was curious about my progress.

"Is the house ready for things to get moved in? With Alex and Lynn helping box everything, I thought I could move a lot of the boxes myself. I'll need a van for the furniture."

"Not just yet, Lily," she replied. "We had a plumbing problem that turned into a much bigger project than I expected. That's what happens when you buy these old, dilapidated buildings."

"Oh, I'm sorry. I hope you're not going to all this trouble because of me."

"Nonsense; I'm used to it. When will you be out again?"

"I have only thirty days to get out of the building, so I'll have to see how the packing goes. I'll give you plenty of notice."

"I'll be here. I wish I could be there to help you. I could

educate you on some things as we packed them."

"I wish you could, too. It's really good for me to touch and examine each item before it's stored away."

"Well, enjoy the process, and we'll see you soon," she said as we hung up.

I went back to the linens, and Alex called. He said I deserved a drink and dinner after my day, so I should come by his place when I was finished. I told him I looked deplorable, but I did think having something to look forward to would be good for me.

I finished the linens and decided a short packing job was in order. Rosie had a shelf above her counter that was lined with vintage cookie jars. They were funny and reminded me of my childhood. Rosie had always tried to get me to buy the red-and-white clown jar, because it was red and white. I told her I hated clowns. I think they are scary.

I got the shorter stepladder and got one jar down at a time to pack. The first one was a chubby chef. The jars made me smile as I removed their heads for packing. The next was Mickey Mouse. When I removed the head, I noticed there was a note inside in Rosie's handwriting. It read, "Lily, I still think you should take another look at the red-and-white clown for your kitchen." How would she have even known I'd be looking at any of these cookie jars? It was an eerie thought. When I finished packing Mickey, I brought down the clown, which was heavier than the others. I opened the jar, and it contained a paper bag filled with something, with a note on top. It read, "Lily, I always kept a little stash for something special. I think you'll find a way to turn this into gold. Love, Rosie."

She'd left something for me? Why hadn't she said

anything? What could it be?

I opened the twisted paper bag, and inside was paper money. There was lots of money, stacks and wads of it! Rosie certainly didn't mean I could have all this cash. What about her family, like her nephew? No one must have known it was there. I quickly twisted the jar back shut. This wasn't happening.

Chapter 37

How did Rosie accumulate all of that money? Was that the reason she was robbed in the first place? Who did I tell? What did I do now?

I took the bag to the back room in case anyone was looking in the window. I put the note inside and then placed the money bag inside a new paper bag so I could take it home. I couldn't risk keeping it here. I needed to leave immediately.

As I left the building, I felt nauseous trying to digest it all. I needed someone to talk to about this. I called Alex and said I was coming early and would explain when I got there.

I could hardly drive, I was so nervous. Luckily, I found a parking spot not too far from Alex's apartment. I hoped I didn't look conspicuous as I walked to his door.

I knocked hard, trying to let him know this was urgent.

"Hey, Lily!" he greeted me with a hug. "You didn't have to bring anything."

"Oh, wait until you see what I've brought," I said as we went up his stairway. "Can I have some wine first before I show you?"

"Geez, Lily," he responded. "You must have had a bad day!"

I stayed quiet while I watched him pour me a glass of wine. I wondered where I should start.

"Are you hungry?" I shook my head. "Okay, so what's up? You look like you've seen a ghost."

"I was packing Rosie's cookie jars and found this note and bag in the red-and-white clown jar. Rosie always tried to get me to buy the clown because it was red and white."

"Wait, slow down,'" Alex interrupted.

"Before I got to the clown cookie jar, I opened the Mickey Mouse jar, and it had a note addressed to me saying I should reconsider buying the clown. So I took the clown's head off, and this was inside." I held up the bag I'd brought. "There was a note addressed to me on top of the bag."

I opened the bag and gave the note to Alex to read. When he finished, I opened the bag so he could see all the cash. He looked astonished, as I'm sure I must have.

"You've got to be kidding me!" Alex yelled as he stood back.

"I can't believe she really meant for me to have this. Is that what you got out of this note?"

"Yes siree! I don't see anyone else's name on this. It's pretty obvious she didn't want anyone else to have it."

"It doesn't make sense. We were just acquaintances."

"Look, she would have left the entire inventory to her nephew if she'd wanted him to have it. Instead, she chose to sell it, and you were the first person she thought of. Did you count it?"

"Count it? I didn't even touch it!"

"Look at all the big bills she's got in here. This wasn't just petty cash. She may not even have realized how much she had in here. Let's count it."

I took a deep breath, wondering if we should touch it. "Make sure you have all the blinds closed," I cautioned. He chuckled and shook his head.

"Let's sort the bills by denomination. Good grief, here's a five-hundred-dollar bill. I've never seen one."

"Here are some twenties, but it appears to be mostly fifty- and hundred-dollar bills. Here are some new ones that are sticking together, like they just came from a bank."

"I always heard antique shops were cash cows, but this is ridiculous," Alex stated.

"She never took charge cards, which I thought was strange. She just said it was too expensive. She did take checks, because I wrote her one every now and then."

"Yeah, a lot of small shops don't take cards. There's a little spice shop I go to that doesn't take plastic either. They claim their sales aren't big enough to justify it. Now we know how Rosie ended up with so much cash."

I poured more wine as I watched Alex add up the bundles. Some of the bills had rubber bands around them. We had to laugh now and then about the surreal experience.

Before we did the adding on the calculator, we washed our hands, commenting on who all may have handled this money.

We counted in silence until the total appeared on the tape. We looked at each other in disbelief.

"Holy mackerel," Alex said. "There's almost fifty thousand dollars here!"

"That is crazy!" I responded.

"I'd imagine she was stashing this away for quite some

time. This was a savings account in some way for her."

"I wonder when she put the note in the jar."

"How long has it been since she encouraged you to buy the place?"

"Quite a while. As soon as she decided to sell, she mentioned it. I think she felt sorry for me for not for having a job."

"I'll say she did. It's interesting how many folks don't want to leave their estates to their family. I think she had her reasons for leaving this to you."

"How did she know I would take her up on the offer to buy?"

"Maybe she was just hoping. So what will you do with this?"

"Oh, Alex, I can't keep this."

"And why not? I don't see anyone else's name on this bag. She knew you would need money to buy that inventory, so there ya go!"

Chapter 38

Alex finally convinced me to eat one of his creative toasted cheese sandwiches, which he always bragged about. It went well with our wine, and I certainly wasn't in the mood to eat out somewhere.

"You've got to deposit this in the bank first thing tomorrow, or even today," Alex advised.

"I can't walk into the bank with this kind of cash. They'd call the police for sure."

"Well, it's not going to be very safe hidden in your apartment."

"I think I have to take it to her estate attorney. I'm not comfortable keeping this unless I am entitled to it from her note."

Alex looked disappointed. "I think you're asking for trouble, but if that's what makes you more comfortable, go ahead."

"Her family had to know she had more money somewhere."

"There are a lot of mattress bankers out there in this

world that don't trust the banks, especially if they've been through the depression."

"Mattress bankers?" I questioned.

"Yeah. Years ago, people hid a lot of money under or in their mattresses."

"Oh dear, well, I'd better get home," I said, putting the piles of money back into the bag.

"Man, I'll never see this much money in one place ever again," noted Alex. "Be sure you pick a safe place in case someone breaks in and suspects something."

"Oh, thanks, Alex. Now I really feel safe."

Alex walked me to the car and watched me drive away.

When I got to my dark, quiet neighborhood, I felt I needed to stay up all night and guard my discovery.

I took the money to the kitchen. When I saw my only cookie jar sitting on top of the refrigerator, I got it down and stuffed all the money inside. If a cookie jar was safe enough for Rosie, it would be safe enough for me. The sunflower-shaped jar had been a gift from Loretta years ago.

When I finally got into bed, I wasn't worried about the safety of the money, but wondered why on earth Rosie wanted me to have all of it. I knew somehow in the back of my mind that once I turned this over to the estate, I'd never see it again.

When morning came, I went into the kitchen and stared at the cookie jar. I called Mr. Willis's office before I changed my mind, and the receptionist said he'd be in at one if I wanted to stop by. I felt relieved somehow. I decided I would not take the money with me, for some reason. I did take a photo of it and slipped the note into my purse.

When it was close to one o'clock, I double-checked my door locks and left.

I had to wait a half hour in Mr. Willis's office before I could see him. When I walked in, he looked surprised to see me.

"You're finished packing already?" he asked.

"Oh, no, not yet. I came to tell you about something I found in one of Rosie's cookie jars with a note addressed to me."

"I see. What was it?"

"Something amazing. I was touched that she wanted me to buy the shop, but this really shocked me."

He stared at me with anticipation. "It appears she was fond of you, and it's not unusual for someone to find a little something addressed to them after folks pass away."

"Oh, I don't think you understand. It wasn't just a little something. It was a significant amount of cash."

Now I had his attention. "How much?"

When I awkwardly repeated the total, he looked like he was going to have a stroke. He sat down behind his desk.

"Are you sure? It didn't look like counterfeit money, did it?" I shook my head. "Did you suspect she had more money somewhere?"

"I really didn't know her very well. She left some savings to her church. What about the nephew?"

"He got something, but I can't divulge what," the lawyer said as he shook his head. "I think he'd had his hopes up for the contents of the shop. He's quite puzzled as to why it was offered to you."

Chapter 39

"I think for the time being, Lily, you need to bring us the money. We need to verify that the note was written in her handwriting and whether there was any other intent for her hiding it there."

"Did she leave a lot of debt?"

"Let's just say that Rosie did okay for herself. To our knowledge, she didn't owe anything in back taxes. If everything checks out, you will be a much richer woman."

I smiled at the thought, but knew it was premature to think about it. I told him I would bring the money over later in the day.

When I got back to the apartment, Harry was walking my way.

"Hey, Harry, I haven't seen you in a while," I greeted him.

He wasn't smiling. "I hear you're moving," he grumbled.

"Someday, but not anytime soon," I answered. "Bertie's in a state about it, isn't she?"

He nodded. "If there's anything you don't want, it's to

get Bertie in a tither," he complained. "I'm sure glad you bought Rosie's business, but I wish you would stick around here where you belong."

"That's sweet, Harry," I said with a smile. "I'll keep you posted on my plans. In the meantime, see what you can do to cheer Bertie up."

"Nobody tells Bertie what to do," he mumbled under his breath. "She's as tough as nails."

"Is that why you're so soft on her?" I teased.

"Hey, get on, would you?" he said, waving his hand.

Before I delivered the money, I took another photo. Something told me that if this money disappeared, I may have to prove it existed. I called ahead to Mr. Willis's office to make sure that when I got there, I could put it directly into his hands and not someone else's.

He was waiting for me and said the money would go directly into the office safe.

"Would you mind signing a receipt for this?" I politely asked him.. "It's not that I don't trust you, but I don't want to be accused of anything."

"Sure. Write down what you want, and I'll sign it."

I simply wrote down the amount of cash with the date and that there was the personal note that was left for me.

"You are a decent, honest friend of Rosie's," Mr. Willis said. "Most folks wouldn't have reported this."

"You'll let me know as soon as possible?"

"Absolutely."

We shook hands, and out the door I went. I wondered if Mr. Willis would tell anyone about what just took place.

I picked up a ham sandwich at Tony's before I went to the shop to continue my packing. Once again, I opened the back door to let in some fresh air.

My next project was to start packing sets of china that Rosie'd had for sale. I had seen the same sets ever since I'd started coming to Rosie's, so knew they must not be selling. Folks weren't entertaining like they used to. One of the sets of china was Haviland. I knew that eventually a collector would make the purchase. Boy, if these dishes could talk!

I happened to glance towards the front of the shop and thought I saw Melanie peeking through the window. I quickly put down my wrapped cup and headed to the door so I could catch her.

By the time I got my keys to open the door, she was gone. She certainly had a right to be curious, I supposed. Why didn't she just knock and say something? Did she have any clue that Rosie had hidden money in the shop? I also wondered what kind of relationship she had with Rosie's killer. They might have known one another, since he may have helped Rosie.

When I finished packing the set of Haviland, I glanced over to where I'd left the cookie jars. There sat the red-and-white clown and two other jars to be packed. One was a gingerbread jar and the other was a Dutch girl. The more I looked at the clown, the more I felt compelled to keep it as Rosie had wished. After all, it held quite a treasure for me if all went well. I went ahead and wrapped it up to take home.

"No, Rosie, I did not change my mind about not liking clowns," I said aloud as if she were watching.

When I finished packing the other two jars, I decided to call it a day. I didn't feel comfortable in the shop after dark.

There was no sign of Bertie on the porch. It was probably best she had some time to digest my leaving. Perhaps when the time actually came, she would be more accepting of the idea and we could part on good terms.

I took the clown to the kitchen and unwrapped the scary character. The colors were perfect, I had to admit. I put him in the sink to give him a good washing. Growing up, I'd never trusted clowns. I always felt their fake smile was a disguise before they reached out and grabbed you. Who knew; I might look back and realize this clown brought me some good luck.

The more I thought about it, the more I felt Rosie's spirit was still around. She had a plan that she wanted carried out. Perhaps she'd play a role in the arrest of her killer.

Chapter 40

Later that night, I got on the internet to see what apartments or houses may be for rent in the wine country region. After a half hour, the attempt was unsuccessful. I could not afford anything appealing. I needed a job; that's all there was to it.

The longer I thought about my finances, the more I wondered if I should just take Carrie Mae up on her offer to buy Rosie's inventory from me. I could rent out there and look for a job when I got settled. Another crazy idea would be to rescue Holly as a roommates. We could open a quilt shop together. I knew the monster would have to disappear before Holly would ever be free. Then there was Lynn. Maybe she would agree to open an art gallery in Augusta and we could live together. I could also think about Alex. He could freelance with his writing, living anywhere.

It was now two in the morning, and I was exhausted thinking of my future. I decided to go to bed and only think of what I needed to pack at the shop tomorrow. That was a lot simpler.

I slept later the next morning without sunshine coming in my window. It was pouring down rain and I wanted to spend the day in bed.

Hours later, I forced myself out of bed, threw my hair into a makeshift ponytail, put on lipstick and my holey jeans, and pulled out an old Fish Creek t-shirt that Laurie had given me years ago. I felt liked I looked. I made my own coffee and toast for breakfast, knowing I would get soaked if I stopped at Tony's.

By ten-thirty, I left, feeling like my day was already behind me. Fortunately, I found a parking spot near the shop's front door. There was an alley behind the shop to drive through, but no one could park there.

I turned on the radio to the station that aired the Cardinals games. I knew there would be a game later in the afternoon. I wanted to pack something fun, so I headed to the shelf containing soneone's perfume bottle collection. They were each amazing, and I was sure Rosie had had to buy them all at once from someone. Some of them still had a little perfume in them, so I emptied them as I packed. In no time, I smelled really good. I wished I knew more about the perfumes. I could tell by Rosie's prices which ones were rare.

All of a sudden, there was a knock at the front door. Of all people, it was Marc checking on me. He wouldn't recognize me. Embarrassed by my appearance, I reluctantly opened the front door.

"Need some help?" he said as he ducked out of the rain. I ignored his question.

"What are you doing here?" I asked in annoyance.

"I took the day off to go look at a piece of property for a client and thought I'd drop by."

"I look awful, Marc," I said. "This is a dirty job. I don't think you know what you're getting into."

"Well, it may be dirty, but you really smell good."

I had to laugh. "I just finished packing some perfume bottles," I explained.

"Well, you may not know this about me, but I'm actually quite handy with tools and all. Do you have anything that needs taken apart or put together?"

I looked at him in disbelief. "You're serious, aren't you?"

"I am. I'll even buy you lunch if I stick around."

"Okay, Mr. Rennels, you asked for it. I have two tables I need to move, and I need their legs removed."

"No problem."

"See those suitcases up there? I need those taken down. Should I keep going?"

He chuckled. "Oh you have some antique typewriters! I'm quite taken by those, and I've often wished I had one. Do they work, and are they for sale?"

"I really don't know, but you can check them out and then put them into boxes. When I set up shop, I'll make sure you get one." He grinned.

Marc found the ladder and immediately started his list of chores. He took them quite seriously, and we engaged in very little small talk.

"Do you like pizza?' I asked after an hour had passed.

"Yeah. Are you buying, boss?"

"I am. Rigazzi's delivers. What kind do you like?"

"I love their pizza. You pick. I'm easy."

"I noticed that."

I went to the back room to order, and when I hung up, the storm had escalated quite fiercely. It was strange being here under these circumstances.

"Wow, we haven't had a storm like this in a long time," Marc noted as he sat on my dirty floor.

"Didn't that last bolt of lightning feel like it hit something close by?"

"Does this place have any water leaks? This is a good time to check so nothing gets ruined."

"Good idea." I walked around, looking carefully.

Chapter 41

The pizza arrived quickly, and I gave the rain-soaked delivery boy a large tip, closed the door, and set the pizza on the counter.

"Wait a minute, Marc," I impulsively said.

I took one of the tablecloths, which I had packed, out of the box and spread it on the legless tabletop sitting on the floor. I went to the back room and brought a large candle that appeared to be for emergencies, as well as two bottles of water, and placed everything on the tablecloth. Marc seemed to be amused.

"Clever. No wine?" he questioned with a grin.

"Are you serious? There are a couple of bottles of wine in Rosie's pantry."

"Well, what are you waiting for?" I couldn't believe this crazy lunch was happening.

The thunder and lightning made us jump several times as we tried to enjoy our lunch. We turned the stress into laughter, and the pizza and the wine hit the spot.

Marc was explaining how he couldn't remember the

last time he had used his tools and how much he'd missed it. Suddenly, the lights went out.

"Oh, no, do you have some matches?" Marc asked with concern.

"No, but I'll bet Rosie has some in the kitchen drawer," I responded as I got up off the floor.

"Be careful, and take this candle with you so you can find me again." We burst into laughter.

The dim daylight from the front windows helped me get back to the kitchen area. It took a while to find some matches, but it made me realize how well-equipped Rosie had been in her little shop. It was something I should remember.

"How about this?" Marc said as I lit the candle. "Man, what I had to do to share a candlelight dinner with you!" The man had a sense of humor.

"Don't read too much into this," I cautioned. "Did you tell Lynn you were coming over here?"

"No, why?"

"I just wondered. What do you make of her accusing Carl of having an affair with someone?"

"As much as I like Carl, I think she's on to something. I'll never forgive him if he's cheating on her."

"Do you think it could be that Kate girl we saw flirting with him at the picnic?"

"I don't know her. You know, I see this going on so much at the office, and it's really sad. It isn't always the man that's cheating, by the way. I'm a rather private person myself, and I actually do know some happily married couples. I thought Carl and Lynn were one of them."

"I feel I'm private as well. My sisters have teased me about it. I don't know very many women, if any, that are happily married."

"Well, I know you have a lot on your mind right now, so I understand your unwillingness to get into a relationship. I just find you very interesting, and frankly, I don't know any other woman who would have the Cardinals game on their radio." We laughed.

"Would you like more wine?"

"Well, we have more work to do, so I'd better pass," Marc said, getting up from sitting on the floor.

"Well, there isn't much we can do here in the dark," I remarked innocently.

"Oh, I disagree. I can think of some things to do, but I think I'll play it safe and try to get these legs off of this table." We both had to chuckle.

"You are such a tease, Mr. Rennels. I do like you, but I have to warn you that I am not a good investment of your time."

"What do you mean? I got a free lunch, and I also realized how much I like working with tools again."

"Okay, okay," I said, putting my hand on his shoulder as he continued working.

All of a sudden, the lights came on again.

"Wah whooo!" yelled Marc.

I blew out the candle and picked up the pizza mess to take to the kitchen. I had to smile about what a nice interruption Marc's visit had been. Had I been alone here in this storm with the lights out, I don't know what I would have done.

Chapter 42

Around six, I convinced Marc to go home. I walked him to the door and impulsively gave him a peck on the cheek.

"Thanks so much. This was a great afternoon."

"I agree. There's a game on Sunday afternoon if you can get away," he suggested sweetly.

"I'll see how far along I am with this packing," I said as I opened the door for him.

"I'll call you."

The rain had stopped, and I felt like I was ready to go home myself. Having a glass of wine in the middle of the day did not help my energy. With the extra help of Marc, I felt like a lot had been accomplished.

When I arrived home, I put away the leftover pizza, which would hit the spot tomorrow. My cell was ringing. It was Alex.

"Did you see the five o'clock news?" he asked anxiously.

"No, I just got home from the shop. What did I miss?"

"That guy confessed to killing Rosie."

"Oh my goodness! Why?"

"He wanted drug money and said he was told that Rosie kept a lot of money in the register. When he found only fifty dollars, he became angry. Rosie told him to get out, and when she turned away, he shot her."

"How awful, Alex! I hope they crucify this guy."

"He said he didn't mean to kill her, just scare her."

"Oh, well, let's forgive him then and move on," I said sarcastically.

"They settled the case, so he gets life in jail. I think they convinced him he would get the death sentence if this went to trial."

"It sounds like someone knew Rosie was hiding cash and talked. Do you think it was that Melanie?"

"It sounds likely. They had to know each other."

"Well, little Melanie didn't know about the cookie jar."

"I guess not. How did things go at the attorney's office?"

"The money is in his safe. He says they need to verify Rosie's writing and decide if there was any other purpose for this money. I guess I'll just have to wait."

"Do you feel he believed you?"

"Yes. He complimented me for being honest."

"Yeah, out of your crazy mind honest," Alex teased. "I wouldn't be surprised if they keep it for whatever reason they can come up with."

I hung up having mixed feelings on the outcome of Rosie's case. When there's drugs involved, people will do anything. I wished I could talk to Melanie. She was probably very curious about me and whether I'd found any money. I would have to look in Rosie's papers to see if I could find a phone number for her.

I stayed up to see the ten o'clock news. It was just like Alex reported. I worried about the killer's life sentence. The shooter would try to get paroled at some point.

Once in bed, I watched the last part of the Cardinals game, which was showing late from San Francisco. I thought of Marc and how he considered me his baseball bud. His offer to help me was impressive. With all of my rejection, he sure didn't have to go this far to capture my attention. I was sure my little peck on the cheek had encouraged him. Maybe I should go to the game with him on Sunday. I certainly owed him something for his help. It might be good for me to get away from the shop.

I decided that tomorrow I would check with Carrie Mae on our moving schedule. I didn't want to book the moving van too soon. This was an unexpected expense for me right now, but it would have to be done. I knew no one with a truck.

I finally fell asleep, but was alarmed to hear the phone ring at six a.m. It was Lynn. What on earth would she be calling about this early?

"Lynn, what's wrong?"

"Carl didn't come home last night."

"Now that takes nerve if he's denying an affair," I said. "Did you try his cell?"

"Yes, but it must have been turned off. It kept going to his voicemail."

"Oh, Lynn, try not to panic. We don't know what happened."

"We're supposed to think they're dead in a ditch somewhere, but I know better. I've had it. I think he wants me to be the one to ask for a divorce."

I finally got her to hang up and try to take a nap. She probably hadn't slept all night. I felt so bad for her. I told her to call me as soon as she heard from him.

Chapter 43

I stayed awake and wondered what excuse Carl could possibly come up with. He had to know this last stunt would likely end his marriage. Lynn didn't deserve this, but I knew she was strong.

I took my coffee to the porch. It was going to be a pretty day after the terrible storm. I wished I could get in my car and drive to wine country today, but I needed to focus on packing. I tried not to think of Mr. Willis and what might happen with the money. I needed to keep busy. I changed the bed linens, put a load of laundry in, and ran the vacuum before I called Carrie Mae. She should have been downstairs in her shop by now.

"Good morning," she greeted me cheerfully. I could just see her smile and that twinkle in her eyes. "Do you have news for me?"

"I'll need another week, I think. How are things on your end?" I asked.

"By then, I'll be ready for you," she answered.

"I've been looking online for apartments for rent, but

I haven't found anything. There are no houses for rent, and even though the prices to buy are reasonable, I can't afford it. Could you possibly put the word out that I'm looking?"

"So you'll come live out here if there's something available?"

"Yes, if I can afford it. I've spent my savings, as you may know. When I get settled, maybe I can afford to open a little shop with my quilts and Rosie's inventory."

"Well, honey, I'll do what I can. I'd love for you to be out here."

I hung up feeling like Carrie Mae wanted me there, so I knew she'd truly put the word out.

Off I went for another day of packing. I hated to admit it, but I was starting to miss my interactions with Bertie as I came and went.

When I got to Rosie's shop, I opened the back door as always. I put the suitcases that Marc had gotten down for me on the counter. I wondered where these had traveled in their lifetime. From here, they would be traveling to Augusta, and who knew from there?

I started packing them, along with the shelves of books Rosie had had for sale. I couldn't help but look carefully at each one of them. It appeared that any hope of me writing a book someday would be going out the door if I moved to Augusta. I heard a knock at the door, and saw it was Lynn. I rushed to the door to unlock it.

"I came to help," she quickly announced.

"You don't have to do that. I'm moving along quite well. Did Carl finally come home?"

"He did. He said he went out for a few drinks, went back to the office, and fell asleep. I've never known Carl to do that, but maybe he was upset."

"Okay, that's weird. Do you believe him?"

"Absolutely not. I can tell when that man is telling a lie. He looked all crumpled up, of course."

"Why didn't he just come home?"

"Good question. It was too painful for me to question him further. I just didn't feel like arguing."

"I'm so sorry, Lynn, but have you thought about what you're going to do next?"

"I wish Carl would agree to counseling. I think he's met someone who has really got him confused. Everyone makes mistakes. We're all human. I love him so much, Lily." She began to cry.

"I know you do," I said consolingly. "Do you want me to talk to him?"

She thought for a minute. "I don't think it can hurt at this point. He's just not himself. Maybe he would open up to you. I wish he would just be honest. If he's done with me, then I don't want him."

"Let me see what he has to say. I'll ask him to go get a drink with me. He'll know what I'm up to, but he may want to explain."

Chapter 44

Lynn stayed and helped me pack some cups and saucers. They were quite charming and beautiful, but I wondered how collectable they really were. Lynn found packing them to be enjoyable and commented on each one. After they were done, there were still some smalls, like the collection of toothpick holders. I tried to label each box so that later I would know what was inside.

Around five, I offered Lynn a glass of Rosie's wine. She gladly accepted, and it was the perfect time to tell her about Marc coming to help me pack this week. She was thrilled and begged me to hang in there and give him a chance.

"I guess I'll go to the game with him," I revealed with a smile.

"Why not? You'll both enjoy it, and you need a little fun with all this work you've been doing."

We finished the bottle, and by the time Lynn left, she was in much better spirits. We were as close as two sisters could be, despite our different lifestyles. I would miss seeing her if I moved to Augusta. She would have gone crazy if I had told her about my discovery in the cookie jar.

I stayed a little longer to look around in Rosie's back room, where her office presumably was. She didn't have a desk, but did have a cluttered card table and antique cabinet, which served for this and that. I saw an old-fashioned Rolodex, so I immediately thumbed through it to see if Melanie's number would show up. The numbers were all handwritten and appeared to belong mostly to antique dealers. Nothing looked like what I was looking for. Where did Rosie keep her bills and receipts? I knew the attorney had taken almost everything to settle her estate. Under some papers was a pocket calendar. I flipped through it, but it seemed to contain only doctor's appointments. There were no notations for birthdays or any social commitments. Who was Rosie, anyway? I only knew her as a customer that she seemed to care about. She'd always wanted to know my job situation. She knew where I lived in the neighborhood, but I didn't know where she lived. Perhaps I'd been her only hope for anyone to buy the shop.

Rosie's building was old, but I couldn't tell how old. There were problems that she had obviously been neglecting. There didn't seem to be an upstairs or attic. The front windows were arched, and above her front door there was a piece of stained glass. Who had been in this building before Rosie?

I was about to leave, feeling I had wasted my time, when I thought I saw Melanie once again peeking in the window. I put down my purse and rushed to try to catch her this time.

When I opened the door, there was no sign of her. She must have quickly ducked inside one of the many businesses lined up along the street. I didn't feel up to searching for her at this point. If she had something to ask or say to me, why didn't she knock on the door?

I wondered if Melanie had a key. I hadn't noticed any changes during my day-to-day visits. Nothing appeared to be missing.

I picked up a corned beef sandwich at the corner deli before getting in my car. On the way home, I wondered about Lynn's situation. I would check on her later.

Bertie couldn't escape when I got to my apartment.

"Bertie, I've missed you!" I said innocently. She gave me a scowl as she straightened the cushion on her rocker. "Are you mad at me?"

She wouldn't say anything.

"Bertie, whatever happens in my life, you will always be special to me. You're like family I come home to every day. You always know what goes on, and we look out for each other."

"So why are you going to move?"

"Because life is taking me in another direction, that's why. I have to make a living at some point. I love quilts and antiques, and I need a new start. You're in your retirement years and I'm not. Don't you realize that you're only forty-five minutes from where I may live? I'm not moving to Minnesota! I will always be there for you. Besides, Bertie, you may get a wonderful tenant and forget about me. I know you can get more rent than what I'm paying. You have been very generous with me. I'll never forget that."

I thought I saw tears in her eyes when she looked away. I told her to think about what I'd said and patted her hand before I went upstairs. I had a good feeling that she would eventually come around.

Chapter 45

Marc seemed delighted that I was going to join him for the baseball game. He picked me up at noon for the one o'clock game. This time, he arrived wearing a red Cardinals baseball cap. I had to chuckle at seeing him look so casual. I had on the same red blazer I'd had on before.

On the way there, Marc had many questions about my progress with packing. He seemed to be serious about helping me on moving day.

Before we entered the stadium, Marc stopped a walking vendor selling baseball caps and put a bright red cap on my head. We both looked rather goofy, but I found it quite fun. I liked baseball caps, so it would be great for my collection.

After we got hot dogs and cheese tacos, I asked Marc if he had talked to Lynn since Carl had come home late.

"Are you serious?" he asked, which told me he didn't know. "He stayed out all night?" I nodded.

I described the incident, and said I wasn't sure what Lynn would do from here.

"He's toast," Marc said. "He's really in turmoil of some

kind."

"I asked Lynn if I should try to talk to him, and she gave me permission."

"Will you?"

"Yes. I hope soon! He may open up to me, who knows?"

"Good luck. Boy, that is such a shame. I've always envied their relationship."

Then we started paying more attention to the game, because the Cardinals were winning big. It was a great way to end the day.

When we got back to my apartment, I asked Marc in. I think he was surprised.

"This apartment is quite spacious and very attractive, Lily," he said spontaneously. "You may miss this place once you move."

"Do you like quilts?" I asked.

"Sure. I grew up with them, but don't use them much. Lynn said that you collect them."

"I have a whole room devoted to them, but I don't let just anyone see it," I teased. "You'll understand my passion if you see it, however."

"I'd love to."

I took him to my quilt room. He stood in silence as he took in the many shelves, racks, and containers of quilts. He then walked over to the quilt on the wall.

"This is really striking!" he said, standing with his hands folded. "Quilts are truly an art form. The few I have are pretty basic, but they have a lot of memories attached to them. We had a special quilt growing up that was in really bright colors. We could only use it if we were sick or had a stayover."

"How sweet," I responded.

"Mom said it would make things better, and I think we believed her. My sister ended up with it."

"You have a sister?"

"Yeah, Meg. She lives in New York. She's an engineer and is married to her work."

"Do you see her very often?"

"Maybe three to four times a year. I usually have to fly there, but that's okay. So, Lily, do you make quilts yourself?"

"No. I'm more interested in antique quilts, and also vintage fabrics. As you can see, I have a passion for red and white."

"Yes, it's a great combination. Lynn pointed that out to me, which is why I sent red and white flowers." I grinned at the memory.

"I'm glad that you appreciate what quilts are all about. Each one has a story. Sometimes when I look at them and run my hands across the stitches, I can feel what they're about, and perhaps what purpose they were created for. Does that sound crazy?" He shook his head and smiled. "You know, there's a patina to fabric, just like there is in wood."

"I didn't know that. You have quite an investment here. Will you sell some of them if you open a shop?"

"Yes, I'll have to, but I'll keep buying for my own collection. I'm always looking for patterns that are more unique. That way, it's easier to let the less significant ones go. Do you collect anything?"

"Can't say that I do. I live a pretty modest lifestyle. I live in a loft downtown. There are times, I miss tinkering around the house like I did when I was married."

"How long have you been divorced?"

"About ten years. Why haven't you married? I guess that's pretty personal."

"It's fine to ask. It's never been on my bucket list, I guess. I've always felt it meant trouble. Now, to be honest, I never met anyone that challenged that thought."

He nodded and chuckled. "You are an attractive woman who shouldn't have any trouble finding someone."

"I worked for a dull publishing company that didn't allow for much fun or opportunity to meet anyone."

"Now that you've left, do you have time to write?"

"I thought I would, but writing requires a lot of thought and a sense of place in order for me to be inspired. I think living in the wine country will do that for me."

"It sounds like you're on your way!"

"Do you want to go out and sit on the porch for a while?"

"Thanks, but I need to get going. I have a busy day tomorrow. This was a fun day, and thanks for sharing your quilt room with me."

As we walked to the door, Marc put his arm around my shoulders. He turned, tipped my chin upwards, and gently kissed my lips.

"I'll be in touch," he said in a whisper.

Chapter 46

It had been a great day. It was the first time a man had asked about my quilt collection, with the exception of Alex.

As I crawled into bed later, I hoped that despite Marc and I getting to know each other better, he wouldn't crowd me into a relationship.

The next morning, I decided I would call Carl at the office and ask him to meet me for a drink. I didn't relish the thought, but if I had any way of helping Lynn, I had to do it.

I answered emails from Loretta and Laurie before I got ready to leave the apartment. I reported to them that if I really worked hard over the next couple of days, I could call the movers.

I took my coffee and toast to the porch until it was the appropriate time to call Carl. His secretary put me right through, which surprised me.

"Lily, how are ya?" he answered.

"I'm good, Carl. I hope I'm not interrupting anything."

"No, you caught me before a meeting. What can I do for you?"

I paused. "Well, I wanted to know if you would meet me for a drink tonight."

"That's a surprise. I suppose it has to do with your sister, am I right?"

"It does. I hate what's going on between the two of you. Are you free?"

"Actually, I'm not, Lily. I appreciate what you're trying to do, but I have a client dinner meeting tonight. Lynn and I will be fine."

"It doesn't sound like it, Carl. It's a pretty big deal to Lynn."

"I don't know what to tell you, Lily."

"Does Kate have anything to do with this situation?"

"Kate?" He was shocked, no doubt.

"If not Kate, who? Whoever she is, she's going to ruin your marriage."

"That's all I have to say, Lily. Thanks for your concern."

When I hung up, I knew I may have gone too far and hit a nerve. Why didn't he try to defend himself? Mentioning Kate's name really threw him. I'd tried, so now what did I tell Lynn?

I went on to the shop, getting a late start with my packing. I walked into a hot, stuffy building that definitely needed air conditioning. Hopefully it had some that worked. I found the thermostat, and something kicked on. I would hope for the best.

I stacked boxes and started to clear an area of boxes that were ready to be put on the truck. The thought of cleaning the place after all this wasn't pleasant.

There was an old toolbox under one of the buffets. When I pulled it out, I noticed that it had been there a long time. Perhaps Rosie hadn't known it was there. I wished that I had found it when Marc was here. I should give it to him for helping me so much. If he also helped on moving day, I would owe him big time.

A knock at the front door made me jump. It was Alex. I hurried to open the door.

"I've got a few hours, so I'm all yours, if there's something I can do," Alex offered.

"Are you sure?"

"If you want to get out of dodge, you'd better step on it, sister!" He then saw the toolbox.

I explained what I had just found and told him I might give it to Marc.

"He's getting to you, huh?" he teased.

"I couldn't believe how much help he was," I confessed. "I broke down and went to the ballgame with him yesterday, which isn't helping to get this done."

"Holy cow, Lily Girl, I can't keep up with you."

"He's very nice, Alex, and he's going to help us on moving day. He knows I don't want a relationship."

Alex looked at me strangely. "Sorry, sister, but you already have one. He does sound pretty cool. Now, what can I do?"

"Count these Mason jars, if you would."

"People still buy these?"

"Not so much for canning anymore, but they use them for candles and as glasses to drink out of."

"There must be four boxes of these," he said as he looked around. "I don't suppose you got any richer since I talked to you last?"

I shook my head. "I wonder how long they'll take to let

me know something."

As we worked alongside one another, I told Alex about Carl staying out all night. He stopped dead in his tracks. Then I told him I had asked Carl out for a drink, and that he was too busy.

"Way to go. Good try!"

"He wanted to dismiss my call, saying they would be fine. Before I hung up, I couldn't resist asking if a girl named Kate had anything to do with all this. He wouldn't respond, but I knew I'd hit a nerve. He didn't even try to defend himself. Don't you think that's odd?"

"Indeed!"

Chapter 47

I hated to see Alex leave. He could talk, pack, and chew gum, all at the same time.

I stayed working later since the days were getting longer. As I packed a collection of old inkwells, I wondered what past writers had to endure to put their words to paper, much less write a whole manuscript. There weren't typewriters or computers back then. They had to write slower with their ink pens, and what did they do when they made a mistake?

I also wondered what the publishing houses and printers were like then. The current chapter of my life might be worth writing about later. *From The Hill to the Rolling Hills* could be a fun title. I had to chuckle under my breath. Who would pick up a book with that title?

Lynn's call brought me out of my silliness.

"So what in the world did Carl have to say for himself?" Lynn quickly asked.

I started from the beginning and told her he didn't deny any of my accusations.

"He was furious that I had told you, of course," Lynn

noted.

"Well, it's not like we are strangers! What are you going to do?"

"I'm going to ask him to leave at some point. I'm not interested in playing detective."

"What if he refuses to leave?"

"I'll know when the time comes, I guess."

"I'm about finished here for the day. Do you want to go meet somewhere? It's such a beautiful evening."

"I'm not very good company, Lily," she warned.

"Anthonino's Tavern has a great patio, and it's casual. How about we meet up in fifteen minutes?"

"Okay," Lynn said with a sigh.

I cleaned up as best as I could and refreshed my makeup. I somehow had to convince Lynn that her world wasn't falling apart.

I got there first, and the patio was crowded. When one couple left, I took their table. I went ahead and ordered a merlot and a glass of ice water.

Lynn was certainly taking her time, so I ordered Antoninos's famous toasted ravioli and the baked goat cheese, which I knew Lynn would enjoy. Hopefully, she would show up.

Just as I was about to give her a call, she arrived.

"I'm sorry. I changed clothes a couple of times."

"For this?" She knew it sounded silly. "I have some good food coming," I said, which made her smile.

I gave her an update on the packing, and then reported how much fun Marc and I had had at the ballgame. She needed something else to think about.

"I guess you're not the only one who needs a new start

right now," Lynn confessed.

"Well, if you have to leave, you can always come with me to wine country. That doesn't sound so bad, does it?"

"That's your dream, not mine," she said. "I can't imagine living without Carl. We planned our whole life together."

"Well then, if he's worth fighting for, do it!"

"I'm not sure how."

"Try to stop thinking about who or what he's involved with. If I were you, I'd tell him to end it immediately with Kate or whomever. Tell him you've invested too much in him all these years, and you're not going to give up everything you love because of some homewrecker."

Lynn looked surprised at my opinion. "It's honestly what I want to do. You wouldn't think less of me if I took him back, would you?"

"It takes a strong woman to swallow her pain, rather than to spit it out."

She chuckled. "That's clever, Lily. Did you just make that up?" We burst into laughter, which was good for both of us. Being together with my sis was the best.

Chapter 48

When I got to the shop the next day, I assessed what I needed to do to wrap things up before moving day. I needed to call Carrie Mae and confirm a date for delivery. My thirty days were nearly up. When she finally answered around ten, she'd been expecting my call.

"I'm so glad you called. Are you ready?"

"I would like to come Monday, if it's okay with you and the movers."

"Sure, just stop by here to get the key and I'll go down the hill with you. Then you can come and go as you like."

"Wonderful. I'll call as we get closer. I don't know how to thank you. Are there any leads on finding me a place to live?"

"Sorry, none so far," Carrie Mae reported. "Do you have plenty of help for the move?"

"Yes, Alex and Marc will be helping."

"I remember Alex, but who's Marc?"

"He's a friend I met a while back. He's very nice and helped me pack one day."

"He sounds like a keeper to me," she teased.

"Don't start. I don't need a man in my life right now."

"Pardon me, Miss Lily, but I think you're going to need as many men as you can right now!" I laughed.

As soon as I hung up, I made the call to the movers to secure Monday. Luck was on my side, and we were all set to move at eight o'clock sharp. The excitement of it all got me going. I opened the back door and started packing the shelves of glassware, which I had dreaded. It was mostly pitchers, vases, bowls, and candlesticks. I had no idea which ones were worth more than others and could hardly tell which were antique and which were Waterford. I gathered a lot of packing materials and began filling the boxes.

All of a sudden, standing at the back door was Melaniel..

"Hey, don't go away. I want to talk to you," I called. "Come in."

"Where are you taking Rosie's things?" she asked with anger in her voice.

"I bought all this and I'm putting it in storage."

"Why did you buy it if you're not staying here?"

"Look, let's start over. I'm Lily Rosenthal. You may remember me as a customer here. I remember seeing you here, and I also saw you looking in the window a few times. I know your name is Melanie."

"I remember you. For the record, I didn't have anything to do with her getting shot."

"I hope not. How long did you work for Rosie?"

She paused, not wanting to warm up to me. "Only a few months." Her eyes kept looking around the shop.

"What can you tell me about the person who shot her?"

"Nothing. That's what I told the cops."

"That's not a very good answer. Did you both think Rosie kept a lot of money here?" She looked at me strangely, and I knew I had offended her.

"I don't know what you're talking about." This girl looked like she was telling a lie, pure and simple.

"Did you and Rosie get along? Were you upset with her about anything?"

"Why would you ask that? Why is it any of your business?"

"Well, I don't know you, and I was devastated by her death. Were you?"

"She certainly didn't pay me well enough, for starters. I deserved a lot more. I saw what folks were paying for her things."

"That was her business. She said the last time I was here that she was experiencing some shoplifting."

"I don't know anything about that."

"Well, Rosie knew her merchandise and would have picked up on any shoplifting that may have been going on." Melanie was ignoring me.

"So what's going in here after you move this out?"

"I have no idea. I move out on Monday and clean on Tuesday. By the way, if you have a key, it would be wise to turn it in."

There was no response.

"Do you live close by?"

"Not far."

"Maybe the new shop will hire you when they move in." Still no response.

"Well, I'll let you get back to your packing," she said as she went out the door.

"Nice to have met you, Melanie," I said as she went out the door without looking back.

There was no "goodbye," "good luck," or "see ya later" from this girl. How very strange that she didn't show any feelings about Rosie's death. Had she wished her dead because she wasn't paid enough? I had a feeling she could have been the shoplifter that Rosie suspected. Perhaps she felt justified.

Chapter 49

With no interruptions, I soon felt I had everything packed that could go into containers. I was exhausted, but also felt a good sense of accomplishment. I got myself a bottle of water out of the kitchen, and my cell phone rang. I was shocked to hear Sarah's voice on the phone.

"Oh my goodness, what a nice surprise."

"I know. I feel badly that I don't contact you nearly enough, but as you know, I was planning a wedding."

"Was?"

"Well, that's actually why I'm calling."

"I'm listening. I was just taking a break from my packing. Tell me what's going on."

"I don't want to go through with the wedding," Sarah stated.

"What happened?"

"Nothing happened. It's not Jerry's fault. He's nice, but the thought of spending the rest of my life with him freaks me out. I shouldn't have let the plans get this far. A lot of money has been spent, and Mom is furious with me."

"You can't blame her. She's been hinting that you were getting nervous about it all. How is Jerry taking the news?"

"I don't know. I'm afraid he's now history. I should be more upset, but frankly, I'm relieved."

"Well, if that's how you feel, I'm glad you did this before you took your vows."

"So, back to the real reason I'm calling. Would you call and talk to Mom about this? You're single, so maybe you can explain to her that not everyone wants to be married. She hasn't spoken to me since she found out I told Jerry the wedding was off."

"She's just hurt and disappointed, Sarah."

"I know that, but I can't get married to make her happy."

"What does your dad have to say?"

"I'm Daddy's little girl. He's taken it really well."

"Won't your mom listen to him?"

"No, that's why I'm asking you."

"Okay, but don't get your hopes up. She's always been more stubborn than the rest of us," I half teased.

"Thanks. I really want to come see you as soon as you get moved. I'm really excited about your new adventure."

"It's an adventure into the unknown, you might say."

"I wish I lived closer, Lily."

"You're welcome here anytime."

We ended our conversation, and I went on home to think about it all.

I picked up a pizza along the way. The smell reminded me of my lunch with Marc. I reminded myself to call Marc and Alex about my definite moving date.

I walked up to the porch, and Bertie was sitting in her chair, knitting.

"Hi, Bertie," I greeted her. "If you haven't eaten, I'm happy to share this pizza with you."

"Thanks, but I eat much earlier, as you well know," she said without looking up.

"What are you making?"

"A scarf."

"Those colors are beautiful. Well, I guess I'd better get on upstairs before this gets cold. See you later."

I went upstairs without another response from her.

I poured myself some wine and took my dinner to the porch. The breeze was delightful and I felt at peace. I thought about poor Loretta, who could not control her daughter, which I knew was upsetting to her. I give Sarah credit for standing up for herself, though. It was an honor that Sarah was asking for my help. Loretta, being the oldest of us, would never take any advice from her youngest sister.

When I finished my pizza at ten, I called Alex and left a message about the moving date. I wasn't sure if it was too late to call Marc, but my wine said to go ahead.

"Hey there," he answered after many rings.

"It's me, Lily."

"What can I do for you at this time of night?" Was that a sarcastic remark?

"I'm sorry it's late, but I wanted to confirm my moving date on Monday at eight, if you're still available."

There was a pause. "Uh, sure. Can you hold for a minute?"

"Sure."

The phone went silent. Was he with someone?

"Monday will be fine. Did you say eight at the shop?'"

"Yes. You're a real gem to do this, Marc. I'll see you then."

I hung up feeling good about the results, but also

feeling a bit odd that Marc hadn't wanted to continue the conversation. Was he glad I'd called or not?

Chapter 50

Sunday was a dark, cloudy day, but the thought of tomorrow's move was a bright spot. After sleeping in until nine, I decided I had to make a last minute sweep of Rosie's shop and make sure everything was ready.

Holly called and gave me another one of her excuses about not being able to help because of the monster in her house. I understood, but wondered where our friendship would be headed once I moved to wine country. When would it ever be okay for her to come see me? We'd always shared so much together. She could make me laugh so easily, but the monster was consuming most of our conversations these days. There was nothing funny about her restricted life.

When I got to the shop, tourists and neighbors were out and about, despite the threatening weather. There was one couple looking in the window with questioning looks on their faces.

I unlocked the door in front of them, and they immediately asked me what happened to Rosie's shop.

"We always stopped by here when we come to the Hill," the lady said. "When did she close?"

"Some weeks ago," I stated. I really didn't want to go into the story of her death.

"We always found something here," the man lamented. "She was always so nice."

"Yes, she was," I concluded with a nod.

I went inside and locked the door. For the first time, I felt a sense of responsibility in continuing Rosie's tradition.

I turned on the lights and decided to put sticky notes on the furniture that needed to go on the truck. I walked into the back room and took Rosie's Rolodex and a pen that had "Rosie's Antique Shop" stamped on it. I wanted a couple of personal things to remind me of her special shop. I hoped she was watching and would give me some advice along the way.

I straightened up her back room, not knowing what the next renter would expect. I thought I heard a knock on the door, and when I went to look, it was Mr. Willis. My heart sank. Was I ready for what he was about to tell me?

"Good morning, Lily," he said when I opened the door. "It looks like you're getting ready for moving day."

"Yes, tomorrow! Come on in!"

"I have some good news."

"You do?"

"Here's a cashier's check for 49,505 dollars. Everything checked out, and it appears this was left for you."

"I can't believe it!" I found myself just staring at the check.

"I think Rosie knew you'd be starting a business when she gave you the first right of refusal on her inventory in the will. I hope you put this to good use."

"I will, I will. Thank you so much for confirming this generous gift."

"You did the right thing. If I can help you with anything in the future, just let me know."

"Do you know if this place has been rented?"

"It hasn't, to my knowledge, but it sure is a good location. Good luck with your move tomorrow."

"Thanks!" I said, letting him out the door.

I went to the back room and wanted to do Holly's happy dance, which she always talked bout. I felt so grateful and immediately said a prayer of thanks.

"Thank you, God and Rosie," I said aloud. "I won't disappoint you."

I sat down to absorb what had just happened. I wouldn't allow myself to think about how I would spend the money. Who should I tell? Alex was the only person I'd told about finding the cash.

I picked up the phone and nervously called him.

"Alex here," he answered.

"It's Lily. Mr. Willis just came to the shop to give me a cashier's check."

"Hallelujah!" Alex yelled into the phone. "It's all legit?"

"That's what he said. I'm still in shock."

"Look, I'd offer to help you celebrate tonight, but because I'm helping you tomorrow, I have to finish this article. Start making your shopping list, Lily Girl, and get your sweet self to the bank as fast as you can!"

I had to smile every time he called me Lily Girl, because that was what Rosie always called me.

"Thanks, Alex. I just had to tell someone. I still can't believe it!" He chuckled.

I grabbed my purse, put the check inside, and headed to the bank. I thanked the Almighty again for trusting me with Rosie's generous gift.

Chapter 51

The bank teller didn't even bat an eye when I gave her the check to deposit. Did this happen every day?

I left feeling more secure now that I had this cushion to help plan the next phase of my life. I could breathe.

When I got home, Harry and Bertie were both on the porch.

"How did this happen?" I teased Harry. "Bertie let you occupy her porch?"

"The old geezer said his knees weren't feeling good enough to make it home, and said that he had to rest a while," Bertie complained.

"That was nice of you, Bertie," I said. "You sure wouldn't want him lying on your sidewalk in front of your house."

"Hey, Missy; how's that packing coming along?" Harry asked.

"The movers will be here in the morning," I announced with a smile. Bertie's face turned sour.

"Then what?" Harry asked, throwing up his hands. "If

you hear anything about who is going to rent Rosie's building, let me know."

"I've heard nothing. I'll still be here, so you can let me know if you hear who rents the building."

"And just what makes you think I'll know, little lady?" Harry joked.

"You know everything!" I teased. "That's why Bertie is so crazy about you."

With that comment, I had to hurry inside. I knew Bertie would be giving me a dirty look.

I made a glass of tea and took it to my porch. I needed to make some kind of plan. Getting the inventory moved was certainly the first step. After making this deposit, I felt I had more options.

I got my phone out of my purse and made a reminder call to the mover, and then one to Carrie Mae.

"Do you think you'll be here before noon?" Carrie Mae asked.

"We may not. I'll call you when we leave here. Is everything there ready?"

"Sure. Stop here to get the key. I hope you don't get too upset when you see all the disrepair in the yellow house. It needs work, but the downstairs will give you plenty of room to store what you have. I turned on the electricity and I even filled your little refrigerator with some bottled water for the movers. I was surprised it still worked."

"Oh, thanks. Well, I guess I'll see you in the morning!"

The phone rang as soon as I hung up. It was Lynn.

"I'm calling to wish you luck tomorrow. I wish I could help, but it's bad timing."

"Not to worry. Alex and Marc will be plenty of help.

How are things going with Carl?"

"I think we'll work through this, Lily," she said with some hesitation. "I think Carl is relieved I haven't asked him to leave. I demanded that he make changes and he seemed to get my drift, if you know what I mean. We'll see. We're going out to dinner tonight. I'll let you know how that goes."

"Wonderful, but be strong, okay?"

"Believe me, this takes more strength than telling him to hit the road."

"You're right. I love you, Sis."

When I hung up, I felt very proud of her. I hoped Loretta and Laurie would feel the same.

Before I went to bed, I emailed my sisters and told them tomorrow was the big day. I knew Loretta would be in bed, but the other two would still be up.

To save time, I laid out my clothes for the next day. When I got in bed, I went over a mental checklist, hoping I hadn't forgotten anything. Finally, I got tired of being tired and went to sleep.

The alarm went off at seven. I rolled over, wanting to finish my dream, but then realized that today my dream was coming true.

I jumped up and rushed to the kitchen to put my coffee on. I went to the porch to check the weather and was delighted to see a warm, sunny day, as predicted. This was the day the Lord had made, so I needed to rejoice and be glad in it.

At seven forty-five, I headed out the door to get to the shop.

The street was quiet. The only place open was the coffee

shop.

I unlocked the front and then the back door. As I looked around, I knew I was ready to go.

Chapter 52

The first to arrive was Marc. He was dressed casually in jeans and a red checked shirt.

"Are you ready?" he asked with a big grin. "I think I saw your moving van come around the corner."

"Great! Alex should be here any minute. I sure appreciate you doing this for me."

Alex arrived minutes later.

"Hey, Alex," I said. "Alex, this is Marc Rennels. Marc, this is my good friend, Alex."

"Nice to meet you," Marc said with a handshake.

"The same here," Alex responded. "Lily, you're driving with me, right?" I nodded.

"I need to drive separately to make sure I get back in time for an event," Marc explained.

The van pulled up in front of the shop, and my heart sank. I went to meet the two strong men who got out of the truck. Their said their names were Rob and Will. I gave them directions to Augusta and then took them inside to see what needed to be moved.

"We'll start with the large furniture first," Will announced.

"I can always take boxes in my car, if it doesn't all fit," Marc offered.

The guys didn't waste any time and assured me it would all fit somehow. They started giving Marc and Alex instructions on how they could be helpful as well. My job was to make sure all the correct items were taken. I was impressed with everyone's strength and efficiency.

The activity caused quite a stir in the neighborhood. Some asked if we were coming or going. Tony stopped by to see if we needed coffee or refreshments, which I thought was sweet.

At eleven thirty, Rosie's shop appeared to be very empty. It was sad, but I couldn't let myself dwell on the sight.

"We'll be stopping to grab a bite of lunch, Ms. Rosenthal," Rob informed me. "We'll be there by two for sure."

"That's great. We may do the same," I said.

We said goodbye and off they went. They knew what they were doing.

"I'm starved!" claimed Alex. "This was hard labor!" We knew he was teasing.

"I know we're all anxious to get to Augusta, but why don't we get a quick bite at the corner deli?" I suggested. "It's my treat!"

"Sounds good," Marc replied.

"You've got a lot of cleanup here," Alex said, looking around the shop.

"I'll do it tomorrow. Let's get going."

We enjoyed a quick lunch on the deli's patio. Marc and Alex made small talk and seemed to hit it off.

Marc of his own, confident he could find my place. Alex and I headed back to my car. We were about to get in when I thought I saw movement in the shop.

"Wait, Alex," I said with caution. "Someone's in the shop." He looked at me strangely. We went across the street to look in Rosie's window. I couldn't believe what I saw. "It's Melanie!" I informed Alex. "That stinker! What is she looking for? I guess she has a key after all."

I didn't wait for Alex and stormed into the shop, catching her off guard.

"I think you're trespassing, little lady!" I shouted. "What are you doing here?"

She gave me a surprised, dirty look.

"I just was gonna see if there was a little remembrance left of Rosie," she said flatly.

"Oh, please, Melanie, don't play games with me," I said with anger. Alex looked on. "I can call the police right now and put you in jail."

"Why don't you come clean with Lily?" Alex suggested. "It would save everyone a lot of trouble."

"You're looking for something, aren't you?" I asked, staring her down. "Maybe I already found it. Could it be money?"

"Maybe," she said sassily. "Rosie kept secrets from us."

"Us? You mean you and Rosie's killer?" Her dirty looks continued.

"She only made cash sales," she stated with anger. "You would never see much money in her cash register."

"And what business is that of yours as long as she was paying you?"

"I'll bet she never reported a dime to the IRS."

"Did she pay you in cash?" Alex asked. She nodded.

"Well then," Alex said with a grin. "I'll bet you didn't report your wages either, did you?"

"I knew she was making a lot of money, but she only paid me a pittance," Melanie complained.

"You know nothing about running a business," I said, shaking my head.

"Do you want me to call the cops?" Alex asked, getting out his phone.

"No, I don't have time," I said, frustrated. "Melanie, I know you're angry about something, but stealing from someone isn't the answer. I think you've already been taking things from the shop, haven't you?"

She gave me a look of "how did you know," but kept silent.

"I think you need to move on," I continued. "The locks are going to change tomorrow. Give me your key." She hesitated, but then took it out of her pocket "Get out and stay out,"I firmly instructed. "I wouldn't advise trying to get another job in this neighborhood, because I'll make sure the word gets out about you."

She went out the door in a huff.

"You let her off pretty easy, Lily Girl," Alex teased.

Chapter 53

Alex and I were running late, so I gave Carrie Mae a quick call to explain our delay.

"You're lucky Melanie didn't get a hankering to look in all the cookie jars while she worked there," Alex teased. I chuckled. "If she had, she could have helped herself a little at a time, and Rosie wouldn't have noticed."

"Oh, I wouldn't be so sure about that, Alex. Rosie was pretty sharp and alert."

As we drove along, Alex kept commenting on the beautiful scenery. When we passed Klondike Park, I told him that was where I wanted him to go hiking with me.

"So, Lily, I can tell you right now that Marc is quite smitten with you."

"Oh, for heaven's sake, you just met him."

"He watches your every move. You may not want to get rid of him just yet."

I looked at him strangely. "He is not mine to get rid of, I'll have you know. You're wrong about him."

"I'm never wrong, if you recall," he teased with a big grin.

The rest of our conversation related to all the charming businesses and houses we passed along the way. Alex completely understood my attraction to this part of the world.

When we pulled up to Carrie Mae's store, I saw Marc's vehicle.

"This little town has changed a lot since I've been here," Alex commented.

We went inside, where Carrie Mae and Marc were engaged in conversation.

"Hey, you guys, what took you so long?" Marc asked with a chuckle.

"I'll explain later," I responded quickly. "Have the movers arrived?"

"No, but I'm sure enjoying my conversation with this gentleman friend of yours," Carrie Mae said. "Here are your keys, Lily. Have fun. There's one for the house and one for the little brick building next to it. I may not have shared this with you, but long ago, a doctor once lived in this house, and he saw his patients in that building. You'll have fun researching the place if you're interested."

"Oh my, yes! Thank you. How interesting. I'm really curious as to how old the house really is."

Alex and Marc spotted the old typewriters, and Marc made an announcement.

"I already made a purchase before you came." He pointed across the counter. "I told Carrie Mae I wanted to buy the little red typewriter over there, but I still want the one you have as well, Lily."

"Very cool," I said. "It's probably from around the 1950s."

"Hey, here's the truck," announced Alex.

"Better show them where the house is, Lily," Carrie Mae

instructed.

We all followed with our cars, and it wasn't hard to see the bright yellow building from afar as we went down the hill.

I stepped onto the front porch and admired the white gingerbread trim at the top, as well as on the porch railing. I could see through the window as I unlocked the stubborn door. I entered the front hallway that led to rooms on each side. The open stairway to the second floor was handsome and in good repair.

"This is like a gingerbread house," Alex said.

"Wow, this is bigger on the inside than it appears on the outside," Marc noted. "You're lucky there are hardwood floors!"

"I think we'll put the larger pieces of furniture in the living room and dining room," I told the movers. "You guys can put all the boxes in one room and leave a walkway in between."

"Come look at this!" Alex called. "This run-down porch could be amazing."

He was looking at the back porch. It was sizable and trimmed in gingerbread like the front porch. The floor was rotten, but I could immediately see potential in the good view towards the large backyard. I occasionally answered a question or two from the movers, but they were moving fast, and I was thankful for their expertise. It was exciting. I knew this house had a purpose, not only for my furniture, but perhaps for my future.

Chapter 54

I couldn't wait to see the upstairs, but it would have to wait, as I was directing traffic. The movers were working quickly. I understood that they had another appointment to get to.

The two rooms of furniture were filling up quickly. The only room that remained empty was the kitchen. As I looked around, it was so strange seeing Rosie's things in a new environment.

Alex came in from the outside and started exclaiming about the outside buildings.

"It's like an overgrown village out there, Lily," he said. "You be careful if you snoop around out there. I saw poison ivy, and the likelihood of snakes is high."

"Thanks, Alex," I joked. "Did you go inside any of the buildings?"

"Are you kidding?" he teased. "I'm a city boy, remember?"

"Lily, it looks like your task has been accomplished, so I need to get going," Marc said, wiping his brow.

"Thanks so much for your help," I said, wanting to hug

him. "Don't forget your new old typewriter."

"It's already in the car," he assured me as Carrie Mae joined us in the front yard. "Carrie Mae, it was a pleasure to meet you. I can see many reasons for Lily to feel at home here."

"I hope you'll return," Carrie Mae said with a big smile.

I walked Marc to his car and gave him a big hug to say thanks.

"Did I score any points today?" he teased.

"Many!" I grinned. "I owe you, big time."

He waved goodbye, and I walked back into the house.

"Did you see the upstairs?" Carrie Mae asked me.

"No, but I want to before I leave," I stated. "Let's go up, Alex."

We went up the beautiful stairs that had a creak or two. Who knew how long it had been since someone had been up here? There were more rooms than I'd expected. To my surprise, there was a small kitchenette, like for an apartment. There was also a porch that was on top of the porch on the first floor. The small bathroom had a sink, a shower, and a toilet. How did that all work? Could someone have lived up here? Carrie Mae had never said anything about it. The room with the three front windows tugged at my heart. We had to chuckle at the very old floral wallpaper on all the walls. Considering its age, the wallpaper was in very good shape.

"These walls are so ugly that they're kind of appealing, don't you think?" I asked, smiling.

Alex nodded and laughed. "The bathroom is so small that you could multitask in there, if you know what I mean."

We laughed at the thought. "If these walls could talk,

man, oh man! Hey, I'm burning up in this heat. Let's get downstairs."

Carrie Mae was once again looking over Rosie's inventory with envy. The movers were getting ready to leave, and they asked Carrie Mae about directions to their next destination.

"Carrie Mae, could the upstairs have been a little apartment years ago?" I asked.

She snickered and looked at the floor. "I hate to admit it, honey, but when I first got married, we lived in that apartment upstairs until I purchased the Uptown Store. It killed me to see this house rot away all these years with no one in it. I'm glad the house is serving a purpose again."

"Good lands, Carrie, that's pretty cool. I think it all could be fixed up once again." She chucked and shook her head in doubt.

We all said goodbye, and Carrie Mae encouraged Alex and I to come back soon.

When we got in the car, Alex said he thought the move went very well. "So, Lily Girl, what's your next move, now that you've got a big pocketbook?"

"It's not that big. I guess I need to concentrate on finding a place to live out here. I could do a down payment on something, I suppose."

"You may want to rent before you buy, to make sure you like it out here."

I nodded. "Tomorrow, I begin the shop cleanup. First things first."

"Okay, I am suddenly very busy the next couple of days," Alex teased.

I laughed. "I know. I can handle it."

"Are you worried that Melanie may return?"

"I've got her keys. I think she knew she got off lucky since we didn't call the police."

When we got back to Rosie's shop, we parted ways. I was exhausted and had no intention of going inside.

When I got back to my apartment, a rainshower suddenly came down. There was no sign of Bertie.

I cleaned up and then put a frozen pot pie in the oven. When I checked my email, my sisters were all waiting for a report about my move. I took time to respond, giving a quick description and saying that the yellow house was quite intriguing. I promised them I would send photos soon.

I took a glass of merlot and the pot pie to the porch. I loved the smell of summer rain. As a child, I always wished I could play in the rain, but I didn't remember that ever happening. I heard my cell phone ring, and it was Holly.

"I thought of you today," Holly said. "How did it go?"

"Very well. Wait until you see that house. We nearly filled up the entire first floor."

"How did Marc do?"

"I think he actually enjoyed himself. He drove separately from Alex and me. Tomorrow I clean the shop. I'll be glad to be done with it all."

"Let me know when you're going out to Augusta again and I'll try to go with you," Holly noted.

"What about the monster?"

"As long as I get home before he needs his din-din," she said with disgust.

"Okay, I'll let you know."

We hung up, and when I finished dinner I headed

straight to bed. I wanted to dream about the yellow house in the rolling hills of wine country. Part of me was almost there, but not quite.

Chapter 55

When I awoke, I dressed in grubby clothes to tackle the job ahead. There was no cleaning equipment to speak of at the shop, so I gathered some things to take with me.

I checked my emails, and Loretta's anger about Sarah spilled over into all of them. I'd have to call her before this got out of control.

While I was on my laptop, I checked eBay to see how quilts were selling and whether there were any new red-and-white quilts for sale. It didn't take long to notice that the patterns on sale were the ones commonly offered. When I went through my collection, I would keep these patterns in mind and put them up for sale.

By ten thirty, I was at Rosie's shop with my cleaning supplies. I opened the back door, hoping no one like Melanie would pay me a visit. In no hurry to start cleaning, I called Loretta.

"Glad to hear things went well yesterday," Loretta greeted me.

"Yup, and now I'm about to get started cleaning up the

shop. I sure wish you were here!" She laughed. "I'm calling about Sarah, Loretta."

"Yeah, I know, it's pretty disappointing."

"She called me."

"She did?"

"She's bothered by how hard you're taking this. She felt that if I talked to you, you would better understand her decision."

"Ahhh! Well, it's not okay, and I hope you told her that. She will regret her decision."

"Maybe not. You surely don't want her to go through with the wedding, knowing how she feels!"

"She's independent like you, and she thinks you have the perfect life."

"That's not fair, Loretta. Not everyone wants a permanent commitment with a white picket fence."

"I think both of you will regret being single when you get older."

"Maybe, and maybe not. I'm still open to a relationship, just as Sarah is."

"Who is going to take care of you?"

"Good question, but I hope it's my own security plan. Look, just let up on her and love her for who she is. She mentioned she would like to visit. It's fine with me if she does so."

"You'd probably influence her to move away from here."

"I would not."

"She idolizes you and could easily be convinced."

"Look, just don't do anything to lose her completely," I advised.

"Okay, you've made your point. I do love that girl and

want her to be happy."

"That's just what you need to tell her."

I hung up feeling like my mission was accomplished.

I didn't know what part of the shop to start with, but my mother always said you should start from the top and continue down to the floors. I started with a dust rag. The place was filthier than I'd expected. Some things I felt needed to be pitched, but that wasn't my responsibility. Rosie had had a vacuum, but something told me it was inadequate, and I soon found out that I was right. The windows needed washed, but again, I felt unwilling to go that far. I did clean the window in the door and was tempted to take Rosie's open and closed sign with me. I decided against it, as it was pretty worn and tattered. I wanted my own fresh one when the time came.

People kept looking in the window. Thankfully, no one knocked.

At five, I looked around to assess my progress. The store looked at least fifty percent better than before. I locked the back door, gathered my belongings, then took one last look and said aloud, "Lily Girl is leaving, but I'm taking you with me, Rosie! I'll never forget you!"

Chapter 56

With little sleep, I was wide awake at four, realizing I had nowhere to go today. I was free to take the next step, whatever that would be. I knew a place to live in Augusta wouldn't magically appear, so I needed to focus on looking for myself or getting a realtor.

While I was in the shower, I decided to make a trip to Augusta, where hopefully I could figure some of this out. There was no point in putting it off.

I took my coffee to the porch and saw that it was a beautiful day to make the drive.

I dressed in shorts, a t-shirt, and sandals for what looked to be a humid, hot Missouri day.

When I checked my emails, there were none from my family, Alex, or Marc. Marc was more than likely going to move on, I told myself.

I passed Bertie talking to another neighbor on the sidewalk and waved hello.

Morning traffic slowed me down until I got to Weldon Spring, where the winding roads began. It was like entering a different part of the world! How nice it must have been for those out here who didn't have to commute in the highway traffic every day.

I always looked forward to arriving in Defiance, because the other towns were not far from there. I hoped no one would be behind me so that I could take my time on these challenging roads. The locals hated getting behind someone like me because passing was nearly impossible.

I wanted to stop at Wine Country Gardens, but it was too early for lunch. I liked seeing the little mom and pop businesses appearing along the Katy Trail. A trendy new spot called the Trail Smokehouse had opened recently. It attracted not only bicyclists, but the locals as well, with good food and a great view.

Passing a sign directing me to the historic Daniel Boone home reminded me of a day's visit I had once enjoyed, years ago. There was so much to see out this way. I passed the road to Chandler Hill Winery, a huge development that attracted weddings and larger parties. When I thought of all the wine drinkers who traveled these winding roads, especially at night, I shuddered.

I decided to stay focused on getting to Augusta instead of stopping here and there. Some of the charming barns and outbuildings caught my interest as possible fixer-uppers for a place to live.

When I arrived in Augusta, I didn't want to bother Carrie Mae just yet without doing some looking around. She had given me a map that was supposed to be helpful, but it was like reading a crossword puzzle the way the short streets connected.

When I drove down the hill to the yellow house, I

decided to park and pay it a visit. I had to give the door a good push once I'd mastered unlocking it. The musty smell hit me once again. I may have brought some of Rosie's antique shop smells with me! I started to give the rows of furniture a look when I saw the old toolbox sitting right in front of me. I had distinctly remembered packing it with some old tin signs. What was it doing here? I'd meant to give it to Marc. I wondered if Carrie Mae had been in here since the move. I ignored the thought until I went down the aisle and saw Rosie's Rolodex sitting on top of the sideboard. That too had been packed with some other things from Rosie's back room. I suddenly felt odd about being there

I continued on upstairs, where the heat was heavier, making it difficult to even breathe. I wanted to open the windows and air the place out, but Carrie Mae had warned me about most of the windows being difficult to open. I had to marvel once again at the unpainted woodwork. Thank goodness it had remained untouched by any paintbrush through the years. Seeing the little doors underneath the attic roofline reminded me of my childhood. We'd had an upstairs like this where I'd played with my dolls. I was tempted to look inside the doors, but the heat was killing me.

I went downstairs, wondering once again who would have been here to unpack those items. I would ask Carrie Mae as soon as I saw her. I securely locked the door and already felt some sense of ownership of the yellow beast.

Chapter 57

I decided to leave my car and walk the several blocks to Carrie Mae's store. When I entered her shop, she appeared to have her hands full with a mother and three wild children running about. When I said hello, Carrie Mae rolled her eyes. The children were picking up merchandise to play with like it was their own. The mother was clueless as she examined some of the antique quilts for sale. I couldn't help but wonder how I would react under the same circumstances.

"I just came back from the house," I informed Carrie Mae.

"Wonderful!" she said as she was trying to concentrate.

"I can help this lady with the quilts, if you want to gather up all the merchandise," I boldly offered. The woman gave me a mean look. I supposed I'd offended her, but better me than Carrie Mae.

"I guess we'd better get going," the lady said, grabbing one of her children by the arm. "Come on, let's go. You all have been so good. Remember what Mommy promised you if you were good?" They yelled and screamed with delight as they went out the door.

Carrie Mae and I looked at each other and burst into laughter.

"Thank you, Lily," Carrie Mae said, clearly relieved. "You saved me from a heart attack! What are you up to today?"

"Oh, I guess I've been snooping around out here for a place to live, but something peculiar just happened when I was at the house."

"What's that, sweetie?" she asked, concerned.

"Has anyone been in the yellow house since I moved in the antiques?"

"Not to my knowledge. I certainly haven't been there. Why?"

"Two items which had been packed away were out in the open for me to see."

"Like what, for heaven's sake?"

"There's an old toolbox that I intend to give to Marc, and I distinctly remember packing it with old tin signs. It was sitting by the front door."

"Well, if that isn't something!"

"Yes, and then Rosie's Rolodex was out of the box and sitting on top of the sideboard. It was packed with other things from her back room."

Carrie Mae shook her head. "You're sure you didn't get them out as a reminder to yourself?"

"Absolutely! Are you sure no one else has a key? I guess I'm just paranoid after what I went through with Rosie's employee."

"You're the only one besides me who has a key. These two items have meaning, don't they?" I nodded with hesitation.

"Maybe it was Rosie. Maybe she's here with you!"

"Well, in spirit, of course. Every time I look at one of her pieces, I think of her. I feel as if she'll be helping me with this adventure."

"I'd say she's already begun!" I gave Carrie Mae a funny look. "Hey, honey, I've dealt with enough old buildings to know that strange things happen."

"You mean like ghosts?"

"Call them what you want. Rosie died a dramatic death. I wouldn't be surprised if she wants to get even or make some of her wishes come true. I don't think you should be too bothered about it all. She is going to be your cheerleader as you move along."

"Do you really think so?"

"You bet! Now, back to a place to live. Did you see anything you want to check out?"

"No, I'm afraid not. I don't know which should come first, the shop or a place to live."

"Well, I can rent you the yellow house for your shop, since everything's moved in. I think the location will work for you. It's nothing fancy, but for antiques, it doesn't have to be. Have you thought about that?"

"I have, but I thought you may need it. It's kind of separated from the other businesses."

"There's always another empty building for me. I'm fine. As for the location, when you have a sign for antiques, people will go anywhere."

"I guess you're right. I know I do."

"I won't charge you rent until you open your shop for business. How about that?"

"Oh, that would be swell. Thanks so much! This is pretty unreal right now!"

"You'll find a place to live as time goes along, but I would get busy on a license and start unpacking." That sounded great.

"I can't wait to tell Alex!"

"You might want to make a stop at our nice library and ask for a sweet girl named Susan. She's real familiar with everything out here and may know of a place to live."

"Thanks, I will."

"Now let me know when you come back out again. I may know some folks who would be willing to help you. There are always folks looking for part-time work."

I gave Carrie Mae a big hug, almost disturbing the pink flower in her hair bun, and happily went out the door to head to the library.

Chapter 58

I rushed into the library just before they closed. I was pretty impressed with its size in this little town. That would definitely be of interest to me as a resident. I asked the lady at the information desk if she could point me to Susan.

"I'm sorry, but Susan is off today," the lady replied. "May I help you with something?"

"No, thank you."

"Would you like to leave your name and number for her?"

"Yes, thank you."

I wrote my name and number and the reason for my inquiry on a notepad. I had so much on my mind that I decided to leave.

I left Augusta with the satisfaction of knowing I now had a shop to call my own. Alex's assistance and Lynn's artistic abilities would certainly help me a lot.

My mind was racing all the way home. I called Alex and asked if he would meet me at Rigazzi's for dinner so I could share my news. He quickly agreed and said we should share our celebration with Lynn. I smiled and called her right away.

She was delighted, because Carl was working late again.

I rushed up my porch steps and saw no sign of Bertie. Cocktail hour was usually a good time to catch her on the porch, since that's when the neighbors were out and about.

I quickly showered and primped my face the best I could. I was almost singing, I was so happy.

When I came out of my apartment, Harry was walking by.

"Say, Lily, have you seen Bertie lately?" he asked, with concern.

"No, I was wondering the same," I responded. I could see he was truly concerned.

"Well, I knocked, but there was no answer. I guess she went somewhere."

"We'll know more in the morning, I suppose," I said, getting into my car. "Have a good evening."

Alex was already enjoying a cold fishbowl of beer when I arrived. I gave him a big hug.

"Do you want to sit outside?" he politely asked.

"No, this AC feels pretty good," I responded.

Lynn came in, and we all hugged in a group. Lynn immediately wanted to know my news.

"I want to make a toast to your shop, Lily, but you don't have a name for it, do you?" Alex joked.

"Oh, you're right. I don't feel right using Rosie's name. I need to make it my own," I stated.

"Well, you're only intending to sell quilts and antiques, right?" Lynn asked.

"Well, say no more, Lily Girl," Alex said boldly. "How does 'Lily Girl's Quilts and Antiques' sound?" We looked at each other.

"Oh, Alex, I love it. Rosie would love it too. That's what she always called me," I gushed.

"It's a darling name, and no one will have one like it, that's for sure," Lynn cheered.

"Okay, raise your glasses," Alex instructed. "Here's to the success of Lily Girl's Quilts and Antiques!" We cheered.

As we drank beer and shared a pizza, I asked them both for input on what I should display and what I could do to make it look inviting.

"Laurie would love to help you with stuff like that," Lynn said. "This is right up her alley!"

"Great idea! I suppose I could take a sleeping bag and hang out upstairs, so I don't have to go back and forth so often."

"Good thinking, Lily," Alex said. "I hate to be the one to plan the rest of your life, but why don't you ask Carrie Mae if you can fix up that little apartment upstairs to live in for now? It's a lot smaller than what you have, and it does need a lot of work, but I can see it looking pretty darn cute!"

I stared at him. He knew what I was thinking. Lynn held her tongue since she had never seen the place.

Chapter 59

"I wonder what Carrie Mae would say about that?" I asked with concern..

"She'll get more rent and her building will get an update," Alex pointed out. "Better yet, Lily, she might consider selling you the building."

"Alex, do you think Lily is made of money or something?" Lynn sarcastically asked.

"Perhaps in time she would sell it, and if I do well with my business, I could actually buy it," I fantasized.

"Well, at least you're thinking positively," Lynn responded. "You just bought that inventory, and I know it takes a while to establish a business." Alex could tell I had not told Lynn about the money Rosie had left for me.

"Look, whatever scenario you come up with, I'm certain Carrie Mae will work with you," Alex said with vigor. "She has everything to gain from your interest in the place."

"You're probably right there, Alex," Lynn agreed.

The rest of the evening was full of silly notions, plans, and ideas, as well as lots of laughs. I was so lucky to have

Alex and Lynn's support with whatever I decided. Lynn didn't bring up Carl's name, which was a good thing. She was working through a difficult situation and I wanted to support her. I did have to wonder where Carl really was tonight.

I got home around midnight. The neighborhood was sound asleep. For a moment, I wondered about Bertie and told myself to check on her in the morning.

Sleep came easily because in one day, I had secured a place to do business and even reside, if I wanted. "Lily Girl's Quilts and Antiques" had a nice ring to it and made me smile.

The next morning, I felt the effect of drinking a large fishbowl of beer and headed for some aspirin. My phone was ringing, and it was Sarah.

"I'm sorry I'm calling so early," she said apologetically. "I was wondering if you minded if I came to see you this weekend. Do you have plans?"

I was half asleep, trying to digest what she was asking. "Yes. I mean, no," I stumbled. "Sure; does your mother know?"

"I just told her I was going. I can only stay a couple of days because of this part-time job, but it's worth it to get away."

"You're flying?" I presume?"

"Yes. I'll come in on Friday night. I could stay with Lynn, but she and Carl are having issues, so I'd rather stay with you."

"That's fine, but I'll have to go out to the wine country to take care of some things regarding my antiques," I warned.

"Oh, the wine country! How cool!"

"Don't get too excited. I'll be putting you to work!"

"Great! No problem. I'll text you my flight information."

When we hung up, I really had a headache. I didn't want to get in the middle of Sarah and Loretta. Maybe Lynn would have some ideas.

I got coffee and went onto the porch to check the weather. I was thinking about how to approach Carrie Mae about the apartment upstairs. Surely she would know who could do the various repairs that would be needed. I should also be sure to check with Bertie this morning in case she needed anything from the store.

Before I went inside, I savored the last sip of coffee and called Holly. I couldn't wait to tell her about occupying the yellow house.

"Oh, I can't believe it!" she responded joyfully. "It's all happening pretty fast, don't you think?"

"I know, but it seems right," I tried to explain. "How is the monster today?"

"He keeps following me around, which drives me crazy. He has nothing to do but interfere in my life. I need to get out of here. Do you want to go to lunch?"

I thought about all I needed to do. "Why don't you stop by here? I need to go through all my quilts to decide which ones to sell, so you could be helpful."

"Sounds good. I'll pick up some lunch and be there around eleven thirty."

"Wonderful!"

When I hung up, I thought about how sad it was for someone to think of any excuse to get away from their house and husband. Surely this was unusual, or did women just not want to admit ttheir abuse?

Chapter 60

When I felt fully awake, I called Carrie Mae.

"Oh, honey, were you coming out today? Because I'm closing the store to go out with my friend, Betty" she explained.

"No, I'm not, but I want to ask you something." I paused. "What would you say about me fixing up the second floor as well, so I can move out there sooner? It will be just until I find something."

I could tell I'd caught her off guard. "Are you sure you want to spend the time and energy for that? It's going to take some fixing that will cost you money. I'm not sure about those old appliances, for example."

"I know, I know. I've thought about all of that. If you can recommend some folks to help me out, I'll pay for it."

"Sure. There's the Stiezer Contractors out here. They do small and large jobs. You can meet with one of them to get some kind of idea about what you would need and the cost of it. Don't get me wrong, Lily, I love the idea of shop owners living above their shops, but I'm not sure it'll be right for your circumstances."

"Well, it never hurts to look into it. I'll probably be out there this weekend because my niece is coming in for a visit. I thought I would put her to work."

She chuckled. "Good luck with that. She may have the wineries in mind."

"You enjoy your day off, Carrie Mae. I'm sure you need it."

We hung up, and I thought that all in all, the conversation had gone well. It would be up to me to make this all work. Holly would be arriving anytime, so I needed to change clothes and check on Bertie.

When I rang Bertie's doorbell, I also knocked. She seemed to be more hard of hearing lately. I decided she truly wasn't there. She might have been a little miffed at me, but not enough to totally ignore me. I finally gave up and went back upstairs.

As I studied my quilt room, I came up with a game plan about how to separate the quilts.

Holly arrived, and we couldn't resist eating the turkey sandwiches she had brought from her favorite deli. She also brought a ruhbarb-strawberry pie, which I wasn't sure about until I tasted it. Holly was a good cook, with very few people appreciating her skill.

After lunch, we went into the quilt room and discussed how best to transport the quilts to the antique shop. It was too soon to put them into containers, but we did refold each one, which I tried to do on a regular basis. As we unfolded them, I decided which ones I could part with.

Holly was in awe as we looked at each one. She hadn't seen many of them before. For me, it was like visiting old friends. I remembered where I'd purchased most of them and from whom.

"Oh, Lily, I remember when you bought this Shoo Fly quilt," Holly noted with a chuckle. "Remember when we went to the antique shop in that little town where the creepy spa was?"

"Do I ever! That was such a nasty old hotel."

"I'm surprised we didn't get electrocuted or catch some kind of disease from there," Holly said, rubbing her arms in disgust.

"When I think back about getting into that claw-foot tub with an electric fan at the edge, I shiver all over. How could they pass any kind of health inspection?"

Holly shook her head. "I kept thinking it was the perfect place for the monster to have me killed."

"Yeah, and I would have been blamed for it," I said. "I had an uneasy feeling when they separated us. You know, I may write about that hotel experience one day. I wonder if it's still there."

"I doubt it, but I'm not going back," Holly firmly stated. "You got a good buy on that quilt because the lady was having a slow day, remember?" I nodded and smiled. "Shame on you, Lily!"

"I never pay attention to the asking price; you know that," I said defensively. "If I decide that I like it, I buy it. They price things to have a little wiggle room, so it never hurts to ask if that's the best they can do. By the way, she laid out the price, not me."

Holly laughed. "I know, because we looked at each other in shock!"

I pulled out the next quilt, which was a red-and-white Irish Chain.

"I think I can let this one go. There are so many out there

to be had, and this one doesn't have very good quilting."

"Hmmm, maybe I'll buy it," Holly said as she examined it. "How much are you going to want for this?"

"I have no idea, but why don't you wait until I get all of my quilts that I'll be selling together?" I suggested. "If you're interested in anything, then we can talk price. I'll always make you a good deal, girlfriend." She smiled at the idea.

"So what are you hearing from Marc these days?" Holly asked, changing the subject.

"I don't know. I haven't seen him since he helped me with the move. Maybe he's thinking I'm going to be needy in the days to come."

"Don't be silly. You should probably show a little more interest. Have you thanked him for helping you? A dinner invitation might be nice."

"I don't know, and I'm really busy right now. Besides, I have an antique toolbox in mind to give him when I see him again."

"Oh, that's romantic!" Holly teased. "That should be a big hint for sure."

I chuckled. "No, it's not like that. He shared with me that he misses tinkering with handiwork, like he did years ago. I know he would love it. These old tools and boxes bring big bucks. Rosie had a two-hundred-and-fifty-dollar price tag on it."

"You've got to be kidding me!" Holly gasped.

Chapter 61

Holly looked at her watch at five and nearly fainted.

"Good heavens! I've got to get home!"

"Oh, that's right! The monster has to have a magical dinner appear at the same moment every night."

"Sorry, you know my drill. I want to meet Sarah when she comes; don't forget!"

"I'll remember, and thanks for your help today," I said as she flew out the door.

I continued with my sorting. My pile for resale was getting higher. Maybe the retail bug was starting to bite. It appeared I was seeing more red-and-white quilts than other colors, which made sense to me, of course.

I took a break and went out on my front porch for fresh air. My mind was once again on Bertie. It had been days since I'd seen her. My cell went off, and it was Lynn.

"I'm so glad you called, Lynn" I greeted her.

"I hear we're getting a guest this weekend." Lynn noted.

"I'm not sure it's a good time for me with all the work I have to do. I hope you can entertain her."

"I'll do my best, but you're her favorite auntie for sure. I'll pick her up at the airport and we can all meet up for dinner somewhere. She just wants to get away for a couple of days, and I don't blame her."

"Thanks, Lynn. I appreciate anything you can do."

"I saw Marc at a fundraiser last night, and he asked about you," Lynn informed me.

"That's nice."

"He's a rather prideful sort and I think he feels a bit rejected, but he didn't say as much. He knows this is a busy time for you."

"He shouldn't feel rejected, and I'm pleased he hasn't been pushy, if you know what I mean."

"I appreciate your not asking about Carl," Lynn said. "I think he's trying to give me more attention, but who really knows?"

"You should know!" I said, raising my voice. "If you feel he still may be seeing someone, you need to address it, no matter how painful."

"I know. Please don't lecture me," Lynn insisted. "Why don't I fix dinner here when Sarah comes? Carl will join us then for sure."

"Fine. What can I bring?"

"I wouldn't refuse some of those great cannoli! That would be awesome."

I went back into the quilt room to continue my mission. I looked at my quilts as friends I had rescued from here and there. I was reminded that some needed repair, and I stored them away to take care of later. I wasn't fond of putting something new with the old. I had a bigger sense of forgiveness when my quilts weren't perfect. Their telltale quirks were part of the life they'd led before meeting me. But if I could do something to keep the damage from getting worse, I wanted to. Holly had a real knack for quilt restoration, so I ask for her for help.

I always checked for fold lines on the backs of the quilts. It told me a lot about their previous storage conditions. A quilt needs love and it needs air, or it likely won't survive, I told myself. I also had a quirky notion that I couldn't mix certain quilts with my other quilts. If I bought two or three from the same estate, I felt they should stay together, like children from the same parents.

I jumped when I heard a heavy knock at the door. To my surprise, it was Harry, and I asked him to come in.

"Sorry to bother you, Lily, but I think there's something out of the ordinary going on in Bertie's apartment. Do you have a key?"

"No, I don't, but do you think she's home?"

"I'm pretty sure, because I just saw Sugar sitting in the window. Bertie would never leave that cat alone while she went out."

"Okay, so what we need to do is call the police and tell them about our concerns," I suggested.

We did just that. I told them I didn't want sirens to alarm the neighborhood. The gentleman on the phone was very nice and said he understood. He said there was someone patrolling the area and that he would send him over right away. I looked at Harry's frightened face and tried to assure him that everything would be okay. I was seeing once again how much he thought of Bertie, and it was sweet.

Chapter 62

In no time, a nice elderly policeman pulled up in front of the apartment. Harry and I waited patiently on the front porch to meet him. He wanted to walk around the back of the building before doing any forced entry.

I stayed on the porch, but Harry followed right behind the policeman. By now, neighbors were alarmed and curious. They were starting to gather, so I went to join Harry to avoid talking to them. The policeman was working on the back door.

"We can see her in her bed," Harry cried in a frantic voice.

"Oh my goodness, does she look okay?" Why hadn't I gone around and looked in her windows?

"He's calling for an ambulance," Harry reported.

I started to run to the back door to enter, but I was held back.

"Stay here, ma'am," the policeman instructed. "The ambulance will be here shortly. It's best they address her needs right away. Does she live alone?"

"Yes. Please let me go to her,"

"Sorry, but we don't know what to expect," he insisted.

"Here comes Sugar," Harry yelled out, and he grabbed the frightened cat that went directly to him.

When the ambulance arrived, I rushed in to see what I could of Bertie. She was as white as a ghost. Her body didn't show any signs of life. I thought I was going to faint. I looked away as the orderlies did their checkup routines. I walked towards the door and prayed for her recovery. It seemed forever until they finally carried her out on the gurney.

"Is she alive?" I asked in panic.

"Yes, she's alive," Harry answered. "The poor thing!"

I asked where they were taking her, because I wanted to follow.

"Here are her keys, Lily," Harry said sadly as he handed them to me. "We need to make sure everything is locked up."

"Why don't you go on home, Harry?" I suggested, giving him a slight hug. "I'll go to the hospital."

"No, siree!" he replied. "I'll have none of that. I'll put Sugar in my house and come with you."

"Okay, I'll run upstairs and get my purse."

In no time, we were on our way.

"Do you know of any family, Harry?" I asked to break the silence. He shook his head. "I may have seen some come and go, but I was never introduced to anyone," I sadly reported.

Driving to the large medical city of Barnes Hospital was crazy. We only knew to drive toward any sign that read EMERGENCY. Harry, in his eighties, hadn't driven in years, and was no help figuring out where to go.

Twenty minutes later, we finally left my car parked by a meter that had limited time on it. I kept stopping folks along the hallway in the direction of where I figured they had taken her. I was beginning to think we'd gone to the wrong place when I recognized one of the ambulance workers. I went over to ask where we could find Bertie. The worker instructed us to go to a certain desk to inquire. I grabbed Harry's hand and moved him along as best as I could.

The receptionist first asked if we were kin to Bertie. When I explained there wasn't any kin and that we were her neighbors who had found her, she seemed more sympathetic. She told us to have a seat and said she would find out what she could.

We took a seat, and I asked Harry if he wanted some coffee, which they had on a table nearby. He shook his head. There were so many distractions from crying babies, folks talking loudly on their cell phones, and soem folks ailing from injuries that were holding temporary bandages on their wounds.

I went impatiently back to the desk again. A different lady looked at me strangely and then said she would send out a Dr. Peters to talk to me. This made me feel better. I went back to the seat next to Harry and told him we should know something really soon. It was another fifteen minutes before someone approached us.

"Are you the folks asking about Mrs. Bertha Maxwell?" I had forgotten Bertie's last name.

"Yes, yes," Harry answered. "Is she going to be okay?"

The doctor looked forlorn. "I'm afraid your neighbor had one or more strokes and didn't recover," he quietly reported.

"What do you mean?" asked Harry in disbelief.

"She has passed on. There was nothing else we could do for her. I'm so sorry. We are trying to find her next of kin.

Can you help us with that?"

I looked at him as if he was talking in slow motion. Did I hear him say that Bertie had died?

Harry looked as if he had just lost his very best friend, and perhaps he had.

"Why don't the two of you sit here for a bit? I know this is a shock," the doctor said comfortingly.

"I'll leave you my name and number," I said. "I live in Bertie's building. If you need a contact, I'm probably it." The doctor nodded as I scribbled on some paper nearby. "Let's go, Harry. We need to get out of here," I said, leading the way. Luckily, my car was still where I'd left it. We got inside, and the two of us could no longer hold back the tears.

Chapter 63

When I got home, I was almost nauseous going up the stairs. My neglect by ignoring Bertie was sure to haunt me.

Sleep wasn't happening as I thought of what all could be ahead. The only good thing about Bertie's death was that I wouldn't have to face her when I moved away. Hopefully, family could be located so I could pay my respects before leaving. Memories of her and Sugar kept rumbling in my head. Would I have been willing to keep Sugar if Harry hadn't come to the rescue? Would there be a funeral for Bertie, or nothing, like there was for Rosie? How could I lose two people I cared about in such a short span of time?

I wasn't sure I slept at all, but at six in the morning, I got up and made coffee before I called Lynn. I hated to wake her so early, but I needed to cancel Sarah's visit. I was not in the frame of mind to entertain anyone.

"What's wrong?" Lynn asked in a groggy voice.

"I'm so sorry to wake you, but Bertie died last night. I need to cancel Sarah's trip and wondered if you would do it for me."

"Of course. What happened?"

"She had multiple strokes and we didn't discover her until days later, thinking she was just away. She died at the hospital yesterday. I feel bad about not checking more closely on her, but I thought she was a little miffed about me moving away and was ignoring me."

"Oh, Lily, don't blame yourself," Lynn consoled me. "Sarah can come another time. I'm worried about you."

"I'll be fine. Harry took her cat. Harry's also devastated, of course."

"Well, just concentrate on your move. The sooner you move from there, the better."

She was right. I hung up, took my coffee to the porch, and sat down to call Alex. I had to leave a message, and then I went inside to get dressed. I wanted out of this building as soon as possible, no matter the state of the yellow house in Augusta!

There were a few extra boxes from the shop move, so I began packing books from my bedroom shelves to keep my mind busy. In no time, I laid on the floor and fell asleep, since I hadn't gotten much sleep the night before.

Around ten that evening, I was awakened by a phone call from Alex. Half-asleep, I mumbled a description of the chain of events surrounding Bertie.

"I need to get out of here," I stressed to Alex.

"I'll help you as much as I can," he promised. "I'm so sorry."

Alex suggested I pack the car with essentials the next time I drove to Augusta so that I could spend the night in order to accomplish more. I was in agreement, but still groggy. I hung up and fell back asleep, not caring when or if I woke up again. I did wake up around eleven the next morning, but it felt like it was a week later. I got up to make coffee and examined the half-empty boxes of books.

Chapter 64

I had just slipped on shorts and a t-shirt when there was a knock at my door.

"Yes?" I answered before I opened,

"Ms. Rosenthal?" a masculine voice asked as I slowly opened the door. "I'm Andrew Collins, Bertie's brother."

"You are?" I questioned.

He smiled. "May I come in and have a word?" he asked politely. "I came to thank you for finding her and sending her to the hospital."

"I should have found her sooner, I'm afraid," I confessed. "I feel so bad, and I hope she didn't suffer."

"We may not really know that for sure. To be honest with you, Ms. Rosenthal, Bertie and I never communicated. I live in Chicago and we just didn't keep in touch with one another."

"I see."

"I've been looking through Bertie's things and can't find a lease naming you as a tenant."

"I never had a lease. I told her I would give her plenty of

notice when I decided to leave, and we let it go at that. I tried to do errands for her and look after her, if you know what I mean."

"I appreciate that. I must also tell you that I'll be putting this building up for sale right away, but I don't want you to feel you have to move. I'm sure the new owner would appreciate a dedicated tenant like you."

"Well, as luck would have it, I plan to move in the next thirty days. Bertie wasn't happy about it when I told her. I knew it would be a big change for her."

He nodded "Well, then, this will work out. I'm sure the building will need some repairs, so it's best that I wait until the entire building is empty."

"Will you be around for a while? Will there be a funeral?"

He shrugged. "Bertie made her will twenty years ago and didn't specify."

"Everyone around here knew Bertie," I said. "The last couple of years she rarely left the house, but folks would come by and visit with her. She was always at my door to tell me the latest neighborhood news."

"I've instructed the funeral home to proceed with cremation. Do you feel a memorial service would be in order?" I stared at him in disbelief. He was asking me?

"Bertie's life should matter and count for something. I know she used to attend St. Ambrose. Perhaps they have a small chapel where a service could occur."

He was thinking. "I'll have to look into what is feasible," he said finally. Feasible? "Here's my contact information. I'll be in town for a bit to get the place listed and do whatever else might come up. I happened to find your number next to her phone. I guess she called you frequently."

I nodded. "Please let me know what you decide, because folks will be asking."

"I will, and thank you again for everything you've done for her. Bertie and I were never close and we had a strange upbringing. It was nice to meet you, and good luck with your new residence."

"Thanks," I responded solemnly.

Out the door he went. I was totally baffled as to how someone's brother could be so distant. How could a simple funeral not be feasible? It gave me pause to think how lucky I was to have loving siblings I cared about and who cared about me.

So now I had to come to grips with the reality of a realtor's sign posted in my front yard. How would I be handling this if I hadn't planned to move? I needed to prepare Carrie Mae for speeding up my moving process. The upstairs of the yellow house would have to do for now.

My phone rang. It was Sarah.

"I'm sorry to hear about your neighbor," she said with sincerity. "I can help you pack anytime, if you want. Mom says it will be fine."

"I appreciate it very much, but I'll have to let you know. I want you to enjoy your trip, but right now, I can't make that happen."

"I understand," Sarah said sweetly. "We love you!"

I felt so overwhelmed that I couldn't get my body to do much of anything. The excitement of leaving here was being overshadowed by guilt.

It was now four, so I called Carrie Mae before she closed her store. I took my phone to the front porch, where a pleasant summer breeze was blowing.

Carrie Mae was pleased to hear from me, as always. When I told her about Bertie, she seemed to truly feel my grief.

"Her brother stopped by today to tell me he's putting this building up for sale," I shared.

"Well, that's quick. Is he forcing you to get out?"

"No, not really. He wants to be fair. If it's okay, I'd like to start moving my personal things upstairs."

"Sure, but it needs a good cleaning, my dear," Carrie Mae reminded me. "It doesn't sound like there will be time for painting and removing wallpaper, which would do wonders."

"No, there isn't. I'll come out soon and start cleaning. Any contact numbers for other help would be appreciated."

"Will do. I'll ask my cleaning lady Korine to try to help you. I don't have her clean that often, but she's quite good."

"That would be great. I'm not worried about the décor right now. I may stay overnight as well."

"Whatever you like! You'd never find a vacant spot in my apartment, but we have many fine B&Bs here that would love to have you."

Chapter 65

The next day, I told myself I had no time to blame myself for what had happened to Bertie. She'd known I cared for her, and I'd shown it for many years.

I went off to Tony's to get more boxes and a cup of coffee. I was greeted instantly with a big hug from Tony, who seemed to know every detail about Bertie's death.

"Any word on arrangements?" he asked as he poured my coffee.

"None. She's been cremated, according to her brother. He was debating whether to have a service. He's putting the building up for sale right away, so it's a good thing I had already planned to move."

"No funeral for that God-fearing woman?" Tony asked with outrage.

I shrugged my shoulders. "I'm sure we'll hear something soon. Thanks for the boxes and coffee."

As I left, I wondered about Harry. He would certainly be the first to hear if there were any services.

While I was dragging the boxes upstairs, my cell

phone rang. It was Alex.

"What's up?" I asked, out of breath.

"I'm just offering my help today if you need it. I finished an article late last night, so I'm free. I can bring some of my chicken salad for lunch, if you like."

"Oh, is it the one with grapes and walnuts?"

"That's it!"

"Deal! I just got more boxes from Tony, so I may start packing in the kitchen today. You can finish up on the books and linens."

"You're the boss!"

I couldn't believe Alex's timing. He was the soulmate that knew me so well. Sometimes we would finish each other's sentences. He was like a brother I could share anything with.

I tried to get organized as well as I could before his arrival. Where to start in my kitchen was puzzling. I started by throwing out expired spices that I never used.

Alex came through the door with a quick knock. After a slight hug, he complimented me on how much I had accomplished. He started unloading his paper bag full of goodies. I made iced tea as he made chicken salad sandwiches on croissants.

"Carrie Mae said I could move in anytime," I revealed to Alex. "I may go out tomorrow and start cleaning. I'm hoping her cleaning lady can help. I just want to get out of here as fast as I can. After losing Rosie and Bertie, I'm done on this street."

Alex shook his head. "I don't blame you," he said. "I've got another assignment due, but I'll come out and help when I can."

"I think Rosie's spirit has moved into the yellow house," I announced. Alex's mouth opened with interest. "Things have appeared that were packed away. They had certain significance."

When I finished telling him about the Rolodex and toolbox, Alex agreed that Rosie's ghost was alive and was there to assist me.

"It could be a good thing, especially if she's going to help you unpack," he joked. "I think it's cool when these buildings have a spirit hanging around. Hey, I'd better get to work here."

"As soon as you're done with those books, the quilt books in the quilt room need to be packed," I instructed.

"I can't believe you have this many books on one topic!"

"They're not on one topic," I argued. "I have books on quilt history, how-to books, and some quilt fiction."

"What are hexies?" Alex asked, laughing as he picked up one of my how-to books.

"They're patterns using hexagon shapes. It's an old pattern, but very trendy right now."

"Why don't you write a quilt book, for heaven's sake?" he asked with sincerity. "You're a writer and a quilt authority for sure."

"Do I need another book?" I grinned.

"But you're a collector. You could title it *You Can't Have Too Many Quilts,* or *Good Eye for Quilts.*" I had to chuckle. "Are there many quilt collectors?" Alex asked as he continued to check the book titles.

"I really don't know. I suppose if someone owns three or more, they might call themselves a collector."

"Is there any kind of quilt you don't like?"

I had to think. "Sort of. I don't like quilts that are scrappy or too fussy. They make me nervous."

"Nervous?" Alex asked with sarsasm.

"Yes, they're confusing. They don't have a message."

"You're crazy, my friend!" He shook his head with laughter.

Chapter 66

Feeling good about how much Alex and I had accomplished, I eagerly packed my things for a productive day at the yellow house. I decided to throw in a change of clothes in case I decided to spend the night.

Missouri in August could easily reach 100 degrees, and this might be one of those days. Thank goodness a fairly new furnace and air conditioner had been installed in the house.

When I got to Defiance, I pulled into the Trail Smokehouse to try their barbeque for lunch. Bikers and cyclists were pulling in from every direction to cool off and have a cold beer. While I enjoyed my delicious lunch, I looked through the many brochures for the area. There were so many towns and places to explore. It was obvious that the tourist business was alive and well in this region.

Between bites, I was interrupted by a handsome, athletic-looking man who said, "Don't I know you from somewhere?"

I looked at him to size up the proper response.

"You must be thinking of someone else, but it's a great line for an introduction." I boldly responded.

"That it is!" he said with a big smile. "I saw you come in and wondered if you were a local."

"No, I'm not, but in thirty days, I will be," I confessed.

"Well, that's interesting," he said, observing my every move. "I'm not a native either. By the way, I'm Nicholas Conrey. Everyone calls me Nick. Your name is?"

"Lily," I simply said as he waited for more. "Lily Rosenthal." I held out my hand for introduction.

"Nice to meet you," he said. "I'm on the bike trail today, unfortunately. It sure was a lot cooler when we started this morning."

"Hey, Nick, we're leaving!" a guy yelled from across the room.

"Okay, I'll be right there," Nick yelled back. "Hey, Lily, I hope I run into you again somewhere."

"Sure! Have fun and stay cool."

Well, that was interesting, I thought to myself. Was everyone out here this friendly?

With that bit of a morale boost, I drove the rest of the way to Augusta. There was a car parked in front of the yellow house when I arrived.

I cautiously walked in the door, feeling the wonderful cool air.

"Hello! Hello! Is anyone here?" I called up the stairs. There was a pause.

"Yes, ma'am," a lady's voice yelled back. "Are you Lily?"

"Yes, and you are?"

"Korine, Carrie Mae's cleaning lady. Didn't she tell you I was going to be here?" Now I remembered.

I walked up the stairs and noticed Korine was surrounded by a lot of cleaning equipment.

"I hope it's alright, but I started with this horrible bathroom up here," she said.

"Oh my, yes! Thank you!"

"You may want to replace that sink. I did the best I could."

"Oh, I will, but my move has to be earlier than expected, so I'll just have to live with it. I'm just thrilled to have air conditioning."

"Isn't that the truth? You could fry an egg on that sidewalk out there!"

"I'll bring my things in and put them in the downstairs kitchen. I brought some cold bottled water if you need it."

"That would be mighty nice, thank you. Just set a bottle on the step for me."

Korine was a pleasant surprise, and with her working diligently upstairs, I could start cleaning the downstairs kitchen. I almost fell over when I noticed Rosie's gingerbread cookie jar sitting on the counter That too had been carefully packed with the others. What else would I find? If this was a joke someone was playing on me, I was not amused. Perhaps I needed to change the locks again.

Chapter 67

The run-down vintage kitchen was at least more current than the galley kitchen upstairs. It had more cabinet space, so most of my dishes could be put there.

I went upstairs to check on Korine. She was a plain sort of lady in her forties, but looked older. She was in good shape, had no makeup, and wore her hair pulled back. She wasn't much for conversation, but I asked how long she had been working for Carrie Mae.

"I've known Carrie Mae forever," she said as she wiped down the woodwork. "I love when I can help her clean her glassware, but that doesn't happen very often. She's letting a lot of her tidiness go, I'm afraid."

"It's hard to keep up with it all and run the shop," I said with concern . "She has so much inventory."

"Oh, lands, woman, have you seen her teddy bears?"

"Teddy bears?' I asked, surprised. "I guess not."

"She's been collecting teddy bears all her life," clained Korine. "I've never seen her sell one of them."

"She has never mentioned teddy bears." I noted.

"Many years ago, like twenty or more, she would have teddy bear teas with the purpose of seeing what kinds of bears other folks had. She hoards them. I saw them by accident one day."

"Interesting," I replied slowly.

"That woman's life is full of stories. Someone should write a book about her."

"Yes, someone should," I responded with some interest.

"So I hear you'll just be staying up here until you find a place to live; is that right?"

"Yes. My landlady passed away and the building is up for sale."

"Well, you'll have a new roof over your head here," Korine teased. "The place isn't fancy, but from the looks of things, you have some pretty antiques for your shop."

"Yes, the shop is my priority, of course. If you have time to help me unpack, I could use the help."

Her face lit up. "Sure, if I have time. I love feeling pretty things. I ain't got much myself. When my husband died, I had to live off of my money from Carrie Mae and my social security, which isn't much."

"Well, there's plenty of work here. You can work today as long as you want. I'm going up to see Carrie Mae for a bit. I'll be back."

"I have her key for her, so I'll return it when I leave."

"You're doing a nice job. I can see improvement already." She grinned.

Carrie Mae was happy to see me, as always. I told her right away how much I appreciated Korine's help.

"She's a keeper. When she gets to know you better, she'll talk your head off."

"I think I'll spend the night out here tonight," I said with a sigh. "I hate the rush hour traffic, and I could keep working for a while. Do you know which B&B in Augusta would be the most reasonable for just me?"

She thought for a minute. "Let me give Kitty a call at her shop. She owns the Cottage Guest House across the street. It's close by, but she may have it booked."

While she went to check it out, I looked around and ended up by her row of quilts, just like always. It was like a magnet. One by one, I pushed the hanging quilts aside to say hello.

"You're in luck!" Carrie Mae called. "It's vacant and it's perfect for one person. Stop by her Emporium Antique Shop to get the key and check in. It's the small house nestled inside a white picket fence with a lot of flowers. You'll love it."

"Great, thanks," I said, feeling excited. "By the way, a cookie jar I had packed away was sitting on the kitchen counter when I arrived today. Korine wouldn't have unpacked that, would she?"

"Heavens, no. She's as honest as Abe. You've got a spirit I never knew to be there, so you must have brought someone with you. Now, there was a doctor that lived there many years ago, and who knows before him. You'll know in time. Too bad they can't do all the unpacking for you." I shook my head. That was not funny.

Chapter 68

Kitty's large antique shop was like a general store. I looked around a bit before I went to check in at the counter. I didn't see any quilts for sale, which I thought was a little odd.

Kitty was a rather petite lady who greeted me with a pleasant smile, as if shoe were waiting for my arrival. She looked about my age or a little older.

"You're Lily,I presume," she said, reaching out to shake my hand.

"Yes, and it's a pleasure to meet you, Kitty. I'm so grateful you have a vacancy tonight."

"I try to just book it on the weekends, but no one can reject a request from Carrie Mae, and I was anxious to meet you. Let's go across the street and see if it will be suitable for you."

When she opened the door to the little house which was surrounded by flowers and a picket fence, I knew it would suit my tastes and needs. The front porch had a white swing and a couple of chairs with comfy floral cushions that made it most inviting.

"Now, it's basically one room with a bath, so prepare yourself," Kitty cautioned.

I couldn't believe my eyes when she opened the door to a vintage paradise. My eyes when in every direction. A small bath was attached to a room that was separated into sections. One corner had a loveseat that created a cozy sitting area and one corner was a kitchenette. A large, fluffy king-size bed took up most of the room. The furnishings were right out of a magazine photoshoot.

"This narrow staircase to the attic is closed, and as you can see, I just put more decorations there."

"It's absolutely adorable," I said.

"I'll bring over whatever you may need and stock your refrigerator. You're on your own for meals. Folks seem to prefer to eat when they want and not be disturbed."

"I agree with that arrangement."

"Word on the street says you'll be opening an antique shop in Carrie Mae's yellow house."

"Yes. It'll be called Lily Girl's Quilts and Antiques." I boasted proudly.

"I love that name. I don't buy quilts for resale, but I do like them."

"Really? That's how I started collecting, and now I need to get rid of some, which is rather timely."

"Good luck. The market for quilts and textiles has been soft for some time." I kept hearing that remark.

We finished our business, and now I had a key. I decided to go back to the yellow house and check on Korine.

I arrived as Korine was about to leave.

"Tell Carrie Mae I did decide to stay at the Cottage

Guest House for the night," I instructed her.

"Okay. So you're going to work here for a while?" I nodded. "Don't be too alarmed if you hear strange noises," she warned. "Do you want me to come back in the morning?"

"Yes. How about eleven? I don't think I'm going to be in much of a hurry to leave that little dollhouse I'm staying in." She smiled.

I went to inspect Korine's progress upstairs. My cell phone rang in the process.

"Lily?" a man's voice grumbled. "It's Harry."

"Oh, Harry, how are you?"

"Making it, I guess. I wanted to tell you what I learned from Tony today. There will be a service for Bertie tomorrow. Where are you?"

"I'm in Augusta, but don't worry, I'll be there. Where will it be?"

"At the parish hall at her church," he said. "By the way, the 'For Sale' sign went up at your apartment today. He sure didn't waste any time."

"Well, Harry, he's here from out of town. I'm pleased he decided to have a service."

"Is he making you get out of your apartment?"

"No, not at all. I'm fine." I hung up, not wanting to tell him too much about my plans.

I started lining all the shelves with shelving paper as I listened for any strange noises. Maybe they were just for Korine. I wanted to hurry and get back to the guest house before dark to enjoy the place.

Traffic was as good as dead and gone when I drove the few blocks to the guest house. It was a pleasant night to sit on the porch, but I thought I would save that for my morning coffee.

I took a long shower and wrapped myself in the plush white robe provided by the guest house. I decided to snack for dinner, so I opened the Nile green vintage refrigerator and saw many goodies to choose from. I couldn't believe the large chocolate-covered strawberries. Yum!

Chapter 69

I got so caught up in that cute little place, I forgot all about why I was staying there. I marveled at the latest magazines, which I hever seemed to be exposed to. Kitty's books had very intriguing titles, but I had too little time to read. I would be up all night absorbing all the ideas I would love to use in my new yellow house.

Alex called at about ten to check on me. I described my productive day and the wonderful B&B where I was staying.

"Tomorrow is the memorial service for Bertie," I informed him. "Do you have any interest in going with me?"

"Sure, what time?" Alex asked.

"I think two, so we could have lunch first, if you like."

"I may not be able to do lunch, but plan on me picking you up for the service."

"Great! By the way, something else was unpacked yesterday at the house," I added.

"You mean like the toolbox and the Rolodex?" he asked with a snicker in his voice.

"Yes, one of the cookie jars that I personally packed with

the others."

He laughed. "Did you look inside? There may be more money from Rosie!"

"Funny, Alex, but what do you make of it?"

"Could it be the cleaning lady you mentioned?"

"No, but she told me there were strange noises in the house."

"Well, there you go! Hey, don't sweat the small stuff, Lily. None of it is harmful."

"Well, I'll see you tomorrow."

What would I do without Alex? I used to have these frequent phone calls with Holly, until her husband put another foot down about our relationship. I would love to get Holly out of that horrible house and get her to move to Augusta.

I got up to get more strawberries and cheese out of the refrigerator. I grabbed one of the quilts stacked at the end of the bed and wrapped it around me on the loveseat, then grabbed another magazine and escaped into a creative world. I jotted down ideas that I wanted to use. My eyelids were getting heavy and it was hard to stay awake. I finally drifted away, feeling happy and content.

I woke up the next morning still huddled in the loveseat. How foolish of me not to take advantage of the huge comfy bed! I stood up, feeling sore all over. I made coffee in the pastel-colored Keurig coffee maker that made me smile. I'd had no idea they were available in colors. I got a cinnamon bagel and headed to the front porch.

Not a creature was stirring at this early hour. It was so peaceful and appeared to be a pretty day. The spa next door was tempting, but it would have to wait for another day. I would love coming to this charming guest house, despite living in the same town.

I finally left the cottage and brought the key across the street to Kitty. I told her I would be back soon.

"Good luck getting your business going," Kitty said. "I know it's a lot of work."

"Thanks. I'll keep you posted." I gave her a wave as I walked out the door.

It was late when I arrived at the yellow house. Korine's car was already there. I was sure she was excited about all the extra hours she could pick up.

"Good morning," I yelled, coming in the door.

"I'm up here washing windows!" she yelled back.

I went upstairs and witnessed her wiping down the windows with newspapers.

"What's this about?"

"Oh, I do this the old-fashioned way. When you have grimy windows like this, I use vinegar and water and then dry them with newspaper so you don't get any streaks."

"Well, I got the right gal for the job. They look great! How long have you been working?"

"Oh, I got here earlier than you told me, since this is such a big job," she explained. "I get up at six every morning. How was your night?"

"Marvelous. That guest house is so cute inside. I got so many decorating ideas."

"Do you have the painters scheduled, by any chance?"

"No, not yet."

"What are you going to do about this outlandish wallpaper?"

"I just can't be bothered with the mess before I move in,"

I sadly replied. "The paper is kind of growing on me."

"I'll do the downstairs windows next," Korine said. "I won't be in your way, will I?"

"No, I'll just be here for a little while. I have to go to a funeral today."

"Oh, I'm sorry."

I went downstairs to get busy with something so I wouldn't think about the funeral. I walked towards the kitchen, but something odd caught my eye. I couldn't believe it until I got closer. There was some cameo jewelry lying on a dresser that I knew Lynn had packed away the day she came to help. She had been admiring the unusual setting. Surely Korine would never unpack it and just leave it here. If this was a prank, it wasn't amusing.

When I walked into the kitchen, the cookie jar remained sitting in the same spot. I took a deep breath, hoping all of this had a sensible explanation. It was time to leave.

Chapter 70

Arriving at my apartment gave me an empty feeling without Bertie sitting on the porch. I hurried to get dressed for the funeral. Should I wear black? I had plenty of black in my wardrobe, but Bertie was such a colorful person that it somehow didn't seem match. She never matched her colors or prints because she felt entitled to be who she was. In all due respect, I decided to wear black slacks with a white blouse.

Alex looked great when he arrived wearing a sports coat. As we quietly drove to the church, we thought there was certainly   lack of cars.

"I suppose with her age, many friends and relatives are gone," Alex explained.

Bertie's brother, Mr. Collins, greeted us as we entered. There were very few people. It was disappointing to just see a container of ashes displayed with a couple of pictures. One photo was of Bertie as a young girl and the other was from later in life, showing her at some celebration.

Alex and I paused for a few moments before we sat

down. Recorded music was playing in the background, and I noticed Harry sitting in the front row.

At two o'clock sharp, a priest came to the front of the room. He told us of Bertie's acquaintance with him and others she'd know at the church. He said he'd witnessed her faith and cheerful spirit. Next to speak was her brother, who thanked everyone for coming. He said he was impressed by how his sister had touched people's lives in the Italian community.

"I want to thank Lily Rosenthal for her love and dedication to Bertie," he said. "Lily seemed to be the daughter that Bertie never had." I thought I was going to break down in tears. "As I talked to others who knew her, they would also mention Harry in the same breath. Harry, I know you'll miss her. I couldn't look at Harry. "Her special cooking and her love for Sugar will be remembered by many."

I swallowed hard as emotion spread throughout the room. When I looked behind me, many more folks had arrived for the service. Many of them were neighbors who only knew Bertie from the street. In closing, Mr. Collins said everyone was welcome at Tony's for some refreshments.

"Do you want to go?" Alex asked in a whisper.

"I don't think so, Alex," I said after some thought. "I don't want to talk about my move and have to say goodbye to some of these folks." He nodded.

We went back to the apartment instead.

"Wow, you are making good progress here," Alex noted as he looked around my place.

"I am, but packing up from two locations has been a bit strange. I guess I'll use the same movers to get me out to Augusta."

"I can't believe this huge stack of quilts here," he observed.

"They are my babies. I'm driving them out to Augusta personally instead of using the moving van. The ones I'm keeping will go upstairs in the apartment."

It was cocktail hour, so I poured some wine to take to the porch. We toasted Bertie, and then I told Alex about finding the cameo jewelry on the dresser. He shook his head like it was no big deal.

"Didn't Bertie have a ghost she called Walter?"

I laughed and nodded. "I wish I had asked more about him. Our conversations were always short."

"What's the latest with Carl and Lynn?" Alex asked, taking another sip of wine.

"The status quo. I suppose they're trying to make it work. I felt bad canceling Sarah's trip, but I couldn't just leave Lynn to do everything."

"So is Sarah rescheduling?"

"I don't know. She'll have to help me work if she comes. Loretta said she idolizes me because I've stayed single."

Alex chuckled. "Yeah, I get that in my family too," he noted. "I guess we're a breed of our own."

"Right now, I think so. Laurie seems to be happy too, so marriage isn't for everyone."

"I'm writing an article about an elderly couple in Clayton. They'll be married sixty years. I've extended the article to include other married couples and what contributes to the longevity of their marriages."

"Now that's interesting."

"What's also interesting is how these close couples sometimes die within hours of each other."

"Yes, I've read about that."

Alex to a stretch and said he needed to be on his way. I was exhausted as well.

As I got ready for bed, I felt jealous of Alex and his writing ability. Writing was part of my bucket list, but instead, I was taking a side road to become a retailer. There was never enough time, even after I'd become unemployed. With the deaths of Rosie and Bertie, I was beginning to realize how short life was.

Chapter 71

I loaded up my car the next morning with the first load of quilts that I intended to sell. I should have been journaling more about this transition and my new career in retailing, but there was simply no time. After several trips up and down the stairs, I answered my ringing cell phone with a free hand.

"Hey, Lily Girl," a familiar voice said.

"Marc?"

He chuckled. "Is this Lily Girl's Quilts and Antiques?" he jokingly asked.

"Why, yes, it is, sort of," I said with a chuckle. "Are you looking for a nice quilt or what?"

"No, I'm just looking for a really nice girl named Lily." he answered.

"Ah, well, that's me. I'm loading my car with quilts today."

"Glad you're making progress," Marc said more seriously. "I talked to Lynn and she told me about the loss of your neighbor. I'm sorry to hear that."

"Thanks, it was a shock. It's escalated my move for sure."

"So I take it you're going to slum it in the yellow house for a while?"

"Yes, it's getting cleaned up, and it's just the thing to do right now."

"I don't suppose you want to take any leisure time with your baseball buddy, do you? I have a good opportunity for tomorrow night's game in our company's clubhouse."

"Oh, wow, tomorrow night?" I paused. "I'll make it work. I've been so busy I haven't even kept up with the games."

"Well, that's not good. Your priorities are out of order." I laughed. "How about I pick you up around five thirty so we can take advantage of dinner in the clubhouse?"

"Sure, that would be great."

I hung up with a big smile on my face. I was actually glad to hear from Marc.

After I filled the car to the brim, I headed to Augusta. I decided to stop at Carrie Mae's first to see if she could contact the boys she used for moving furniture around her shop.

"How's it going, Lily Girl?" Carrie Mae asked when I walked in the door. It seemed everyone was picking up on my new shop name.

"It's going fine, I think, but I need some more help. I need a sign painter, some muscles, and some carpenters."

It looked like Rosie's Rolodex. "I'll have to call the two brothers when you're ready for them. They'll jump at the chance to make a few bucks."

"Tha415nks. I brought out a carful of quilts today. I don't want to leave them in the hot car, so I'd better get going."

"Oh, I can't wait to see them. By the way, I'm supposed to give you this note from Korine."

I was puzzled. "Korine?" I questioned. "I thought she might be working at the house right now."

"I'm afraid not. You need to read this."

It read, "Dear Lily, sorry I had to leave your place. When I came down the stairs, your rocking chair was rocking. There's something creepy going on in that house. Maybe I'll reconsider when you get all moved in. Korine."

"Did you read this?" I frowned.

"I didn't have to. The woman came in here scared to death."

"I just don't understand it all."

"Well, it's a shame. She's a good worker. She was pleased that she had finished all your windows before she quit."

"Let me leave some money for her," I suggested. "Will you see her soon?"

"Yes. Tomorrow she does laundry for me." Carrie Mae revealed.

I pulled out what cash I had and left it with her. I said goodbye and got back in my car. It took me four trips to the car to get all the quilts into the yellow house. I stacked the heavy trash bags and placed them on top of the kitchen counter. I was exhausted.

I went to the other room to check out the mysterious rocking chair. It was an ornate Victorian rocker that I had seen for many years in Rosie's shop. It had inlaid pearl in the headrest. Rosie's price tag was four hundred and fifty dollars, which I thought was a little high, but what did I know? I stared at it as if it was going to start rocking in front of me, but that didn't happen.

Chapter 72

As I looked at the progress Korine had made, I got a text from Laurie asking whether I needed her to help set up my business. She was always so thoughtful, and yet scatterbrained at times. I wanted to do this my way, so I politely turned her down and invited her to come when I was officially open for business. I tried to visualize where I wanted all the furniture to go. I could move the smaller pieces into place by myself.

"Hello, hello!" a voice came from the front door. To my surprise, it was Carrie Mae. "I just had to take a break and see what you were up to here," she confessed. "Can I do anything to help?"

"Actually, you can," I said with some relief. "Where should I put my checkout counter? This is the counter Rosie used."

Carrie Mae walked around a bit as she sized things up. "With that size, you're going to have to place it on this side of the room, close to the door," she advised. "You'll want to be able to see what folks are leaving with."

"Makes sense." I nodded. "It has an old-fashioned cash drawer that I may use instead of Rosie's cash register. Would that be crazy?"

"Oh, I used one for years myself. Sure liked it a lot better. You can certainly give it a try. Does yours have a bell that rings when it's opened?"

"It does!"

"Things are shaping up, Lily Girl. You should do well, once folks know you're here. We have no rules about displaying merchandise outside, so your quilts will be a draw. Merchandise attracts."

"Yes, Rosie always had something different on display on her sidewalk every day," I replied. "Do any of your things ever get stolen? You have so much that you leave out overnight."

"Well, my shop's on the corner and out in the open, which helps. I rarely have anything taken."

"I guess I'll have a freestanding sign," I said. "There isn't a place on the house that will work."

"I think you're right," Carrie Mae said. "What's happening upstairs?"

We went up the steps, and she marveled at how clean everything looked.

"You may want to sand those wooden floors now that the linoleum is up," she suggested.

"I was thinking the same thing."

We walked into the kitchenette, and she told me she had a newer refrigerator that she could put in. I gladly accepted.

"Why do you have this lovely cake plate up here?" Carrie Mae wondered.

I couldn't believe my most valuable glass cake plate from downstairs was unwrapped and placed on my dresser! I just stared at it.

"I have no idea. I know it couldn't have been Korine."

Carrie Mae gave me a strange look and shook her head.

"Oh, Lily Girl, you are going to have some fun here!" Carrie Mae teased. with a chuckle. "It's best that you have a sense of humor about all of this."

"That reminds me to take the toolbox with me today to give to Marc."

Carrie Mae went on her way, and before I headed home to my apartment, I checked my email on my phone. Lynn was telling the sisters that she was going to have an art exhibit at the Foundry Art Center in St. Charles. I was so proud of her. How she could do her painting and deal with Carl at the same time was admirable.

Loretta reported that she was helping out with her church's Vacation Bible School.

I responded to all of them by giving an update about my move. I ended by telling them I was going to a game with my baseball buddy. I knew that would make them happy.

I arrived at my apartment, and the neighborhood seemed exceptionally quiet. I fixed a grilled cheese sandwich and poured a glass of wine to take to the front porch. I saw Harry coming down the street, so I quickly set down my wine and ran down the stairs to talk to him.

"Harry, how are you?" I greeted him. I could tell he was glad to see me.

"I'm fine, Lily. How about you?"

"I've been busy packing to keep my mind off of Bertie," I explained.

"I see her brother didn't waste any time putting her house up for sale," Harry said, shaking his head.

"That's true, but you wouldn't want it to sit here vacant, either. Mr. Collins said he was going to do some renovations after I move out."

"Things won't be the same around here without you, Lily," Harry stated sadly.

"I'll still come around, and if you need anything, just let me know."

"You'll have a whole new life, and I wish you the very best," Harry said, as if it were his last goodbye to me.

"Thanks, Harry. Bertie would want you to keep checking on everyone, remember." He smiled.

I gave him a big hug and went back to the porch to finish my dinner.

Chapter 73

I heard thunder and lightning in the early hours, which woke me up. It was baseball day. This couldn't be! The good news of the day was that I wouldn't be driving out to Augusta. I planned to pack all day until Marc picked me up for the game. I turned over my pillow and slept another hour.

As luck would have it, I woke up to sunshine coming in my window. As soon as I got up, I wanted to lay out my clothes to wear to the game. Remembering that Marc's law partners would be there, I wanted to look as nice as I could for baseball. I laid out my red blazer and the red Cardinals hat Marc had given me.

After coffee and toast, I began going through my clothes, deciding what was going to charity and what I'd be keeping. My little closets upstairs in the yellow house would be a challenge. I filled trash bags very quickly.

Next, I began taking art off the walls. I had several of Lynn's paintings, and I wanted to use them in my new place. As I wrapped things for travel, it stirred up many memories. I'd had so many boring days in this apartment. It was mostly because I was so unhappy in my job. My quilts were my only joy, and I couldn't wait to take them into the world of retail.

Time passed quickly, and before I knew it, it was time to get ready for the big game. I began thinking more about meeting Marc's friends and associates. What would I say if they asked what I did for a living? I didn't want to embarrass Marc.

Right on time, Marc knocked at my door. I was pleased to see he was wearing his baseball cap as well. He seemed glad to see me. "Are you ready to rock and roll?" he asked teasingly. "Hey, Lily, this place is looking pretty bare!"

"Yes, I got a lot of packing done today," I boasted. "Before we go, I have a thank-you present for you." He looked at me questioningly. "I found this antique toolbox with tools in Rosie's shop and thought of you. You said you miss tinkering with tools."

Marc's eyes brightened when I showed him the box. "How cool is this? This is old, and I know collectors relish these kinds of things. Thank you so much." I could tell he was thrilled.

"Well, you were a big help, and I didn't know how else to thank you."

Off we went, and with complimentary parking, our arrival was a breeze. We went up the elevator to the clubroom, where everyone was already helping themselves to an amazing buffet. Introductions began immediately, and there was no question that I was being sized up by one and all. Marc went to get us a drink and an attractive woman joined me in small talk.

"You must be pretty special to Marc. He never brings women to these kinds of events."

"Really?"

"You make a really cute couple. How long have you been an item?"

"I didn't know we were an item," I replied, scanning the room for Mark.

"Well, you appear to be one," she persisted. "He's a good catch!"

"I see you've met Sharon," Marc interjected when he returned with our drinks.

"Marc, you've not shared anything about your lovely friend." Sharon said mockingly.

"Well, she's a pretty serious baseball fan, so we'd better get to the outdoor seats so we know what's going on."

"Sharon? Nice to meet you," I said as we walked away.

When we were seated, Marc apologized for Sharon's interference.

"She does that to everyone," he explained. "She thinks the law firm belongs to just her and her husband, and that she's the social director. She's caused many uncomfortable situations over the years."

"She said you usually don't bring anyone," I said. He laughed.

"Not anyone like you," he said, giving me a wink.

He was so darn cute!

The game began with a whopping home run by Molina, everyone's favorite player. It seemed to set the tone for the rest of the game. The Cardinals were playing their key rival, the Chicago Cubs, so the excitement was intense.

I think you bring good luck to the games," Marc said. "You should come with me more often."

We had such a good time with small talk and lots of

food that Marc kept bringing from the buffet. After the game, I could feel Sharon's eyes on me as we left. Marc was in a grand mood.

"You know, I'd love to visit the Baseball Hall of Fame in Cooperstown someday," he shared. "It's on my bucket list."

"That would be awesome," I agreed. "I've only seen pictures."

We continued talking about it as we approached a sports bar nearby. Marc wanted to wait to drive until the downtown traffic was clear. I had to admit, I wasn't in a hurry to get home.

Chapter 74

It was quite late when we got back to my apartment. I didn't ask Marc to come in, as we were both ready to call it a night.

"I'm so glad you decided to come with me tonight," Marc said as he put his arm around me.

"Me too. Remember, I'm your lucky charm."

He chuckled and nodded. He took me in his arms and kissed me gently. It was sweet. Not too long or too short. "Thanks for the toolbox and tools. I can't wait to have some fun with it."

"You're welcome. It had your name on it."

I went upstairs feeling happy. It was good to feel so comfortable with another man besides Alex, who was like a brother. As I undressed, I had to laugh at some of Marc's remarks. He had a great sense of humor. We hadn't discussed Lynn and Carl at all. It was just about us and baseball. Once in bed, I fantasized about the idea of going with Marc to the Baseball Hall of Fame. I thought I could really enjoy that trip with him.

Before I left for Augusta the next morning, I loaded my car with accessories and boxes of clothing. I had planned to stop at Robins Nest on the Katy Trail in Defiance to get a cup of coffee. It was a clever place that had a sense of the community coming from every direction. The drive was beautiful, but I looked forward to not having to do it quite so often. I would miss The Hill. There wasn't a better place for restaurants.

I pulled into Robins Nest. The woman who worked there was always so friendly. I took my coffee and muffin and sat outside to watch the activity on the Katy Trail. I was checking emails on my phone when I heard a familiar voice.

"Lily?" I turned around and saw that it was Nick, the man I'd met at the Trail Smokehouse.

"Good morning," I said with a big smile. "Are you out riding today?"

"No, I'm on my way to Augusta to unload some artwork at the Gallery Augusta," Nick explained. "I really like the coffee here, so I made the stop and saw you sitting here."

I suddenly felt very bare without any makeup. "I'm going to unload more boxes in Augusta myself."

"So you're still not quite moved in?"

"Almost. Where do you work, or should I say, paint?"

"I have a barn on my property that I call a studio, just to keep my house in some order. I'm retired now, so I have the luxury of golfing and riding the trail."

"That sounds nice. You must have retired pretty young."

Nick grinned. "You think so?" He chuckled. "Where are you going to live out here? I think the last time I saw you, you were looking."

"Well, because I have to be out of my city apartment, I'm

going to live in the upstairs of the house for now." *I shouldn't be telling him this.* I thought.

"Can I join you? I'd like to hear more."

"I suppose, but I have a lot of work I need to accomplish today."

Nick walked away to the counter. I had to admit, I was flattered that this good-looking man paid any attention to me, especially with the way I looked. His sandy-colored hair, tanned body, and blue eyes were hard to ignore.

Chapter 75

When Nick returned, he asked me more questions, which made me a bit uncomfortable.

"I'm feeling a bit guilty with all I have to do."

He smiled and shrugged his shoulders like it didn't matter. "What's the name of your shop, so I can find you?"

I paused. "Lily Girl's Quilts and Antiques. I was called Lily Girl by a good friend who passed away. I knew she would love the name."

He nodded like he understood. "Now that's a mouthful. So you're Lily Girl?" I nodded. "I love quilts and antiques." "Do you have a sign yet?"

"No, I need to find someone to make one. I have someone's card."

"I could take care of that for you," he offered.

"You could?"

"I've done it before, although it's not my usual thing. It sounds like fun. What's your address?"

"I don't know." He laughed. "Well, it's on the corner of Chestnut and Public."

"Sure, that's easy."

"It's a yellow house on the corner."

"I'll try to stop by after my delivery and take a look at what you'll need."

"That would be great. I'll pay you, of course." He laughed and nodded.

We shortly went our own way. Something told me Nick wasn't the sign-painting type, but was just trying to get to know me better.

I decided to stop at City Hall to see if I could apply for my business license. A friendly woman behind the counter had forms right there, as if she were expecting me. It appeared I would need approval for my sign as well. I filled out what I could, asked a few questions, and left for the house. I got in my car with a sense of this was really happening.

Carrie Mae was calling me on my cell, telling me she had the two boys that would be available to help me in her shop and was sending them down.

"Yes, yes, perfect!" I responded. "I sure wish I hadn't lost Korine. Oh, by the way, I have a man coming to plan my sign this morning."

"Who did you get?"

"Well, he's really an artist by the name of Nick Conrey, but he offered to do it for me," I explained.

"My goodness. Yes, he's an excellent artist. Glad you met a new friend."

I welcomed the boys, Kip and Tom. I described to them where I wanted each piece of furniture to go. I was using the living room and the dining room as my show rooms. Two hours later, the house looked like an antique shop. The boxes of merchandise would now have to be unloaded at my leisure. This was exciting! I paid the boys generously, and they offered to come back if I needed them.

I fixed myself a glass of iced tea and saw a yellow Mercedes convertible pull up in front of my yellow house. It was Nick. I was already a mess when he'd seen me this morning, so I sucked it up and went out to greet him.

"I'm glad you found me," I said.

"Sure, I've gone by this house many times," he note. "A little landscaping and paint will make this a showplace. It has character for sure."

"I think so, too. I can see red geraniums, maybe in some flower boxes, to contrast the yellow and white."

"Good eye, Lily," he said. "Now, where did you have in mind to put your sign?"

"I think it'll have to be freestanding on this corner so traffic can see it from all directions."

"I agree," Nick said, standing where he thought it should be placed.

"Can you build the post and sign as well?"

"No, but I know a guy who can," he assured me.

"What do you think it will end up costing me?"

He grinned. "Perhaps a nice dinner?"

"No, if I'm going to go into business, that won't work."

"I'll think about it. Give me your email address and I'll send you a mockup for your approval."

"Great. Come on inside. Please excuse the mess."

Chapter 76

"You've got some nice pieces here," Nick commented as he walked between the aisles.

"Where do you live, Nick?" I asked.

"It's out on Schluersburg Road," he said, like I would know where that was. "It's a small, secluded place where I can do my work."

"I'm not familiar enough with the area to know any of the roads yet," I confessed.

"There's plenty of time for that. I can certainly be helpful."

"Well, right now it's not important. I have to get this shop open."

"I guess I'd better let you get back to work, then," Nick said apologetically.

"I'm glad I ran into you today. I hope I'm not putting you in an awkward position doing this sign for me."

"I'm the one who offered, remember?"

We walked to his car, which I admired. He said he rarely took it out, but when he'd retired, he felt he'd earned a new toy. I couldn't help but wonder about his circumstances, but I didn't want to go into further conversation.

"You'll be hearing from me soon," he said before driving away.

The thought of getting the sign made was exciting. As I walked back inside, I wondered where to start unpacking. I needed to get the counter organized, so I'd start with the boxes related to it.

Rosie's inkwell, which served as a pencil holder, had sat next to the antique school bell that Rosie had had on her counter. Since she was in the back room a lot, customers would tap on the bell to announce they were there. I took out the Rolodex as if I were really going to use it. I unloaded boxes of paper bags Rosie'd had under the counter in hopes that I would use them up quickly for sales. I couldn't help but wonder if Rosie was watching me. Since I'd left behind her open and closed sign, I would have to make or buy one.

Rosie had kept her glass cases of small items close to her counter so she could keep her eye on them. I positioned them the same way. I was getting a good handle on things as I piled empty boxes on the back porch.

Carrie Mae surprised me when she walked in the front door.

"Well, ain't this lookin' nice?" she teased. "I just had to see how you were doing. You have good, easy in-and-out access. Very nice."

"I can't take the credit, Carrie Mae. I remembered the way Rosie arranged her shop."

"Good idea. How about your sign?"

"Nick was here, and he's going to email me a proof before he starts."

"That man is smooth and quite a looker," Carrie Mae said, shaking her head. "I don't know much about him, other than his paintings. You just be cautious, Lily Girl." I smiled and nodded. "So when is your upstairs furniture arriving?"

"Next week. My place is looking pretty bare. I'll miss that neighborhood for sure."

"I would think so. Well, you get back to work. You're doing great."

She turned to go out the door, but suddenly turned back around.

"Did you see that?" she asked in shock.

"What?"

"That rocking chair was rocking."

I walked from behind the counter to take a look, but the chair was standing still.

"It's not rocking," I said calmly.

"Well, Lily Girl, you have company," Carrie Mae said as she waved goodbye.

I was getting tired and felt my day had been productive, so I decided to drive back to the Hill.

My thoughts while driving home were about Nick, my sign, and the active spirit at the yellow house. When I pulled in front of the apartment, I smiled when I saw Harry talking to the neighbors on the sidewalk. His life was getting back to normal, despite missing Bertie.

Chapter 77

My cupboards were bare, so I called Lynn to see if she would meet up with me for dinner.

"It's good to hear from you," she responded. "I didn't want to bother you right now with all you're doing."

"I just got home and I'm famished. Have you had dinner?"

"Not really. I was hoping Carl would call and say he was free, but it doesn't look like that's going to happen."

"He's still working a lot of nights, I take it?"

"Yes, and I'm trying not to be critical because they have a big case going on."

"I need a decent meal. Why don't we meet up at Charlie Gitto's?"

"Good heavens, without reservations? It's way too formal. How about J. Smugs? It's close and casual, and we can sit outdoors."

"Sure, that's fine. I love their barbeque. I'll meet you there in thirty minutes."

I showered and changed into a sundress. I felt my jeans

were molded to my body from wearing them so often. I sure was hoping to hear some good news from Lynn, but I had to be prepared for whatever she shared.

She was ten minutes late to dinner and apologized. She seemed nervous.

"It's delightful sitting here, watching the people," I said. "I'm going to miss this."

We placed our order, and to calm Lynn down a bit, I started the conversation by talking about my progress. I told her about meeting the artist Nick Conrey. She said she had heard of him. She was surprised when I told her he was going to do my sign.

"Do you think you'll go out with him?" she asked, catching me off guard. "What about Marc? You said you had a wonderful time at the ballpark."

"I did, but we're not an item. I'm his baseball buddy." She gave me a strange look. "Lynn, what's wrong tonight? You should be happy for me. I thought you were supporting my new adventure."

"I'm sorry." She teared up. "It's Carl. Nothing has really changed. I want so badly to keep this marriage together. He's stopped any intimacy. He says he's too tired and too busy. I feel like I'm hanging on by a string."

"Oh, Lynn, I'm so sorry. At some point, you'll have to decide what you want and deserve."

Our barbeque arrived and I encouraged Lynn to eat. I would have bet she hadn't been doing that. As we took our first bite, she dropped a bombshell.

"I promised Loretta I wouldn't say anything, but we're too close to keep this a secret."

"What? Is she okay?"

"It's Sarah."

"Now what?"

"She's pregnant."

"You have got to be kidding!"

Lynn shook her head. "The father is the guy she doesn't want to marry. Loretta is about to kill her, of course."

"I wonder if he really is the father. I hope she won't have an abortion."

"Oh, it's too late for that. She's going to have a Christmas baby."

"Oh, Loretta will be a grandmother. That's pretty cool when you think about it. I'll bet that's why Sarah wanted to stay with me for a while. All in all, Lynn, I think we need to embrace the good side of this."

"I figured you'd see it that way," Lynn said with a smile.

Chapter 78

In bed that night, I wondered what kind of baby quilt Sarah would want. I couldn't help but smile at Loretta's next generation coming about. I hoped Sarah would remain in college, but how in the world would she support herself?

It appeared that Lynn's hope for Carl was wearing thin. Just like Holly, however, she had to decide how bad her treatment would become before moving on. *Perhaps there are more women out there in the same boat,* I realized.

The next morning, I arranged for the movers to come in a couple of days. There wasn't any reason to prolong my move now that I had a place to go.

I walked into my empty quilt room and felt a sense of loss being without my quilts. My babies had moved on, and now it was time for me to join them.

I loaded the car with more clothing and a few small pieces of furniture. I could feel the eyes of the neighbors watching. Some may have been sad, while others probably thought less of me for leaving them. After my last trip to load up, I went inside to check my emails. There was a sister group email from Laurie.

"I miss you guys. When I close at Christmas, I definitely need to see all of you. Lynn, are you planning Christmas like you said when you were here for my birthday? I'll have it if no one volunteers."

I knew that question would rattle Lynn, and what would Loretta's family think of coming here to St. Louis, especially with the due date of the baby being around that same time? We sisters were never apart at Christmas. It was like we had made a promise to each other.

My response was, "I miss everyone, too! The movers are coming soon. I'll be anxious to show everyone my new shop and make-do living quarters. I promise there will be lots of wine!"

I jumped in my car and began my drive. I began thinking about Christmas. I should be open by then and have a bustling business. Fall to Christmas was the prime time for retail, and I didn't want to miss it.

After I unloaded my things at the yellow house, I was ready for some coffee, which I planned to get from Kate's Coffee. The more I brought in the house, the more I had to chuckle at how crowded the rooms were becoming. Some things would have to be stored elsewhere. Perhaps one of the outbuildings would be suitable.

When I came down the stairs from one of my many trips, I noticed that something was different. It was something red and white. My red-and-white Hearts and Gizzards quilt was unpacked and lying on top of the others! Of all the quilts, why was this one being shown to me?

"Okay, Rosie. It has to be you," I said aloud. "Don't frighten me. I can accept that you're here, but don't give me cause to be afraid or concerned, please! I love this quilt, so I presume you want me to use this one, or else why would it be out of the bag?"

Feeling strange, I started hauling all of the quilt bags upstairs. I thought the smaller bedroom could be devoted to my personal quilt collection. I put the special quilt aside and placed it in the room I intended to make my bedroom. Goodness knew there wasn't a color scheme anywhere in the floral wallpaper! When I brought up my bag of smaller quilts, I took them out one by one to see if there was a crib quilt appropriate for Sarah's baby. My appliquéd 1920s Humpty Dumpty quilt seemed to be in the best condition. I loved the nursery-rhyme-embroidered quilt, but it had a lot of pink, which would only be suitable if Sarah had a girl. Again, the idea of Sarah's baby made me smile.

Since the day was getting away from me, I decided to spend the night. I thought that with all these quilts, I could certainly make myself comfortable for a few hours. I decided to place a pile of quilts by the triple windows so I could easily look outside. It would give me a view of the street and my vehicle, just for security reasons. I decided not to change into nightwear, since I didn't know what to expect on my first night here. I found it humorous stacking the quilts as if I were on an adventure. Welcome to my first night in wine country!

Chapter 79

I had no cable service yet and it was too early to turn in, so I decided to take a walk. I made an assumption that it was safe to walk in this little town. I took my keys and left on the overhead hall light. If I walked to my right, the road was very dark and narrow and curved into an area I was not familiar with, so I walked in the direction of the streetlights. In the future, I really wanted to walk every day on the Katy Trail. Perhaps I would have more encounters with Nick.

There wasn't another soul walking around the darkened streets. Occasionally, a car would pass that was most likely leaving or going to a winery. I passed the Cottage Guest House and saw lights on inside. Had I asked for the night's room, it would have already been booked. I couldn't help but envy those lucky folks inside.

The blocks were short and somewhat confusing if you weren't paying attention. I turned around and went toward Locust Street, where Carrie Mae's Uptown Store was located. Across the street was the Silly Goose restaurant, which seemed to be crowded, judging by all the cars parked along the street. I was about to turn the corner when I stopped, recognizing a familiar face. It was Nick. He was coming out of the restaurant with his arm around an attractive woman. They were laughing about something. Carrie Mae had told me this guy was smooth with the ladies in this very small town. I had to remember her advice. I hid in the shadows, hoping they wouldn't see me and would drive in another direction once they got in their car. Once it was all clear, I headed down the hill toward the house.

When I was a block away, I saw lights flashing inside. I hadn't installed a security system yet, so what could be wrong?

I ran the rest of the way and unlocked the door. When I got inside, the lights stopped. My heart was beating so fast. Was someone in here and my spirit was trying to warn me or chase them away? Was that crazy thinking or what? Should I call for help? Did Augusta have its own police department? I took a deep breath and decided to go from room to room to see if anything looked out of the ordinary. After checking out the first floor, I slowly went up the stairs. It didn't feel like anyone was there, and nothing looked out of place.

I told myself to calm down and decided to call Carrie Mae in the morning. I would ask her to install a security system. I knew deep down that was a lot to ask, unless I paid for it.

I lay down on my pallet of quilts, feeling like I was at a sleepover somewhere. I turned off all the lights except the one that lit the stairs. This was a strange first night in the yellow house.

I remained very still. Everything was so quiet. In my old neighborhood, there was always traffic noise at any time of the day or night. Cars would honk and the occasional siren would go off, since I was located near the firehouse.

My mind went back to seeing Nick coming out of The Silly Goose. I'd bet there was a lot to know about the cyclist who was painting my sign. I had to remind myself to keep that friendship very professional. Things got groggy, and off to sleep I went.

The next thing I knew, bright daylight pouring through my bedroom windows. My pallet was a mess, like I had been wrestling most of the night. When I got up, my muscles ached all over.

Where was my coffeepot? I realized it wasn't at the house, and that meant getting dressed to go out for some much-needed caffeine.

I washed my face, grabbed a clean top out of one of the boxes, and headed down the stairs to the front door, leaving my messy quilts in a pile.

I headed to Kate's Coffee. There were folks already sitting on the patio, so I ordered a pecan muffin and a cup of hazelnut coffee to take to a table outside. The Oaks pwned other places, which they collectively referred to as Oak's Crossing. The couple was always friendly and very ingrained into the community.

I sat there alone, glancing at the large stone turtles in the garden. It was a reminder of how much I wanted to do a bit of gardening now that I had a yard.

"Good morning, Lily," a voice said from behind me. It was Kitty from the guest house.

"Good morning," I awkwardly responded.

"You must be all moved in, since you're here so early today," Kitty observed.

"No, tomorrow is the big day," I replied. "I didn't bring

my coffeepot, so here I am."

"You stayed in the house?"

"Yes, but don't ask me how that went," I said, giggling a little. "I saw you had guests last night."

She nodded. "Mind if I join you?"

"No, of course, please do," I happyily responded.

"I love those pecan muffins, don't you? This place has been a godsend for my business. Some folks want breakfast, so they come here."

"Are you opening your shop today?" I asked with interest.

"Yes. I have a furniture delivery coming, so I need to get back soon. When do you think your shop will be open?"

"I don't know. I'm still unpacking and getting my business set up. It will be an adjustment. I know very few folks out here. I'm especially going to miss my sister who lives in my old neighborhood. I'm afraid my friends and my sister probably won't come out here as often as I'd like."

"That's a shame. It's such a charming area with lots to do."

Chapter 80

I was in a much better mood after visiting with Kitty. I wanted to share my experiences with the spirit in the house with her, but decided against it.

When I got back to the house, I made sure I had room upstairs for the furniture that would be arriving. I sent a text to Alex to remind him about helping me on moving day. He quickly answered back that he would be at the apartment as early as seven that morning. He offered to bring donuts and coffee, to which I replied with a smiley face. My next call was to Holly to give her a heads up on the move.

"Already?" she said, surprised. "I thought you would be here until the end of the month."

"My apartment is bare and I'm tired of running back and forth."

"I'll come over in the morning to help, but I won't be going out to Augusta with you. You know I'm Miss Scrubby Dutch, so after you leave, I'll clean your apartment. How about that?"

"Oh, Holly, how generous of you."

"It'll be a piece of cake, as clean as you are."

"Thanks, and I hope you'll come out to Augusta soon."

"You know how Maurice is, so I can't promise anything. He hasn't been feeling well lately, so he's around the house all the time. He won't say what's wrong and frankly, I don't care. He hates doctors, so there's no point in telling him to go see one."

"That's a shame. What an unhappy man!"

We hung up. Once again, my best friend was coming through for me, despite the challenges she faced each day.

I left Augusta in time to beat the traffic. I had gone without lunch, so I picked up a pizza from Rigazzi's on the way home. I would certainly miss this place.

I had finished most of my pizza and a glass of wine on porch when Marc's name showed up on my phone.

"Where are you?" he asked.

"I'm having my last meal on the porch at the apartment."

"And how's that going for you?"

"It's a bit sad, but good at the same time."

"So tomorrow is the big day?"

"How did you know?"

"Lynn told me. I called the house to talk to Carl, but he wasn't there."

"I don't suppose she knew where he was?"

"I didn't have the heart to ask. It seems things aren't any better."

"I know, and I don't know how to help."

"I think she needs to get away for a bit. She's been sitting around waiting for the other shoe to drop. She should go see one of your sisters or come out to help you."

"You have a point there, so I'll ask."

"Call me when you're settled. I'll take you out to your favorite winery, if you have one."

"I've been too busy to check them out. I'd love the company."

"By the way, I had a little repair job in my kitchen this week and was able to use some of the tools you gave me. I cleaned them up, and they're as good as new."

"That's great. Maybe I can find a job or two for you in the yellow house." Marc chuckled, but I was serious.

"Anytime. Good to hear your voice. Good luck tomorrow!"

Chapter 81

I could hardly sleep during the night, but when six o'clock came, I jumped out of bed ready to start the busy day. I tore the sheets off the bed and put them in the washing machine before it would be moved away. It appeared to be a very hot day, so I dressed accordingly.

In no time, Alex appeared at the door with much-needed coffee and Krispy Kreme doughnuts. We took them to the porch and devoured them before the moving van arrived.

"Now, Lily Girl, I hope this is your last move for a while," Alex said kindly.

"I'm sure it is, but I've been thinking."

"That's dangerous."

"I'm going to ask Carrie Mae if she will sell me the yellow house."

"Oh my, don't you want to live out there for a while before buying?"

"Perhaps, but there's so much that needs to be done, and I can't expect her to do all that while I'm a tenant. I think there will be great benefits to me living upstairs, and it's within walking distance to everything but you!"

He laughed and nodded. "You aren't worried about those crazy happenings?"

"You mean Rosie? She's not going away anytime soon, and I could use her help."

Alex shook his head in disbelief. "Well, you've got the money to invest, or else you're going to have to pay capital gains tax. No harm in asking, I suppose."

That was the end of the discussion because the movers pulled up in front. I recognized one of the movers as one I had used when I took the antiques out to Augusta.

"Are you sure you're going to have room for all of this?" one of them asked.

"It will all go on the second floor, so I hope it will all fit up the stairway."

Holly arrived with her vacuum and cleaning supplies. She helped herself to coffee and the last doughnut. Alex kicked into gear and ran up and down the steps with smaller furniture.

"I want to cry and cheer you on at the same time," lamented Holly. "It won't be the same around here, but I am so proud that you're taking steps to start a new life."

"I'm hoping you'll do the same one day," I noted.

"So is there going to be a [arty of some kind?" Alex asked.

"Only you would ask," I teased. "I'll have an open house for the shop for sure."

"Glad you brought that up, Alex," Holly inserted. "I have a little going-away present for you." Holly was always giving gifts to everyone.

"You do?"

Holly opened her large purse and pulled out a wrapped package with a little card attached. I unwrapped the tissue and was totally delighted with what I saw. It was a needlepoint open and closed sign. I knew right away that Holly had made it. The letters were in red on a white background, but it also had a bright yellow border and a yellow ribbon hanger.

"I really need this!"

"I know, and I almost didn't get it finished in time."

"I love it, girlfriend. Thanks so much." I gave her a hug.

It was noon before every piece of furniture was loaded into the van. Holly had already started cleaning my bathroom.

"We're ready, Ms. Rosenthal," one mover yelled. "Are you ready to leave?"

"Yes, just give me a few minutes," I responded with some anxiety. "I need to say some goodbyes." I turned to my friends. "Here's my key, Alex," I said with a deep breath. "Just hang onto it for me. Thanks for all your help. Both of you are the best." Holly wiped tears from her eyes. I hugged them both.

"Don't worry," Alex said. "You have until the end of the month if you've forgotten anything. You take that next step you've been planning."

Holly only nodded, too choked up to speak.

I checked each room and said goodbye. Flashbacks of memories came, especially when I went into my quilt room. I turned around with sadness and headed out the door. I looked up and down the street, hoping Harry would be around. It was probably too painful for him. I gave Bertie's house one last look, hoping to seal it in my memory. Taking a long, slow, deep breath, I then exhaled and climbed into my vehicle.

All the way to Augusta, I was anxious and melancholy. Had I done the right thing? Would I regret making this move?

Chapter 82

When I pulled up in front of the yellow house, the sun was beating hard and the heat was overwhelming. I felt sorry for the movers, so I immediately made some iced tea. I gave them instructions, and they moved quickly in and out of the air conditioning.

Getting my bed up the stairs was challenging for them. Once they succeeded, they were kind enough to assemble it. I was shocked by how much room it took up! It was strange to see my personal things show up in this location. I could see right away that some of the pieces would have to come down to the antique shop for lack of space.

It was four o'clock when the movers finished. I too was hot and exhausted. I sent Holly and Alex a text that I was now all under one roof. I teased the by telling them I may have changed my mind. Alex texted back, "Nooooooo!"

I took my tea upstairs to put linens on the bed and unpacked a few clothes. I then saw through the triple windows that Carrie Mae had pulled up in front of the house. I couldn't wait to see her.

"Welcome to my home!" I said with a big grin.

"Oh, honey, why did you decide to move on the hottest day of the year?"

"Come on in and have some iced tea."

"It feels wonderful in here!" Carrie Mae exclaimed as she fanned herself.

"Excuse all the mess, but the good news is that my bed is ready for me to crash in it for the night."

"You'll need it! I won't go upstairs. I sure wouldn't want anyone to see what my living quarters looks like."

I couldn't wait to show her the sign that Holly had given me. We sat on one of the small loveseats I had for sale, and I caught her up on my day. She claimed the day was too hot for shoppers, so she'd closed early.

"Why don't you let me buy you some dinner, Lily?"

"Oh, you are so sweet, but I'm much too tired to move out of this house. I'll take a rain check."

"I understand. Rome wasn't built in a day, so don't knock yourself out. Take your time and smell the roses out here. This is a lovely community."

"You are so right. This may not be the best time, Carrie Mae, but I told Alex this morning that I was going to ask if you would sell this building to me."

"Seriously?"

"I'm serious."

"Lily, you've bitten off a lot lately," she began. "You moved a shop to a place you're not familiar with and you've never owned a business. You have no idea what it'll be like or how much money you'll be able to make. You have utilities, not to mention feeding yourself."

"That's a mouthful to digest," I joked. "I know what

you're saying, but paying rent isn't a good use of my money."

"Living in the same building is economical, but the downside is that you never really get away. As you get older, it gets harder and harder."

"Just think about it. I'll pay for an appraisal."

She looked at me like I was crazy.

"I know you think I can't afford it, but I can."

"You can?"

"I'd like to remodel some of the rooms and bring the porches up to good standards. I can't expect you to do that. There's also a lot of landscaping I would like to have done."

"Girl, when you decide to get into something, you go all out," she said, shaking her head. "Okay, I'll think about it."

"Thanks, that's all I'm asking."

"You scare me, Lily, but in a way, we're lot alike," she said with a smile.

Chapter 83

My first night was most interesting. After Carrie Mae left, the heat of the day turned into a horrific thunderstorm. Thank goodness everything was moved, since I hadn't known it was coming.

The house had different sounds from my old apartmet. The pounding on the roof was very loud, something I'd never paid attention to there. The lightning and thunder had me jumping continuously. My biggest fear was that the electricity would go out. I then remembered the large candles under Rosie's counter, which I'd brought with me. I had used them when the electricity had gone out at her antique shop. I quickly went to get them. I left one by the door downstairs, and the other I decided to keep by my bedside.

I felt like I needed to talk to someone while the storm raged, so I first called Alex, but got his voicemail. I called Lynn next, and she was shocked to know it was storming because it was only cloudy on The Hill.

"Are you scared?" Lynn asked, concerned.

"Not really, but I don't know what to expect. The sounds

are much more dramatic than they were at the apartment. Even when it's quiet, it's loud. I guess I'll find out if this new roof leaks. When will you be out to see me?"

"Alex has been encouraging me to go, and I know you could use some help. How about tomorrow afternoon? I can bring sandwiches from the corner deli. You're probably missing some of the food by now."

"Oh, that would be scrumptious! Would you mind getting some of Tony's bagels as well?"

She laughed. "Okay, but don't ask for pizza!"

With that good news, I felt I could relax and go to sleep. The day had been physically and mentally exhausting.

At four a.m., I awoke to a tremendous noise of thunder. It was still dark and I had to get a grip on where I actually was. Then, my biggest fear happened. The electricity went off. That meant sleeping with no air conditioning and light.

I wanted to light the candle by my bed, but the matches were in my purse downstairs. Why hadn't I brought them up? After all, I lived up here now, not downstairs in the shop!

I got up and guided myself with the flashes of lightning tp get myself down the steps. Trying not to run into anything, I found my purse and the matches. I lit the downstairs candle and began to go upstairs when I noticed a dim light out of the corner of my eye. Was something on fire?

I took the candle to the center showroom, and there sat one of the lamps I had packed! It had a dim light and its cord was loose and unplugged. I turned it off and wondered if I were dreaming. I proceeded back to the stairway. I couldn't get to my bed fast enough! I decided to leave one candle burning by the stairway in case I had to rush down the stairs. I wouldn't let myself think about the weird light. I had to get some sleep. The rain turned to a light patter on the roof, which sent me into dreamland.

I awoke to very bright sunlight in the room and realized the storm was over. I blew out my candle and was pleasantly surprised to hear the air conditioner kick in.

"Thank you, Rosie," I said aloud. "I'm so glad I brought your candles. Please stop the scary pranks."

I got up and dressed with excitement to see my sister. She would be my official first guest. I quickly made my bed, putting the red-and-white Hearts and Gizzards quilt on top.

When I came downstairs and saw the lamp sitting where I'd left it, I moved it to the entry hall. If this was going to be a safety measure provided by Rosie, I wanted it in the hallway!

I made coffee in the kitchen downstairs. Making it there would give me access to coffee all day. I took my first cup to the front porch, where I enjoyed cooler fresh air. Limbs had blown everywhere from the storm. I picked them up slowly and discarded them in the wooded area along the side of the house. I tried to open the door of the doctor's brick building as I passed by, but it was locked. I remembered Carrie Mae saying she had the key for it. I wondered how much property actually belonged with this yellow house. Some of the outbuildings were creepy, yet charming.

Lynn drove up as I was going back indoors. I greeted her with open arms as though I hadn't seen her in weeks. She had packages and a big green fern in her arms.

"Happy house! My, this is a very yellow house!"

I laughed. "Thank you! Please come in. I left all my pathetic plants behind, but I'll do my best to keep this alive. I've never had a green thumb, but I'm determined to try gardening out here."

"So this is Lily Girl's Quilts and Antiques!" Lynn said as she walked between the furniture and boxes.

"Yes, it's the beginning, anyway."

"You know, this looks a lot like Rosie's shop," Lynn observed.

"I'll take that as a compliment. After all, it's her furniture. Oh, this fern will be lovely on this plant stand by the window!"

Chapter 84

As Lynn walked around, she commented about how much bigger the house seemed on the inside. I then explained that the upstairs was not organized or decorated.

"Are you sure you're ready to see it?"

She smiled and nodded.

It took a while for her to respond as she went from room to room. "This could be a charmer, Lily. I adore this wallpaper. How did it stay in such good condition?"

"It's so ugly, but I'm getting attached to it. It will be changed, but it's not a priority right now."

"Well, I'm ready to get to work!" Lynn stated as we went back downstairs.

"Not before I have one of Tony's bagels. I'll get us some coffee."

Lynn's excitement was contagious. She had to comment on everything she unwrapped as if it were Christmas.

"I'm going to have quilt racks made for this wall to hold all the quilts, but Carrie Mae said she'd have one to loan me in the meantime. All the rooms will be very crowded, but I like to shop in crowded stores, don't you?"

"I suppose, but I think you should make this kitchen a showroom as well. There are many kitchen related items that you could display in here. Your cookie jars, that old scale over there, and some dishes would work in this room. Are you going to cook in here at all, besides using your coffeepot?"

"No. What a great idea! You have such an eye, Lynn. Remember, as you unpack, see if everything has a price tag."

"Hey, boss, I think you're getting company," Lynn announced as she looked out the front window.

I looked out to see Nick arriving in his yellow convertible.

"Do you know that hunk of a guy?"

I nodded. "He's my sign man."

"Of course he is."

I giggled. "Hi, Nick," I said, opening the door.

"I see you have company, or is it a customer?"

"Meet Lynn, my sister," I said. "Lynn, this is Nick."

"A pleasure," Lynn said, reaching to shake his hand.

"I see that good looks run in the family," Nick teased.

"Oh, you should see our other sisters, Loretta and Laurie!" Lynn joked. "It's nice to meet you, sign man."

"Is that what she told you? I'm retired and doing some art work. Your sister needed a sign design, so I offered to help."

"Lynn, this is the artist I told you I'd met. Lynn is an artist as well and has her own gallery on The Hill near my previous apartment."

That took the conversation to a whole new level. It was like I wasn't in the room. Artists lived in a world of their own. It was all about who you knew and where you sold your work. After about twenty minutes, I interrupted and asked if he had any sign designs to show me.

"That's why I stopped by."

He got out his phone to show me what he had come up with. It was exactly what I'd envisioned, and Lynn also gave her approval. I was still feeling like the third wheel in the room. It appeared to me that Nick was hitting on Lynn, and she was definitely responding. I hadn't seen that side of her in a long time.

"When do you think you and your carpenter can get this done?" I interrupted.

"Is she always this pushy?" Nick asked, smiling at Lynn.

Lynn laughed. "Yes, she is, and if I don't get back to work, she'll fire me."

"Okay, I'll be on my way. I'll get right on this. Nice to meet you, Lynn," he said flirtatiously. "Maybe I can take the two of you to dinner sometime."

"Thanks, Nick. Nice to meet you, too," Lynn replied. "Stop by the gallery if you get into the city."

"Thanks, I will."

As the door closed behind him, Lynn and I looked at each other.

"Did you hear yourself?" I teased. "You fell right into his hands. Just like putty!"

"He's another artist, for Pete's sake. I'm actually familiar with his work. I had no idea that he lived out here. If he's shown an interest in you, why haven't you responded?"

"Carrie Mae warned me about him, and I saw him with another woman the other night."

"So what?" Lynn asked with her hands on her hips.

"Let's get back to work. You concentrate on the kitchen. Here's a box of embroidered hand towels that could go in there."

An hour later, we took a break to eat our sandwiches while we sat on the front step.

"No lawn chairs?" Lynn asked as she looked around.

"No, I had the clunky wicker furniture on my porch at the apartment, but I left it there. Some of it was Bertie's. I want to rebuild these porches, so I'll need to get some furniture. There's always such a nice breeze here."

"What do you mean about rebuilding the porches? That's expensive! What will Carrie Mae think about that? She's already been pretty generous, not charging you rent until you open your business. That's amazing, if you ask me!"

"I know, but I've also asked Carrie Mae to sell me the building."

"Are you out of your ever-loving mind? You've already drained your savings to buy this inventory! You'll never get a loan unless Carrie Mae finances it. What are you thinking?"

I took a deep breath and realized it was time to share with Lynn about the money Rosie had left me. I watched her face go into disbelief as I described finding the money in Rosie's cookie jar. I knew Lynn was about to instruct me to give it back until I told her that the estate attorney said it was legally mine.

"So, Miss Worrywart, I do have a cushion to invest with," I explained as pleasantly as I could. "I know Rosie wanted me to buy her shop, and in a roundabout way, she's accomplished it. It will be economically good for me to live here as well."

Lynn shook her head. "You always were the lucky one in the family. Or maybe I should say the spoiled one. That is unbelievable."

"Rosie and I had a nice relationship. She taught me so much about antiques, just like Carrie Mae taught me all about quilts."

"I didn't mean that you didn't deserve it," she said apologetically. "Do you think Carrie Mae will sell it to you?"

"I don't know. She said she would think about it. I think she'd rather have rent every month, but whatever she decides, I can live with it."

"She doesn't need the money, does she?"

"Carrie Mae owns most of the property around here. Korine, the cleaning lady that we shared, said Carrie Mae has a teddy bear collection above her shop that's worth a fortune."

"Teddy bears?"

I nodded. "She has a huge inventory of most everything, but she's a bit of a hoarder, I think."

"Wow!" Lynn responded.

"I love that woman. She'll do anything for anybody. She has a heart of gold. She hires folks who need money and truly cares about this community."

"Well, Lily, I need to be on my way. I'll finish this box and go. Are you going to find a place for my paintings or are you going to sell them?"

"Lynn, are you crazy? Never! They go perfectly with the wallpaper upstairs! I may hang them yet today!"

She laughed.

"I will never part with them. Thank you so much for the goodies and all your help. I love you, sister!"

Chapter 85

Lynn's visit certainly lifted my spirits, and every time I went into the kitchen, I smiled and admired her creativity.

I still hadn't heard anything from Carrie Mae about my suggested purchase, but she sent her boys over with a good-sized rack to display my quilts on. Since I'd never sold quilts, I had to price those that were coming from my collection. I scanned the internet, seeing much higher prices than I knew I could get here in the Midwest. As I attached the quilts' tags, I talked to them like they were my children. I was sending them away to unknown families in hopes that they would be taken care of. I hoped Holly was still interested in buying some so I would know they were in good hands.

I had high hopes that my sign would be coming soon, and I was expecting my business license in the mail any day. The inspection had gone well and my internet was up and running. The yellow house was starting to feel like home. I still wanted a security system, but until I knew the building would be mine, I had to wait.

Folks were starting to recognize me when I did get

out and about. My next-door neighbors chose to keep to themselves, and I wanted to respect that. Not many folks would like to have a business located next to them, so I wanted to keep a low profile. I took a break to sit on the front porch step when I saw Kitty walking her dog. They were coming my way.

"Good to see you!" I greeted her. "And who is this?"

"This is Patches, and she's old, so she won't hurt you," Kitty explained.

"Would you like to have a glass of wine or some iced tea?"

"You know, wine sounds really good," she stated, keeping Patches close to her side.

"I'll be happy to show you around inside, if you'd like."

"Yes, I've been anxious to see the inside of this place for a long time. Do you mind Patches coming in?"

"No, not at all," I said, patting Patches on the head. Showing Kitty the shop was exciting since she owned a shop herself. I asked her a few questions, and she was surprised by the quantity of my merchandise.

"How could you possibly own this huge of an inventory without previously owning a shop?"

"I bought a shop and basically relocated it," I began. "I knew the owner because I had shopped there so often. She wanted to sell the inventory and kept hinting for me to buy it. One day, she was shot and killed. There were many things that guided me to purchase her inventory after her death."

"That is a sad series of events for your poor friend."

"It was hard losing her, but fortunately, she gave me right of first refusal on everything. I couldn't let her down, and I didn't have a job at the time. So, here I am." I handed her a glass of wine, and Patches suddenly starting barking like crazy.

"Patches! Patches! Stop it right now!" Kitty commanded. "Are you here alone, Lily?"

"Sure, why?"

"She acts like this when she's around a stranger that may do harm to me. Let's go outside. I'm sorry. This is odd behavior for Patches."

We went to the front porch and sat on the step. Patches kept whining and wanted to stand by the door like she knew there was someone inside. I have always felt that animals could see and feel things we can't. Perhaps Patches saw the spirit I'd brought with me.

It was getting dark, and Kitty wanted to get on her way. I was tired and ready to end the day. After she left, I went upstairs hoping there wasn't really anything in the house. I undressed and was about to turn off the lamp when my phone rang.

"I'm just calling to see how you're doing," Marc said. "I just got home from a meeting and am watching the end of a great game. Yay, Cardinals! Are you watching?"

"No, but I take it from the tone of your voice that they're winning! I had a neighbor stop by, and we sat on the front porch and shared some wine."

"I thought that was what all those wineries out there were for," he quipped.

"True, but I have a pretty good stock of wine myself. Carrie Mae said there's a really old wine cellar in the basement, but I haven't been brave enough to check it out."

"That would be cool! I'd love to have a cellar of my own. Have you thought about growing some grapes in that big backyard of yours?"

"Don't give me any more ideas, Marc," I joked. "I think I have plenty to do right now without tending grapevines!

Before we hung up, I told him about Lynn coming out to help me. Our observations on her marriage seemed to line up. He thought Carl was waiting for Lynn to make the first move to separate. That made me so sad. Marc made no mention of coming to see me. I had a feeling this would be true of many of my friends.

Chapter 86

As I sat on the front porch drinking my coffee the next morning, I thought how nice it would be to call a contractor to refurbish the porches. As I pictured how the end product would look, I could almost feel the cool breezes when my cell phone rang. It was Sarah. "How is my favorite niece doing?" I asked cheerfully.

"I guess you've heard about my pregnancy by now, so discounting the morning sickness that refuses to go away, I'm fine," Sarah sighed.

"I'm sorry I haven't called, but moving and getting this shop open has taken up all my time."

"It all sounds wonderful, Aunt Lily," she remarked. "I'm calling to ask if I could visit for a few days, just to get away from the drama around here. I'd be happy to help you."

"Well, I don't have much room, but I do have a pretty comfortable couch," I replied.

"No problem! I promise not to overstay my visit."

"You'll have to call Lynn and arrange the transportation out here. What does your mother think about this visit?"

"Frankly, we're both ready for a break from each other," she admitted. "Thanks so much. I'll call Aunt Lynn right away."

I hung up and went in for another cup of coffee. What had I just agreed to? I sure didn't want to get between Sarah and Loretta. I thought the world of Sarah, and we'd all loved watching her grow up, since my other siblings and I had no children. It was no wonder she was spoiled.

I emailed Loretta right away and told her I would be happy to see Sarah. I got an immediate response.

"Don't say I didn't warn you! Make sure she's back home for her doctor's appointment and make her earn her keep." She sounded like a typical mother. Sarah would always be her little girl. I had to admit that I felt Sarah was a bit immature. I was glad she hadn't actually married for that very reason.

After lunch, I rewarded myself by walking up the hill to see Carrie Mae and planned to stop at a few shops. On the way out, I met the mailman. "Welcome to the neighborhood," he greeted as he handed me the mail.

"Thanks! This will be my residence as well as my business."

"Good luck to you!" he said as he walked away.

I looked down, and there it was. My business license had arrived, and it was addressed to Lily Girl's Quilts and Antiques. It was my first official mail here at the yellow house. It would have to be framed. I placed it on the counter, hoping Rosie was watching from above.

When I arrived at Carrie Mae's Uptown Store, I saw her helping a customer.

"Hi, Lily!" Carrie Mae greeted me. "I want you to meet Lisa. She comes in here a lot, like you used to."

"Hi, Lisa, I'm Lily Rosenthal," I said. "I'm opening a shop on Public and Chestnut. I got my license today, so it will be open soon!"

"That's great!" Lisa responded. "You must mean the bright yellow house."

I nodded.

"I'll be sure to check it out."

"She loves quilts like you, Lily," Carrie Mae added. "Lisa comes in from Dutzow to shop and eat."

"Oh, that's great." I smiled. "I'll have a lot of quilts for sale."

"I'll check them out sometime, but now I need to run, Carrie Mae." Lisa gave Carrie Mae a big hug.

"Thanks again, Lisa," Carrie Mae replied.

When Lisa left, Carrie Mae bragged about how she could count on Lisa spending at least a hundred dollars every time she came to her shop.

"I really do need to get to know her!" I said, chuckling.

"Now that you have the license, when will you open?"

"I don't have a sign yet."

"Well, you can't wait on Mr. Nick who's just making that sign as a favor to you," she teased. "There's more than one way to skin a cat. I'd hang an open sign on your door. Then I'd pull out some merchandise, like a couple of colorful quilts, and arrange them in front of the house. It will get attention, and I can tell people to call on you."

"You have a good suggestion there, Carrie Mae," I said thoughtfully. "It would be a soft opening like some businesses do. I have that open sign Holly made for me. It would be perfect."

"You know, the fall festival is coming up. That Friday

night is called Swingin' in the Vines. It's always kicked off the season around here. Shops decorate up a storm. You may want to take advantage of all the traffic it attracts." I totally agreed with her.

I went on my way feeling very energized and with a plan. My next stop was one of my favorite shops from past Augusta visits. It was the Gallery Augusta. Vic and Ruth Ann had owned the business for many years. I always admired their fine art and gorgeous furniture. I assumed the owners of all those beautiful new homes in the wine country purchased many of their things. Before they saw me in the store, I browsed around and saw a couple of Nick's paintings. When I saw the price tags, I knew I could never afford one of them. I said a brief hello and went on my way.

I decided a yummy snack would be nice to have, so I headed to the Cookie Doe Cookie Shop. It was no bigger than my bedroom, but the smells of the bakery got my attention. I purchased a bottle of tea, a dozen cookies, and a blueberry muffin for the next day's breakfast. This shop was going to be too close for comfort and become habit-forming.

Chapter 87

After talking to Carrie Mae, I made a mental note to have my soft opening the next day. I was sure I'd learn a lot, and there was no use announcing it to everyone. I'd put Rosie's rocking chair on the front porch with a bright, attractive quilt. I had a single quilt rack that I could display on the side of the porch as well. It sounded exciting. I was putting my display things aside when I got a call from Lynn. She was verifying that I had agreed for Sarah to visit. "It will be good for everyone," I stated. "I appreciate your getting her from the airport and bringing her here. It sounds as if she won't be staying long."

"I can't help but wonder if she's really feeling up to the trip."

After we hung up, I called Carrie Mae to tell her about my plan. I told her my account was set up with the Bank of Franklin County and that I'd be heading over there to get money for the cash drawer.

"Well, that's good news, and I'll be sure to send folks your way. At some point, you may want to have a coupon with a discount for those who visit from my shop."

"Well, that's a thought. I'd better be thinking about some advertising in general."

"I gave you a copy of the *Boone Country Connection* community newsletter. Folks read every word, and it has all the latest information about everything going on in the area."

"I'll have to design an ad. Before I forget, my niece will be visiting soon. She's pregnant and not married, which means she needs a break from her mother and the drama at home. I don't know how long she'll stay."

"Well, that's really nice of you. I can't wait to meet her. Let me know if you need anything."

"Thanks, but you know I'm not here alone. Rosie has my back!"

She laughed.

The day was slipping away, and I had to plan for Sarah as well as get my shop ready to open. I decided Sarah could have my bedroom since she was pregnant. I had slept on my couch before, so it wouldn't be a big deal to me.

I looked at a photo of myself and my siblings on my dresser and a light bulb went off. I took the photo out of the frame and slipped in my business license. It would look great hanging behind the counter.

I left to get some cash from the bank and some lunch at one of the local restaurants I wanted to try. The Ashley Rose Restaurant and Inn was located in the middle of Augusta and was known for good German food. They seemed to always have cars parked around the place, so I gave it a try. Carrie Mae said they had good, simple food. It sounded fine, but I was starting to miss my Italian fare. After looking over the menu, I decided to get what everyone else was eating and ordered the schnitzel with potato pancakes and red cabbage. I was famished and hoped it would be delicious.

There wasn't anyone to strike up a conversation with as I took bite after bite. It was good, but I wondered what the fuss was all about. The young waitress was anxious for her shift to end, so I asked for my bill. She bragged about the coconut créme pie, so I ordered a slice to take home. The folks I observed in the place appeared to be riding the Katy Trail. As I left the place, I admired the long front porch. I wanted to just stay there a while. What was it about me and porches?

When I was a block away from the house, I saw lights flashing inside once again. What was the deal? I quickly got out of my car, and as soon as I opened the front door the lights stopped flashing. What in the world must the neighbors have though about this oddity? I didn't even bother looking about the house for anything unusual. This house had a mind of its own, and I was just lucky to be living here.

Chapter 88

I woke up very early to start my new career as a retailer. Lily Girl had to be up to the task. I realized I hadn't thought of store hours, so I decided that ten would be when I'd open. The day was cloudy and there was a possibility of showers, so I was cautious about putting any merchandise outdoors.

As I drank my morning coffee, I checked my email and saw that Lynn had emailed my sisters with glowing remarks about my shop. They each responded and requested photos. I took the plunge and told them that today was my dry run at being a shop owner, despite not having my sign ready. Loretta was the first to reply by saying, "Congrats, baby sister!" Laurie emailed, "You can do it!"

I smiled, wishing they were here. I proceeded to turn my sign on the door to open, as if it were an everyday occurrence. I took a pretty yellow-and-blue Dresden Plate quilt to display on the rocking chair, and chose a colorful scrappy quilt to put on the quilt rack. The cloudy day kept the sunlight away from the quilts, which was good. I went inside and brought out a small red bench and a watering can with a bright sunflower painted on it. It was fun making a small display that would hopefully draw attention as people drove by.

I stood back by the street and decided I needed some noticeable sign announcing that I had quilts for sale. I knew I could come up with something, so I walked to the backyard and wandered around to the red wooden shed that was about to fall down. I saw the perfect board I had envisioned barely hanging on to one of the doors. I gave it a yank, which nearly took me to the ground, but the board was just what I wanted. I could paint "QUILTS" vertically on the board and lean it against the house or porch. I got up and took it to the back porch, where I used a broom to brush it off. Next, I just needed some paint.

I was interrupted by a car pulling in front of the house. Was it a customer? I brushed myself off and went to see who it was.

"Good morning, Lily," Carrie Mae's friend Betty greeted me. "I hear you're open today."

"Yes, yes, please come on in. I was just in the back for a bit."

Betty slowly walked toward the front door, looking at my display.

I opened the door for her. She appeared to be ailing from something, but she had the prettiest smile.

"Lily, this is amazing," Betty said. "I remember coming in here years ago when Carrie Mae lived upstairs. What lovely things you have. If I could just sit here a bit and gaze about, I'd appreciate it." She sat down on a velvet piano stool I had near the door.

"Sure, take your time. There's a lot to see. My sign should be here any day."

"Carrie Mae said you've been working so hard, and when she told me the name of your shop, I had a good laugh, because my grandmother always called me Betty Girl." She smiled, fondly remembering the name.

"That's so sweet. I named the shop that because of Rosie, the previous owner of all these antiques. She always called me Lily Girl, which made me smile."

"Well, she would be honored, I'm sure!" Betty said, nodding.

"Yes, her spirit is here with me," I confessed.

"There's nothing wrong with that! Some folks around here talk about their ghosts, and some don't want any part of such things."

"I feel it's a blessing."

"Say, Lily, is that teapot a piece of Haviland?"

"Yes, it's the Moss Rose, which is one of the more common patterns." I carried it over to her.

"You're right. I have some of this pattern, but I've never seen a teapot. How much is it?" I showed her the price tag. "Lily Girl, this is way underpriced," she said, shaking her head. "You're not going to make any money that way."

"It's what Rosie had on it," I explained.

"Carrie Mae said Rosie's prices were too cheap, so you'd better take another look. I'll buy that if you add on another thirty dollars."

"What? Oh, I can't do that."

"I'm still getting a bargain. You want the sale or not?"

"Okay, Betty. You will be my very first customer!"

"Tou hold onto it while I check out the other room."

Chapter 89

A half-hour later, Betty left with the teapot, a vintage embroidered towel, and six butter pats. I was thrilled. I helped her to her car and noticed three girls were walking down the hill, heading straight for my shop. I thanked Betty and greeted the threesome. "The owner of the Uptown Store sent us down here," the redhead announced. "What a cute yellow house."

"Thanks. Please come in and look around." I encouraged them.

When they entered, they separated immediately.

"Is there more upstairs?" the shortest one asked.

"Oh, no, sorry," I explained. "That's where I live. I need to get that blocked off."

"Oh, how nice to live above your shop," the short girl commented.

They had so many questions about things that I didn't know who to help first! Rosie had once told me she'd had to be aware of group shoppers who tried to create a distraction so that one of them could shoplift.

"Oh my lands!" the redheaded girl yelled to the others.

"That rocking chair on the front porch is rocking by itself!" They rushed to the window. That was not what I wanted to hear.

"Betsy, you're crazy," the darker-haired friend responded. "No more wine for you today." Obviously the chair had stopped its movement. The redhead's friends dismissed her comment and went back shopping, despite the fact that she continued to argue that the chair had been rocking.

"Maybe a good breeze came along," I said to reassure her.

By now, the redhead was ready to leave and hurried her friends along. Thankfully, the dark-haired friend purchased a small needlepoint footstool. She also remarked about how inexpensive it was.

The day went surprisingly well until three, when a big clap of thunder startled me. I rushed outdoors to rescue the quilts and the other items. When I carried the chair inside, I wondered if I should keep it upstairs instead of on the first floor. It may get me into big trouble one day! I closed the door, feeling my first day had been successful. Let it rain, let it rain!

I didn't waste any time going behind the counter to tally the day's sales. I recalled seeing Rosie's daily voucher on her sales record, so I decided to do the same. I knew all this should be computerized, but for now, I would enjoy the manual process.

It wasn't quite cocktail hour, but I poured myself a glass of merlot to celebrate. I sat on the piano stool and sent a few pictures to my siblings, as well as to Alex and Holly. I was tempted to include Marc, but decided against it.

As I listened to the rain, it was much more comforting than the first storm I'd lived through here at the house. I looked at the board leaning against the back porch. Should I dare go in the basement to look for some old paint? Hearing another fierce crack of thunder, I decided against it. I'd ask to borrow some paint from Carrie Mae.

I gave her a call to report on my day, and she said she too had locked her doors when the storm arrived.

"Did Betty tell you that she was my first customer?" I asked with excitement.

"Yes, she really loved your shop and thinks you'll be quite successful."

"Really? I had such a good time. I only had one man come in all day. He was looking for old tools. I thought about the toolbox I gave to Marc."

"Oh, I'll bet that was Old Man Kotz," Carrie Mae noted. "He's got money, so don't let him talk you down on your prices. He's been known to do that."

I laughed.

"Honey, I've been thinking. I told Betty today that you wanted to buy the house, and she asked me what I was waiting for."

"She did?"

"She reminded me that us old gals aren't getting any younger. She thought it would be a good idea for me to sell you not only the place, but also some of my stashed antiques. She thought you'd be the perfect one to help me out with all of it. Now, I'm not totally sold on the notion yet, but if you want to come by in the morning, I'll show you what my lawyer and I have talked about. You may not agree with my thinking."

"Oh, Carrie Mae, that would be great! There's so much I want to do here. I feel like I can really make a go of it."

"Well, that's all fine and good, sweetie, but just wait until you experience those days when no one comes in the door. Those days can get to you."

Chapter 90

How was I supposed to sleep that night? I was trying to think positively about Carrie Mae's notion of selling. I hated being so naive when it came to matters like this. There was only one professional I could think of to ask for advice, and that was Carl. I called him at home and Lynn answered. She immediately expressed her happiness about my first successful day in retail.

"Thanks, but I called to talk to Carl. Is he home?"

"No, he's working," she sadly said. *Of course he is,* I thought.

"Carrie Mae has agreed to meet with me about selling her house, so I had some questions to ask Carl."

"Well, just call his cell," she suggested. "Just don't be too anxious and think it through."

"I will. We'll talk later."

I called Carl's office, but he wasn't there. I tried his cell, and it went to voicemail. I thought how sad it was for Lynn not to be able to reach him if she needed him. This was not the Carl I used to know. I left a message requesting a return call. I explained what I was about to do and that I valued his opinion. I also wanted to add that he should go home to his wife, but didn't.

I went upstairs and noticed the rain had finally stopped. I opened one of the windows to get the breeze and that fresh after-the-rain smell, then put on a nightgown before getting my notepad and pen from the nightstand. I wanted to make a list of questions for Carrie Mae,

I was interrupted by a call from Alex.

"Way to go, Lily Girl!" he responded when I described my successful first day. "That wasn't so difficult, was it?"

"No, not at all. I really enjoyed it. Of course, Carrie Mae's best friend was generous, knowing it was my first day. I had one strange incident, however. I had a group of young women in here, and one of them claimed she saw the rocking chair on the front porch rocking on its own."

He chuckled into the phone. "I would have loved to have seen how you handled that one," he teased.

"Her friends thought she was nuts, so I didn't have to handle it at all."

"When is your niece coming?"

"Any day now. I can't decide if I'm looking forward to the visit or not."

"Hey, I drove past your old apartment this morning, and it looks like there's a lot of activity."

"Well, that's a good thing, I suppose. I haven't checked on Harry since I've moved out here. I hope he's doing okay."

"I'm sure he's adjusting. He has many friends in the neighborhood."

"I got good news from Carrie Mae about buying her house. She wants to meet with me tomorrow morning about it."

"Hot dog!" Alex said, laughing. "You're still game, right?"

"Oh, yes. I can't imagine renting this place with all that needs to be done. I called Carl for some legal advice, but I haven't reached him yet."

"Well, what about your baseball friend?"

"No, I don't feel comfortable with that."

"Something tells me you're going to do what your gut says anyway. Am I right?"

"It's all I have to go on. I haven't regretted buying Rosie's inventory and moving out here. It seems like buying this place will complete the picture, don't you think?"

Alex paused. "I'm not an expert in that field, but I think you need to get an independent appraisal," he advised. "That house has been vacant for some time. I think you're in for many surprises, and not all of them will be good."

"Good advice. I'm happy to pay for it. I'll let you know what happens."

I always felt good and secure after talking to Alex. We shared everything. He would make a great husband for someone, but his attitude about marriage wasn't very good. When he did go out with someone, he was always so critical of them afterwards. He also mentioned that some women had reacted negatively when they found out he was a freelance writer. He interpreted that as them thinking he may not be quite wealthy enough for them.

When I got back to my to-do list, I put the appraisal down as number one. I added another and then another concern. By midnight, I was yawning way too frequently to concentrate.

Chapter 91

"Good morning, Lily Girl," Carrie Mae greeted me. "Are you ready for another shop day?"

"You know, I really am! I think I can do this."

We chuckled.

"I have to tell you, Lily, I talked with my daughter, a couple of friends, and my attorney about me selling you this place."

"You did?" Did I want to hear the conclusion?

"As you know, we have a unique situation here."

"I know, I know."

"I think we've come up with something to make a transaction as easy and as inexpensive as possible. As you recall, I paid nearly nothing for the place because I was going to use it for storage." I nodded. "You then came along, and I agreed to let you store your things there, so with that I had to invest in a new roof and furnace."

I kept nodding.

"I have no intention of making any money off of this sale. I just want to recoup what I've put into it. A house with this amount of land is going to make your appraisal quite high. You really don't need all that ground, so my proposal offers you about a half-acre that includes the house, a small yard, and the brick house next to it. For historical purposes, they should stay together. I can't imagine you trying to maintain all that ground. Now, if you can agree to the amount of the down payment, I'll be happy to carry the rest until you get it paid off." Her proposal sounded fair, and Carrie Mae had a good point about not owning the excess ground.

"That sounds great!" I responded.

"Now, honey child, you look this over first. You're going to need a few dollars to yet that place looking decent. It has a lot of problems."

"I suppose there are things I haven't thought of."

"I think there's quite a bit you haven't thought of, like taxes, for instance," Carrie Mae teased.

"Perhaps, but I think this is a perfect investment for Rosie's money."

"Well, here are your papers. Look at them carefully before you sign."

"I will. You've been so cooperative and generous. I don't know how to thank you."

"You may not thank me one day!" she said with a chuckle. "If you have a lawyer, you may want to have him look at it for you. There are a few appraisers out this direction that you could use."

"Thanks, I will."

"Take as long as you need. Now, would you care for a cup of tea or coffee?"

"Oh, coffee would be great," I said as I took the papers.

"Before I forget to tell you, there's a dealer from Kentucky who comes by every now and then looking for quilts. He's a broker for businesses on the east and west coasts. Since your quilt inventory is so heavy right now, you may want to give him a call. He won't want to pay much, of course, so be mindful of that. Stay with your prices if it doesn't feel right. It would give you some startup capital, which is why I'm mentioning it."

"His money's good, right?"

"Oh my, yes! That I can guarantee you."

"Oh, the time has gotten away from me. I need to go. Thanks for the coffee. I'll be in touch."

Just as I was about to go out the door, the mailman came in.

"Good morning, ladies!" he greeted us.

"Good morning, Snowshoes!" Carrie Mae said with a chuckle.

"Snowshoes?" I asked.

They laughed.

"This man will walk anywhere in the wintertime," Carrie Mae explained. "You know how hilly it is around here? There are some winters when we get a lot of snow, and he's gotten stuck with his vehicle too many times, so Snowshoes here will start putting on snowshoes to get to some places, and he's had that nickname ever since." The mailman chuckled with embarrassment.

"Don't you get cold?" I asked, just picturing the scene.

"You get really used to it, and I know where to get a hot cup of tea to get warm, if I need it."

"I'll have to remember that," I said with a smile.

Snowshoes delivered the mail, and off he went. I had to chuckle to myself. Snowshoes's face was round and friendly like the rest of him. He'd make a good Santa Claus if one was needed in a pinch.

When I got back to the shop, I still had thirty minutes before it was time to open the store, so I sat at my desk, looking over Carrie Mae's proposal agreement. There were many details, but the number I was searching for was the down payment. When I saw it, I was pleased, because it would still allow me to do some repairs. I was sure I was looking at all of this through rose-colored glasses because I wanted it to work. Carrie Mae was right. I needed fresh eyes on this matter.

Chapter 92

I took the rocking chair and two different quilts to display. If anyone was paying attention, I had something new to show. I thought again about the quilt sign I wanted to paint on the barn door wood. My phone rang, and I saw that it was Lynn.

"Sarah's arriving tomorrow. Are you ready for her?"

"Sure. It'll all work out!" I said optimistically. "Let's plan an early dinner with her before you head home. There's a cool restaurant close by that I know you'll like."

"Okay, and I'll bring some goodies from The Hill for you to enjoy."

"Oh, that would be such a big help," I replied. "I don't plan on doing any cooking. We both need to experience what's available out here. I still want to talk with Carl. Is he home?"

"No, and he mentioned you'd called. He said he didn't want to get involved, and that you should call Marc."

"Oh, great. That's not the Carl I used to know."

"Well, you really should ask Marc for help. He would be thrilled!"

"We'll see. So I'll see you tomorrow afternoon, then?"

"Yes. I'll take Sarah to lunch before we drive out."

When I hung up, I realized I had a lot to do before the next day.

It was twelve-thirty before I had my first customer of the day. "Well, looky here!" the elderly woman said as she entered. "You must be really new out here!"

"I am! Today is only my second day to be open."

"Well, a sign sure would have been helpful, I must say," she complained in a crackling voice. "If it weren't for your quilts on the porch, I wouldn't have noticed the place."

"My shop sign isn't quite finished yet," I explained.

She didn't respond, and went up and down the aisles examining everything.

"Can I help you find anything special?"

"I'll be fine," she answered curtly.

I got the message to leave her alone. I was kind of that way when I shopped. I did things behind the counter so that I was close by. Out of the corner of my eye, I saw the woman pick everything up and set it back down again.

"Missy, where did you come from? Do you have kin around here?"

"No. I moved here from St. Louis. Carrie Mae Wilson from the Uptown Store told me about this place." The woman suddenly had a different look on her face. I didn't know if it was a good or a bad thing.

"I should have known," sh sarcastically replied. "Where do you live?"

"Right upstairs, here" I stated with a smile.

"Well, I don't see anything in here, but I'll buy that rocking chair you have on the front porch." I was shocked, but delighted. "What's your price on it?" I shrugged my shoulders and headed out the door to to check while the woman stayed inside.

When I looked at the tag, I saw it read "NOT FOR SALE" in large letters. I couldn't believe it. I'd seen that rocking chair in Rosie's shop for many years and assumed it was for sale. Should I make up a price or tell the woman it wasn't for sale? She was so rude, I decided I didn't want her to have it.

"Oh, ma'am, I'm so sorry, but I forgot the cane.,

"Now, that doesn't make a bit of sense, young lady. You cant stay in business that way. I'll pay whatever you want."

"I'm so sorry, but I can't."

"You will not, or you cannot?"

"I cannot."

"Well, then, I'll be on my way, and I don't plan to come back here again. That's false advertising, if you ask me."

Out the door she went, and she gave the door a good slam. I was just as shocked as she was! Why hadn't Rosie wanted to sell the chair? I wondered if the woman would have bought it if I had told her it was haunted. My retail days were not starting out too well.

My only sale of the day was to Kitty, who closed her shop early to check out mine. She said she'd spotted a round walnut clock when she was here last and decided to come back for it. I was delighted and offered her a ten percent discount. Kitty said the clock was for her home, but that the price was so reasonable, she could easily resell it. Why was everyone talking about my low prices? Was that a good thing? I was grateful either way, because that sale made my day.

Chapter 93

The next morning, I prepared as well as I could for my first overnight guest. It was only eight when someone knocked at my front door. I looked out the window and saw it was Nick, who had arrived in a pickup truck. I reluctantly opened the door, knowing I looked unkempt.

"Good morning, Lily Girl!" he said with a big grin. "I've got your sign ready to go!"

"Wonderful! I opened without it for a couple of days, so this is great! Do you need me to help?"

"Not unless you've changed your mind about where you want to put it. You may want to watch to make sure it doesn't interfere with that weeping cherry tree you have on the corner."

I did watch as he proceeded, and at the same time, I put out the rocking chair and a couple of quilts. I didn't want to engage in conversation; he'd be here forever. When he attached the actual hanging sign, I got chills. It was official, and Rosie would have been so proud.

"What do you think?" Nick asked.

"There are no words," I said with a smile.

"Well, how about words like 'awesome,' 'love it,' and 'perfect?'" He chuckled. "Now, you know, you have to go to dinner with me for payment."

"Sorry, the timing is bad. I have an out-of-town relative coming to stay with me today. I really do need you to send me an invoice. I can deduct it!"

Nick smiled, shaking his head. "Well, I won't forget!" he said, giving me a wink. "Are you seeing someone else, by any chance?"

"No, no, I'm just very busy right now. Would you like a cup of coffee?" I felt it was the least I could do.

"No, I'm actually on a delivery to Gallery Augusta."

"Oh, I saw a couple of your paintings there," I mentioned. "You are quite good."

"You should encourage Lynn to put some of her work there," he suggested.

"Thanks, I'll tell her. She's bringing out my guest this afternoon, and we're all having dinner tonight."

"Sounds like a good dinner to crash!" he joked.

I remembered how he'd flirted with Lynn when she was out here. "Sorry, my friend," I replied. "Don't forget to send the invoice."

When Nick drove off, I quickly got my phone to take pictures of the sign to send to my sisters, Alex, and Holly. I sure wished Rosie and Bertie could see it. As a car drove up and honked, I turned around to see that it was Kitty.

"Way to go, Lily Girl!" she shouted from her car window. "It looks great! Who did it for you?"

"Nick Conrey."

"Really?" she asked in disbelief. "How did you manage

that? I guess he's taken a fancy to you, right?"

"Me and many other women around," I joked.

"That's the word! Good luck today! I hope we have customers!"

I gave her a wave and went inside, feeling very pleased.

After a short time, a car pulled up with two women inside. They got out and looked around.

"Welcome, ladies!"

"You must be new," the one with the baseball hat commented.

"I am, so please look around. If you need any help, let me know."

We made small talk, and they truly did check things out.

"Is the price correct for this glass pitcher?" the baseball hat lady asked. "It looks like Waterford."

I honestly didn't know if it was Waterford. "That is the correct price," I answered, trying to sound confident.

"I'll take it," she said quickly, putting it on the counter.

"I'm looking for old postcards," the woman with the ponytail requested. "Do you have some I can look through?"

"Sorry, I don't," I replied.

"You sure have a lot of quilts!" the baseball cap girl said. "Do you sell a lot of them?"

"I just opened, so I can't answer that," I explained.

"Can I open some of these?" she asked. She had already made a pile of some she had wanted to look at.

"Are you thinking of your jackets?" the ponytail girl asked her.

"Yeah, they're cheap enough," she said, pulling some aside.

"You mean you cut quilts up for clothing?"

She nodded, not offering any further explanation. "These three will work great," she said, handing them to me. "Is there a discount for buying all three?"

"Sorry, no discount," I said, not wanting to picture the horror of my quilts getting cut up. The girl left a mess of unfolded quilts behind, not even attempting to put them back.

Chapter 94

My stomach churned as I folded each quilt and put them back on the rack. I felt I had just given permission to slaughter some of my beloved quilts! Two of the three were in really good condition. Should I have educated the girl about cutting up quilts? Should I have refused to sell them to her?

Both girls went out the door as happy customers and said they'd return again. These kinds of sales were not making me happy, but I guessed that was the nature of any business. Rosie had once said, "Do not fall in love with your inventory!"

Lynn called shortly after they left and said she and Sarah were on their way. She said Sarah had survived the flight just fine and was feeling well.

I decided to leave my display for Lynn and Sarah to see. I kept thinking of Carrie Mae's papers sitting on my desk. They needed attention. Should I just go ahead and call Marc? I hated to involve him. I didn't like others knowing my personal business. However, I picked up the phone impulsively and let it ring. I was about to hang up when he answered. "It's Lily!" I said awkwardly.

"Well, hello! How are things going out there?"

"Good, really good. I was wondering if you could give me some professional help."

"Sure. Shoot!"

"I'm about to sign some papers to purchase this building from Carrie Mae," I began.

"Well, congratulations!"

"I need to have it appraised and then have someone take a look at the sales contract. It appears fine to me, but I'm out of my league with these things. I called Carl, and he suggested that I give you a call. He doesn't want to get involved."

"I see. I do know a good appraiser in Washington, Missouri that you could call. After you receive the appraisal, I'll be happy to give you my opinion."

"I would appreciate it very much and would be happy to pay you."

Marc chuckled. "We'll work that out. When is a good time for me to come out?"

"Lynn is bringing Sarah out today. She'll be here for several days, but that's not a concern. How about we make it tomorrow afternoon?"

"Sure! I can take you ladies to lunch if you like."

"I'd better not arrange that, Marc, but thanks. It's going to be difficult to close the shop, now that I've just opened."

"Under those circumstances, how does three o'clock work?"

"Great."

Marc handled the request very professionally, which I liked. I wondered what he thought about it.

I didn't waste any time calling the appraiser that Marc had suggested. He said he would stop by within a couple of days. Was I getting the cart before the horse? I was moving forward, which was the important thing.

When Lynn and Sarah arrived, I grinned from ear to ear. I went out to greet them with big hugs. Sarah certainly appeared pregnant, which was a strange sight for me.

"Oh, Aunt Lily, this place is adorable!" she exclaimed. "Look at your sign with that darling name! Can you believe it?"

"Thanks; it is surreal!" I admitted. "Thanks for driving her out, Lynn. Come on in. I made some tea and I have cookies from the local cookie shop."

"Sounds good to me!" Sarah responded.

They were delighted to see how the shop looked and remarked how much bigger the place looked on the inside. I showed them around, and before we went upstairs, I tried to prepare Sarah for the look of the vintage décor. Her response was almost giddy. She loved the wallpaper and gushed over each detail. I thought if I'd lived in a cave, Sarah would have loved it. She didn't like the idea of taking over my bedroom, but I insisted.

I closed the shop so we could be on our way to dinner. I was still affected by the customers from earlier in the day, so I shared my experience. Lynn and Sarah both shrugged it off like it was no big deal.

We got in my SUV so I could show them around

Augusta. Sarah was overwhelmed.

"This is like living on a movie set," she claimed with delight. "I can see how you fell in love with this little town."

When we drove by Carrie Mae's Uptown Store, I told Sarah how excited Carrie Mae would be to meet her.

Chapter 95

The Silly Goose restaurant was very welcoming. The place was nearly full, so I was glad I'd made a reservation. Their décor was simple and tasteful. I explained to Lynn and Sarah about their limited menu and how it was geared primarily toward seasonal options.

"This all looks so healthy," Lynn said as she saw their dinner choices. "This is great for our little mama with us this evening." She grinned at Sarah.

We all chose the special of glazed chicken on rice with steamed vegetables. The salad was spinach with strawberries, roasted nuts, and feta cheese.

Sarah was full of questions as we enjoyed our dinner. She had a wonderful sense of humor, unlike her mother. She had many stories to share that she knew we would enjoy. Sarah was the only one to indulge in dessert, which was the restaurant's special bread pudding with lemon sauce.

It was getting dark when we got home, so Lynn was anxious to be on her way. After Sarah and I said our goodbyes to her, we decided to sit on the front step for a while.

"It's so quiet and peaceful here," Sarah said as she took in a deep breath of fresh air.

"Have you thought of any baby names?" I asked spontaneously.

She looked at me oddly. "My mother did tell you I was having a girl, didn't she?" Sarah asked, grinning.

"No! That's wonderful! I guess it should be no surprise, with all the girls on our side of the family."

"I can tell you for sure that her name won't be starting with the letter L," she said, emitting a little giggle.

"I know. Your grandmother thought it was pretty clever."

"I think I need to wait and see what she looks like," Sarah decided.

I wanted to ask about the baby's father, but we'd had enough conversation for the evening.

We were upstairs unpacking Sarah's suitcase when she asked, "There's someone else in this house, isn't there?"

I wasn't sure I'd heard her right. "I'm not sure what you mean. It's just you and me," I reminded her.

"The house has a ghost, doesn't it?" she asked in a teasing manner.

I took a deep breath and told her about Rosie. I was surprised how casually she reacted to my thinking a spirit had followed me here.

"Please don't be alarmed," I reassured her. "I just think she hasn't moved on and really wants to see me set up this business. There have been too many signs that this is her mission."

"I always heard that when someone dies a dramatic death like your Rosie did, they stick around for various reasons."

I nodded in agreement. "I shudder when I think of her

awful death. She didn't deserve it. I hope she didn't suffer."

"Do you talk to her?"

I nodded and blushed at the same time. "Yes, and I hope my customers never catch me at it," I said with a chuckle in my voice.

"I frankly think you should pay close attention to what she's trying to tell you."

"What do you mean?"

"She can see things you can't. Maybe she'll try to warn you of a shoplifter or a shady character that's trying to harm you. Don't be too quick to dismiss what she's doing."

"You are so wise for your age, my dear," I teased.

We hugged and said goodnight. I wrapped one of Rosie's quilts around me and got comfortable on the couch. For now, it felt good, but I hoped I wouldn't roll over onto the floor during the night.

I was almost asleep when I thought I heard Sarah talking to someone. I got up and went close to her door. She was talking on her phone. Who could it be at this hour? Perhaps she would share it with me the next day.

I surprised myself by how well I slept on the couch. Other than a sore muscle here and there, I felt rested and ready for a full day. I went downstairs to make coffee and get the bagels that Lynn had brought from Tony's. Summer was at its end, and it was a beautiful day. I decided that I needed to spend it with my niece and keep the shop closed.

When Sarah came down to the kitchen, I suggested that I show her around the wine country. I told her about Wine Country Gardens and how I'd frequented the place many times before I moved out here. "I loved their chicken salad, and it was a great place for me to take a book to read or just stare out at the spectacular view. They're always so kind to me. Sometimes I just walk around the lake or sit on their porch and stare. It sounds crazy, doesn't it?"

"No, not at all. Please take me there!"

As I filled Sarah's coffee cup, I told her about Defiance, where we'd be going for lunch. I had to chuckle to myself thinking I'd see Sarah's huge appetite kick in. "Sarah, did the doctor say anything about watching your weight?" I asked.

She shook her head with her mouth full.

"I'll bet you're excited about having your baby in time for Christmas!"

"Mom sure is!"

"I guess I shouldn't ask, but how is Jerry taking the news about your cancelling the wedding, especially since you're pregnant?"

"He's disappointed, but it's best for both of us."

"Is he excited to become a father?"

She looked perplexed. "It's complicated," she said as she refilled her glass.

"I'm sorry. It's none of my business. Your aunts, however, are simply delighted that there is going to be a baby in the family."

She grinned. "I knew you would be."

Chapter 96

We began our day's adventure by scoping out the wineries. Sarah said if she were not pregnant, we would be having a glass of wine at each one.

We arrived at the Wine Country Gardens around one and ordered lunch. As Sarah gazed at the awesome view, she said she would marry anyone if she could get married at this spot. I told her that many weddings took place here. I introduced her to Chris, the owner, who seemed to be interested in Sarah's situation.

"Well, if you lived around here, I would offer you a job for next season," Chris claimed. "We've lost so many who have gone back to school and won't be able to return. Some have been working here for many years."

"I would love working at a place like this!" Sarah said as she looked around. "I'm taking some hospitality classes and would love having a restaurant like The Silly Goose that only serves healthy options."

"Some folks have that natural chemistry with strangers, and you seem like one of them," Chris said. "Our staff has their own clientele, which really helps."

"It's because of you, Chris, that I ended up living out here. You always made me feel welcome, and I saw how much you and Bill have put into the community. You've captured the beauty out here with your business," I said.

"Thanks, Lily," Chris said, blushing.

"It's been nice to meet you, Chris," Sarah said as Chris went back to work.

Our lunch was fantastic, and Chris sent us a complimentary dessert, which completed our day.

"We'd better get back." I reminded Sarah. "I have to be ready for Marc at three."

Sarah was in no hurry to leave and wanted to walk around the lake before getting in my vehicle. We arrived back at the house just in time to see someone peeking into one of the windows. I unlocked the door and asked her in. She said she'd heard about the shop from a friend. She headed straight to the rack of quilts. Sarah immediately went to help her unfold some of them. I tried to provide information on each one, if I had any. Sarah was listening more than the lady was.

"We'll let you look around," I suggested after a while. "Let us know if you need some help."

I saw Marc pull up and went out to greet him.

"Well, look at this," he said, pointing to my sign. "The sign looks like it's been here a long time."

"Thanks! Sarah is with a customer inside. We can't discuss many details until the customer leaves, I'm afraid."

He nodded. "It's good to see you," he said, giving me a wonderful smile. "I'll look around your shop for a bit, if you don't mind." We went inside, and Marc nodded hello to Sarah and the customer.

"Aunt Lily, she would like to buy this Log Cabin quilt," Sarah informed me. "I took her check and got all her information. I hope I did it right."

"Well, that's great!" I responded. "Everyone loves a Log Cabin quilt, so I hope you enjoy it. Sarah, the bags are underneath the counter, and one of them is big enough for a quilt."

Sarah quickly bagged up the quilt, and I thanked the lady for stopping by. She simply smiled and went on her way. Shoppers sure came in all sizes, personalities, and styles!

Sarah quickly gave me a high five for making the sale. I had to chuckle at her enthusiasm.

"You've trained this gal pretty well," Marc said.

"Sarah, this is Marc. I told you about him," I said.

"The baseball guy, right?" She smiled.

Marc nodded.

"He keeps me up to date with the Cardinals, since I've been so busy," I explained.

"Nice to meet you, Sarah, and I hope you're enjoying the wine country," Marc said.

"It's divine, except for not tasting the wine," Sarah replied. "I love Aunt Lily's shop, too. I can't believe that lady paid five hundred dollars for a quilt without batting an eye!"

"That was a fluke, my dear. It doesn't happen very often. Sarah, would you mind giving Marc and me a little privacy while I talk with him about my contract?"

"Absolutely!" She nodded. "I need to go upstairs and make some calls. It was nice to meet you, Marc."

"Don't forget to check in with your mom!" I reminded her. "Tell her hello for me."

"I will," she said reluctantly.

Chapter 97

Marc and I had a seat near an antique desk. I began to explain how Carrie Mae had arrived at her offer, then remained silent as Marc carefully read the papers. I told him I had an appraiser coming, but he nodded and kept reading. We were interrupted by Snowshoes, who brought the mail inside.

"You're late!" I teased.

"You can thank the Millfords for that!" he said, shaking his head. "Long story. Have a good day!"

I looked back to Marc, and he had a teasing smile on his face. I looked to him for a response.

"Of course, without the appraisal I can't give you my total opinion, but it appears that so far, this is a very generous proposal. It's as if you were family."

"That's what I thought. I'm glad we agree."

"Worst-case scenario is you get the whole place in shape, but your business flops or it isn't what you thought. You can always resell it."

I paused at what he'd just proposed. "I can't think in

those terms, Marc. I need to make this work, for many reasons."

"And you will, I'm sure! Look, I know you've been busy getting settled, but if you ever want to take time for a nice evening out, I hope you'll think of me."

I smiled at him. "How sweet, Marc. You know I will. I'm not very accessible out here. I can only ask so much of my friends and family. You will send me an invoice for your time, I hope."

"Are you kidding? You don't mean that. I thought we were friends. That's what friends do for each other."

Now I felt crummy.

"I'd better get going so you and Sarah can sell more quilts."

"Marc," I said, and paused. "I didn't mean to insult you. I value your opinion, and I really like being with you."

He nodded and smiled, but looked as if he didn't quite believe me. "Tell Sarah goodbye for me," he said, moving toward the door.

"Thanks. I'll call you when I know the appraisal amount."

"Something to look forward to."

I walked with him to the car. As he pulled away, a young couple parked to come into the shop. They told me they were looking for four matching chairs for their dining room table, so I had to give them the bad news that I didn't have any such thing. I encouraged them to come in and look around anyway.

Sarah was now downstairs and immediately engaged in conversation with them. She certainly wasn't shy. In five minutes, the couple was on their way, but said they'd return.

"Aunt Lily, what is it with you and that handsome

lawyer? Why aren't you dating him?"

"We've gone out a few times," I explained. "I asked him to do a professional favor. It makes a difference now that I'm living out here. Who would want to make that drive to go to dinner?"

"Now that's a cop-out. Distance has never kept two people who like each other apart."

"Okay, I get the hint. Now, I want you to take a look at the crib quilts on the end of this rack. If you like any of them, I want you to have one."

"Seriously?" Sarah asked with a big smile. "I saw one I loved when I was showing the one lady those quilts."

"Which one?"

"The pinkish nursery rhyme one," she said, going over to pick it up.

"I like that one too, and thought of giving it to you, but I didn't know if you'd be having a girl or boy. Now that we know, it's perfect!"

"Oh, thank you so much, Aunt Lily," she said as she gave me a hug. "I haven't purchased one baby thing yet."

At five, I turned the sign to indicate that the shop had closed, and Sarah and I decided to get some exercise by walking around the town before getting dinner. On our way, she received a call on her cell phone and said she'd call them back later. I could overhear a masculine voice on the phone.

We walked to the Augusta Winery. I hadn't visited it before, so we found a seat on the lovely patio. We decided we'd be happy with a platter of cheese, sausage, and fruit. I tasted a couple of their red and white wines and settled on a white wine called River Valley White. It was a dessert wine, but very refreshing. I told Sarah that I hoped to learn more about wine now that I lived out here. There was a pleasant breeze, and we were very relaxed. Sarah had many questions about the area, and I couldn't answer them all.

"Do you think you'll like being a mother?" I asked to change the subject.

I caught her by surprise. "Oh, sure," she said simply.

"How do you feel about Jerry and his role as the father?"

She paused and looked away from me.

"Your mother said he's a really nice guy."

Chapter 98

"I guess I should have said something before now, but I was afraid you would say something to my mom. I hope I can tell you something in confidence."

"For heaven's sake, what?"

Sarah paused again. "Jerry is not the father of my child."

"Oh, Sarah, what do you mean?"

"I've been seeing someone else for quite a while," she said in almost a whisper. "Of course, it took its toll on the relationship I had with Jerry. I just couldn't marry him."

"That I can certainly understand! Why didn't you just break up with him? Who is the father?"

"One of my professors."

"Sarah!"

"I know, but he's an amazing man."

"Does he know he's the father of this baby? Will he marry you?"

"He's already married."

I sat in stunned silence trying to collect my thoughts. My mind was racing. I had to choose the right words. "Sarah, you know this is a no-win situation, don't you?"

She nodded. "I do, and I've always known he never planned to leave his wife. We were very honest with each other. I am perfectly happy to have this baby alone."

"But were you honest enough to tell him about the baby? By the way, you may think you are going to raise this baby alone, but your parents, by no fault of their own, will also be raising this child in some way."

She shook her head. "They'll never forgive me if they find this out, so I'll have to leave home. I know Jerry would marry me anyway, but I don't love him. I won't consider that option."

I took a big swallow of the white wine, wishing I knew the right words to say without ruining her trip. "This has to be so stressful for you, Sarah," I said, taking a deep breath. "That is not good for your pregnancy."

"Please don't think poorly of me, Aunt Lily," she pleaded. "I didn't plan any of this. I think my baby and I will be just fine."

We sat there talking and talking until they chased us out at ten. I was so engaged in the conversation, I didn't realize I had consumed three glasses of wine. I truly felt sorry for Sarah. Scolding was not what she needed right now. She said she'd never seen herself as being married with children. I now understood why she'd had to leave home for a while. She was right about her mother. This news would be a tremendous blow to her.

We hardly passed any cars walking home. Sarah had to be exhausted. When we walked into the house, we were dead tired. I wondered if Sarah would still return that phone call.

I reclined on the couch, trying to absorb all Sarah had

revealed to me. How had all this happened to my sweet little niece who came from the most perfect home ever? What in the world could I do to help? I would have to stress that she needed to get rid of the married man. If he had any sincere interest in Sarah, he would have left his wife by now. He could also lose his job. I did think she did the right thing by not marrying Jerry. Two wrongs don't make a right.

The next morning, I woke up much later due to the wine and worry. Sarah was still asleep, which was good. I dressed and started coffee. The appraiser was due to come today. I placed my rocker on the porch and displayed two red-and-white quilts, showing the world I was open for business.

Sarah finally came downstairs as the appraiser arrived. While she had her juice on the front porch step, I had a conversation with the appraiser.

While the appraiser checked out the house, I checked my email. Loretta was eager for an update on Sarah. I quickly responded, saying we'd had a great lunch at the Wine Country Gardens. Little did she know what I knew.

Sarah walked inside. "If you don't need me today, I'd like to go out on my own and do a little shopping. I want to bring back some things for a few folks. I saw some cute places that we passed last night."

"That's a great idea!" I encouraged her. "Don't forget to bring something back for your mom."

"You think I don't know that?" she retorted. She was right. I should have known that she knew better. I had to begin thinking of Sarah as an adult and not treat her like a child.

"Well, that was quick," I said to the appraiser as he came inside.

"I had all the dimensions on the computer, so I just needed to verify some things," he explained. "Is there anything else you want to tell me about the place?" Did he mean like whether a ghost came with the building?

I don't think so," I innocently answered.

Chapter 99

Sarah went on her way, as happy as a lark. What was it about youth, to be so optimistic and carefree? Neither one of us mentioned our conversation from the night before. Lynn was coming tomorrow to pick Sarah up. I had to admit I'd enjoyed having her with me, despite what I had learned from her.

It was a slow day in the shop, so I dusted like crazy while I did a couple loads of laundry. There were perks to living and working in the same building. I happened to glance out the front window and saw Nick get off his bicycle. Was that a good thing or not?

"Hey, Lily Girl," he said, coming in the front door. I had to admit he looked pretty handsome in his khaki shorts and white polo shirt.

"Hi there!"

"I thought I'd come by and see if the sign was still standing."

"Yes, it is, and I'm getting many compliments on it."

"That's what I wanted to hear."

"Did you bring me an invoice?"

He chuckled. "I can write on a piece of paper that a dinner date is owed for production and installation of the sign, if you like."

"You just don't want to take me seriously when I say I refuse to do business that way," I complained.

"Admirable, my friend, but I felt I was helping out a nice lady who was starting a business. I am capable of being a nice guy."

"Of course you are. I do appreciate it, but it's not necessary."

"The Gallery Augusta is having a champagne reception this weekend for an artist friend of mine. Would you be interested in going with me? There will be many locals there that you could meet. If your niece is still here, she could go as well."

It sounded tempting. "She leaves tomorrow. It does sound very nice, but if it's okay, I'll just meet you there. I really don't want anyone thinking I'm dating someone right now."

Nick couldn't contain his laughter. "Okay, I wouldn't want to give anyone a false impression."

"What time will you be going?"

"It's from five to eight, so how about six?"

"Can I count this as our dinner date?" I joked.

"Okay, Ms. Rosenthal, play hard to get. You aren't my first rodeo."

"See you then," I said as he left.

Nick was so right. I wasn't his first rodeo, nor was I going to be his last. That guy was not for me, but it didn't feel right to be rude to him.

Around two thirty, I finally had a customer. It was Judy, who worked at Kate's Coffee. She was sweet and bubbly and happened to be a quiltmaker. She said she'd grown up in Augusta but lived in Marthasville. She went straight to the rack of quilts as she shared stories about coming from a long line of quilters. She pulled a scrappy Double Wedding Ring quilt off it's hanger and admired all its work. I told her it was reasonably priced and that everyone always admires the pattern.

"Oh, I can't afford to buy anything like this right now," she stated as she caressed the stitching.

"To be honest, Judy, this pattern is not my favorite. I purchased it with some other inventory, so I'd be happy to take less for it."

"Oh, you shouldn't do that. This price is already very reasonable. You're in business to make money, and I know how hard that is to do around here with all these shops."

"Well, how about this? I'll knock one hundred dollars off the price and let you make payments whenever you can. You can even take it with you. I know where to find you." I chuckled.

"You're serious, aren't you?" I nodded. "But I'd feel bad taking advantage of you," Judy admitted.

"Look, that quilt needs a home with someone who will love and cherish it."

She finally agreed and gave me a twenty-dollar down payment. She was very happy and told me she'd pay me another twenty dollars next month.

sI wished all my customers were like her instead of the ones who wanted to cut up my quilts!

My phone rang, and it was Holly.

"It's so good to finally hear from you," I said with concern. "Is everything okay?"

"I'm sorry I haven't been out to see you. Maurice would have a fit if I left for that amount of time. He's really not feeling well. He makes me feel guilty if I even leave to go to the store."

"What's the matter with him, besides being unstable?"

"He won't tell me much, but he finally did go to the doctor. He's losing weight and looks horrible. He's not eating so I'm not cooking, which I'm thankful for. There is something serious going on."

"I'm sure whatever it is, he'll blame you for it."

"How did you know?" she chuckled.

As always, there was nothing I could do for my friend. She hadn't reached the point of wanting to give up her financially comfortable life. It would be up to me to go see her when I got back to the city.

Chapter 100

Sarah didn't return until five thirty that evening. She was carrying all sorts of packages. She was very tired and complained that she hadn't expected to feel so fatigued.

"You go up and rest. I would be tired, too, if I did what you did! You need to put your feet up. We'll stay in for dinner tonight. I'll pick something up for us."

She looked relieved. "Perfect," she said as she went upstairs.

I decided to go to Ashley Rose and get us a couple of veggie burgers and fries.

I let Sarah sleep until about seven, when I decided to wake her. She was hungry, so I reheated our dinner and took it upstairs to the living room.

"I don't want to go home," Sarah stated bluntly as she shuffled around in her chair to get comfortable.

"You don't have much choice, Sarah, but I've truly enjoyed having you here."

"I love this little town. It would be a wonderful place to raise my little girl."

"Sarah, you must finish school," I insisted. "You'll need all the help you can get to support your child."

"I know that. I think what I'm saying is that I need to get away from Jerry and the father of the baby."

I nodded.

"I don't want my mom raising my child, and if I stay at home, that's exactly what would happen. You know how controlling she is. She was a wonderful mom for me, but now I need to be the mother. I can always get my degree later."

"Whatever you decide, it's going to take money, Sarah," I reminded her.

"I know I could find a job out here, and when the baby comes, I could get some assistance so I could live on my own. I've done a little research, and my folks have put aside what I would need financially to finish school."

"Oh my goodness, I don't know how to argue this. Go home and rethink everything."

"I suppose I can do that," she said, smiling. "Don't count me out on coming back here, Aunt Lily."

I could hardly finish my dinner after hearing Sarah's wish. I changed the subject by asking about her purchases.

"I brought you a little thank-you gift," Sarah revealed.

I took her tissue-wrapped package and looked inside. It was a brass pineapple doorknocker.

"The pineapple represents your hospitality. Thanks for letting me stay here. I thought it would look nice on your front door. I will always be thankful for this visit."

"Oh, Sarah, this is touching and quite beautiful. Thank you so much. You shouldn't be spending your money on me."

"Trust me, my mom will ask me right away if I bought something for you. I sure was hoping I would meet Alex or

Holly while I was out here."

"That would have been nice, but Holly's husband isn't well, and Alex is a very busy writer with deadlines, so it's hard for him to take much time off."

"Do you miss them and The Hill?"

"Sometimes, but now this is home. I couldn't have stayed in that building after Bertie died. I still think about her every day. She was depending on me more and more as she got older. It was hard enough getting over Rosie's sudden death."

"I think I got a glimpse of Rosie the other night," Sarah shared.

"What?"

"I was reading quietly upstairs and felt her presence again, like on the first day I got here. I looked in the hall and something seemed to disappear."

"You didn't say anything. What kind of something?"

She shrugged her shoulders. "It's no big deal for me. I feel the supernatural all the time. I've been able to do that since I was a little girl. Don't worry. Whoever is here is harmless, but curious. You should embrace it."

"How did you get to be such a wise young lady?" My cell phone interrupted us. It was Lynn confirming her arrival the next day. "I really hate to see her go," I said to Lynn.

"Well, the airline ticket is purchased. I thought I would bring out some pizza from Rigazzi's for lunch."

"Oh, that would be wonderful, Lynn. From what I can tell, there's no pizza delivery out here. Can you believe that?"

"I'm sure you'll survive. By the way, I had lunch with Alex today," Lynn shared. "He's so busy, and he misses you."

"I was just telling Sarah about him."

"Did you get Marc to help you with your contract?"

"Yes. We're just waiting for the appraisal before he gives his opinion."

"How has business been?"

"I don't know how to answer that. Only one sale today so far. I'm hoping for the best. What else can I do?"

Chapter 101

The next morning, I baked some canned cinnamon rolls for breakfast. We sat with somber faces at my small kitchen table.

"You know, Christmas will be here before you know it," I said to break the silence. "Not only will my sisters and you be all together, but we'll have a little baby girl with us."

"You wouldn't leave this precious town at Christmastime, would you?" Sarah asked seriously.

"Well, I don't want to get snowed in here. Christmas is all about family, and we have never been apart at Christmastime. My shop and Laurie's will likely close up for a while."

I saw Snowshoes coming towards the shop, so I met him at the door.

"Good morning!" I greeted him.

"Good morning! It looks like you're officially in business with all these bills," he said with a chuckle as he gave me a handful.

"I'm afraid so! Have a good day!"

Right on top of the six envelopes was my appraisal. I

couldn't open it fast enough. There were three pages, but the only thing I was looking for was the bottom line of the value. I held my breath, and to my surprise, it was better than I had hoped.

I told Sarah I needed to make a phone call to Marc, so I would be on the front porch. After many rings, he finally answered. "Am I calling at a bad time?"

"I was working out. Sorry if I sound out of breath. What's up, Lily Girl?"

"I have the appraisal. I received it today and I'm quite pleased with it." When I revealed the bottom line to him, he didn't react. He said he'd rather give his opinion when he had my contract in front of him. I agreed.

I followed Sarah upstairs to help her get her things together. She was very quiet.

"Try to think of the bigger picture, Sarah," I advised. "Once the baby comes, life will no longer be about you. You'll be thinking about what's best for your baby."

"I already have, and I shared that with you. I will continue to try to make you all happy."

"You have three aunties who want nothing but your happiness," I assured her. "I probably shouldn't add this piece of advice, but you are right. You're not a child, so don't let someone talk you into something you're not comfortable with."

"Thanks, Aunt Lily," she said with a big smile.

I kept the closed sign turned on my door so that we could have a nice, quiet lunch when Lynn arrived. When she pulled up, I was pleasantly surprised to see Alex with her. I ran to the car and hugged both of them.

"I'll go anywhere when I can have a Rigazzi's pizza for

lunch," Alex teased. "You're lucky I didn't help myself on the drive out here."

We went inside, and Lynn introduced Alex to Sarah. They hit it off immediately, which was what was so unique about Alex. We sat down to share the pizza and enjoy Alex's humor. I had to pinch myself over having these special folks all in one place.

Lynn looked at her watch and reminded Sarah about her plane departure. Sarah ignored her at first, but when she knew it was time to leave, she got all teary-eyed.

I hugged her tightly and reassured her of my support. I told her to keep me posted on her progress. "Give the rest of your family my love," I said, weeping a bit myself. After I hugged Alex and Lynn, I was left alone waving at the curbside. At that moment, I wanted to be back in the city where I was closer to all of them.

I went back inside and turned my sign to open. I brought out the rocking chair and quilts, hoping to do business so I wouldn't think about my loved ones. I put the precious leftover pizza away and sent Loretta a text that her daughter was on her way home. I'd bet Loretta didn't realize how mature Sarah had become recently. She would always be her little girl.

Chapter 102

After a very slow afternoon in the shop, I turned my sign to closed, still feeling rather lonely. I wanted to think of something positive, so I sat down at my desk and made a list of things I wanted to do when I closed on the house. I had to get a security system. After that would be the porches. There were many minor things, but I told myself that for now, the floral wallpaper would stay. It was sort of growing on me. I got ready for bed early and was happy to receive a phone call from Marc as I turned down my bed.

"Somehow, I knew you would still be awake," he joked.

"You're right," I acknowledged.

"You're all worked up because the Cardinals are tied with Cincinnati, right?" he teased.

"Oh, yeah, right!" I chuckled.

"Well, if they don't change pitchers soon, this game is a goner."

"You're not a very positive thinker, Marc," I teased. "They'll pull off a win, you'll see! Are you really calling to give me some advice, or just the Cardinals' score?"

"It depends how you look at it," he joked. "Okay, back to the yellow house. From what I'm seeing, it's obviously a reasonable value because you basically have no land to speak of. With all that vacant land so close to you, do you realize you could have someone come along and develop something that you may not approve of? There are no restrictions against someone doing that."

"I understand, but Carrie Mae wouldn't let something like that happen on her property."

"Carrie Mae is not a spring chicken. She'll have to sell it one day, or else her daughter will inherit it and will likely make a quick sale to settle her estate."

"Okay, so any other bad news?"

"Well, your resale possibilities will be limited. For instance, it's unlikely a family would ever be interested in the house without a yard. It would almost have to be sold for commercial use."

"I see," I said, feeling confused.

"Okay, I'll stop there. I know your mind is already made up, anyway."

"Yes, it is. I was going to call Carrie Mae right after I heard from you. By the way, Lynn just left with Sarah to take her back to the airport. I am feeling a bit down."

Marc paused. "Well, I hope you took my advice in the right spirit. You know I wish you the very best with all of this. I hope I'm included in your celebration."

"You'll be at the top of my list," I assured him. "Thanks so much for your help. I'm hoping there will be an invoice, of course."

"I don't charge my friends, especially the really close ones," he said sweetly.

"Thanks, you are a real sweetheart. I'll have to think of another way to show my gratitude."

We talked for another half-hour. I wished Marc lived closer so I could see him more often. He was a good catch, but like Carl, he was exposed to young, beautiful women every day.

The next night was the reception at the Gallery Augusta. Somehow, I dreaded having to be with Nick, but I would get through it somehow since other people would be around.

I tossed and turned most of the night. I kept remembering the negative points that Marc had pointed out to me about the house. It was a financial risk, and my slow retail sales wouldn't cover my expenses right now. I had to be sure to make my payments to Carrie Mae. Now was the time to advertise, which would take more money. Why did the world come crashing down at nighttime?

Out of frustration, I went downstairs to make some tea. As I came down the stairs, I noticed there was a flickering of light coming from one side of the yard. Was it a patrol car? I opened the front door and saw a light flickering from the brick doctor's office building. How could that be? I could see light coming through the little window at the top of the door. Could a homeless person have broken in? I wanted to call Carrie Mae and ask questions, but it was two in the morning. I shut the door and told myself to wait until morning. What would happen next?

Chapter 103

I ended up falling asleep on the loveseat downstairs. As soon as I was fully awake, I looked out the window to check the brick house. No light was evident. I put on a pot of coffee and stretched my sore muscles. I couldn't help but wonder if Rosie was trying to tell me something about the doctor's building, or if it was the doctor himself acting up. Sarah had advised me to start paying attention to these happenings.

It was a cloudy day with sprinkles on and off, so I didn't put anything on the front porch for display. I really needed that board that I planned to paint out front. When I went to Carrie Mae's, I would ask her for some paint. As soon as I was dressed, I gave her a ring.

"Good morning!" she greeted me. "I was thinking about you today."

"I hope that's a good sign," I responded. "I've done my homework, and I'm ready to sign your contract."

"Well, that is good news!" she replied happily. "I'll set up a closing date with my attorney."

"Say, Carrie Mae, I have something to ask you," I began.

"I saw a light flickering in the doctor's building last night. Has that ever happened before?"

She laughed. "Honey, that's impossible. I don't think that building has ever had electricity. He probably practiced medicine by candlelight. I think you may have been dreaming."

"No. The light flickered like candlelight. No one can get in there, can they? I wondered if a homeless person got in."

"Now just forget that nonsense," Carrie Mae insisted. "There's only one door to that little place. Come on up and get the key today and you can check it out for yourself."

"Okay, I will. I don't suppose you have an open can of paint that I could borrow, do you?"

"What color?'

"Any color."

She chuckled.

"Whatever is handy. I'll get it when I get the key, if you have some."

"There's gray and white on the back porch," she replied.

"By the way, I'm going to a reception at the Gallery Augusta tonight. Are you going?"

"I didn't get an invitation, but that's okay. I'm glad you're getting out and about."

"Nick asked me to go with him, but I told him I would just meet him there."

"That's smart. I have to cut you off, sweetie. Someone's at the door."

I was about to leave the house with a hoodie over my head when my phone rang.

"Lily!" a familiar man's voice said.

"Harry, is that you?"

"Yes, honey. Am I calling too early?"

"Absolutely not! How are you?"

"Well, I'm kind of sad this morning."

"What's wrong?"

"Bertie's cat died last night. She hadn't been eating much lately, so I figured something was wrong. I was going to take her to the vet today, but I couldn't find her. She was behind the couch, already gone."

"Oh, Harry, I'm so sorry. You were so good to her. Maybe she died of a broken heart, missing Bertie and all."

"She missed her, alright. I was afraid to let her outside anymore because she took off for Bertie's place one day. I found her on Bertie's front porch."

"Oh! Are they still working on Bertie's house?"

"Yes. Everyone sure misses you."

"How sweet of you to say, Harry. I miss everyone, but I've been so busy getting my shop open, I haven't had time to come into the city."

"When you come in again, I'll treat you to lunch at Tony's."

"That would be swell. Thanks for letting me know about Sugar."

I sat down to reflect. Now Harry wouldn't have anything to remember Bertie by. I took a deep breath and prayed for Harry. He had the kindest heart ever!

Off I went in the rain to Carrie Mae's place. The rain was coming down harder now, so I had to drive. When I walked into Carrie Mae's shop, there was Lisa, the quilt customer. She called me by name, which was impressive.

"Will you be open today?" she asked me.

"Sure! I'm just here to pick up some things from Carrie

Mae."

"Here you go, sweetie!" Carrie Mae said as she handed me the key. "The paint is under the bench on the back porch. I hope it's still good."

I said goodbye and went out to search for the paint. There were about six cans that looked like they had been there for many, many years. I chose a can of white and shook it as hard as I could. I didn't have a paintbrush, but I would think of something to use.

Chapter 104

The rain did not let up as I dashed into the house. I turned my sign to open, but Lisa would likely be my only customer. The minute the rain let up, I walked outside with the key to unlock the little brick building. I was delayed by Lisa pulling up to visit my shop.

"Holy cats and dogs," she exclaimed as she closed her umbrella in the shop. "I may be the only one out today!"

"You're probably right. Would you like a cup of hot tea or coffee?"

"I already had a sip with Carrie Mae, thank you. My goodness, you are well-stocked here for such a new shop!"

"I purchased another shop's inventory and brought it here."

Lisa was immediately drown to the quilts filling the next room. "I see. Look at all these quilts. You have more than Carrie Mae!"

"I've been collecting quilts for a long time. I feel I know a lot about quilts, but I'm new at knowing my antiques and how to price them."

"I love quilts, too. I love the Civil War-era quilts."

"I have some. As you can see, my passion as a collector is for red-and-white quilts. I do have this postage stamp style in marvelous Civil War prints. It reminds me of a hired hand's quilt since it's so narrow, or it could have been a youth size."

Lisa's eyes were big when she took the quilt in hand. "This is amazing! I love this little print on the back, too, with that touch of Prussian blue. You don't usually see a print like that in such a big piece like this backing. How did you get so hooked on red-and-white quilts, Lily?"

"I love how bold they become with just the two colors. The red dye process was developed in Turkey and remained dye-fast, which was a godsend after the fugitive green dyes from earlier times became so undependable. Quiltmakers started leaving out the green after 1870 because of it, so between 1880 and 1930, the red-and-white trend became very strong."

"I have a green Pine Tree quilt that is early, and the green is fading, but the tree trunk is still a lovely red."

"It's so nice to talk to someone who likes quilts as much as I do. My friend is quite knowledgeable, but now that I live out here, we'll barely see one another."

"I'll talk quilts with you anytime you want! Tell me about this crazy quilt. It's not my cup of tea, but it's different than ones I usually see."

"It's dated 1893 on the back, which I think was the completion date. There's an embroidered ribbon on the front that's from 1890. It needs to be repaired badly and will only get worse as time goes by. Some folks are quite enamored with quilts like this."

"Well, this storm is getting pretty bad and I have to go

home and let my dogs out, so I'd better get going. One of my dogs goes nuts when there's a storm. I definitely want this postage stamp quilt. Your price is quite reasonable for something so rare."

"Sure. I'll get it bagged up for you in a plastic bag so you don't get it wet."

"Sometime you'll have to come and see all my quilts."

"Oh, I would like that very much. I need to see what Marthasville is like, too."

Off Lisa went, dashing to her car with her umbrella. It was a fun sale on such a crummy day. Now that I was seeing folks purchase quilts every now and then, I'd have to do what Carrie Mae did and give them a care sheet. I turned my sign to indicate that the shop was closed and called it a day. I sure had no interest in going out in this weather, but I'd told Nick I would come to the open house.

I thought again about the light in the brick building. I would have to wait until the next day to unlock the door. I wondered what other folks thought if they saw the light.

Chapter 105

I got dressed in all black in case I got wet going in and out of the rain. I had a red paisley-print shawl that gave me an artsy look for the occasion, and some wild dangling silver earrings. Hopefully my umbrella would keep me dry.

Cars were parked everywhere and no spaces were available close to the building. It was six o'clock on the dot when I got in the door. A nice young woman welcomed me as she took my umbrella. The place was packed, and I didn't recognize a soul, not even Nick.

Vic came up to me to say hello. "Nice to see you, Lily. Have you met our guest of honor, Mr. Martin?"

"No, I haven't, but would like to do so," I politely said. Thank goodness someone had told me his name, because Nick never said who the artist was.

"I think you purchased a print of his from me awhile back," Vic reminded me.

I nodded. "Have you seen Nick Conrey here tonight?"

"No, I haven't. How is the shop coming along?"

"Fine, considering I didn't know what to expect. I'm

in the process of buying the house from Carrie Mae."

He looked surprised. "Well, how about that! It's good to know that someone will take care of it. Over the years, Carrie Mae has let a lot of her properties fall into disrepair."

I didn't know what to say. "Yes, I need to have a lot of things done to it."

"Keeping the yellow paint?" I knew he and others disapproved of the bold color.

"I can't picture it any other way!" I answered. After that comment, he went on to help another guest.

I made my way closer to the artist to examine his work. I picked up a few appetizers, as I hadn't had dinner. Where was Nick? Why would he not call or text if he wasn't going to be here? I then saw Kitty enter. She picked up a glass of champagne from the wandering waiter, as I had done, and came my way.

"Good to see someone else doesn't mind getting out in this weather," she said with a friendly smile. "My husband hates these kinds of things, so I usually go by myself."

"Are you familiar with this artist?" I asked. "Look at all the people around him."

The two of us finally got close enough to introduce ourselves. Mr Martin looked exhausted, so I wasn't going to ask any questions. He nodded and smiled as we complimented his work. We were interrupted by his assistant saying that it was time to wrap things up. It was eight o'clock, and there were no signs of Nick.

Kitty and I parted ways as we headed to the door to say goodbye to Vic and his wife. The rain had stopped, and I remembered my umbrella before I headed to the car.

It had been a strange evening, and I had obviously been stood up. Thank goodness I hadn't told very many people I was going to meet Nick there.

Chapter 106

When I arrived home, I noticed the light was on again in the brick house. Because the rain had stopped, I decided this was an opportunity to unlock the door and see where the light was coming from. The key looked ancient, but hopefully it would work. I calmly approached the door and inserted the key. It would barely turn to the left, but with a push I had the door open. The room was dark with no light at all. Go figure! The only light I had was coming from the corner streetlight.

I felt crunching glass beneath my shoes. I could barely make out the objects inside the building, but there were shelves to my right with bottles on them, which I presumed were filled with old medicine. This was not the time to touch anything, due to the darkness. I took a step back and went out the door to lock it back up. When I got back inside the house, I looked out the window to see if the light had returned. The brick building remained dark, which somehow made me feel better. I would check it out again in the daylight.

I had a lot to digest that evening, starting with why Nick

hadn't shown up. I certainly wasn't going to call him to find out. My mind then went back to the little brick house. Was Rosie trying to tell me something about the house, or was it a message from the doctor who had spent so much of his professional life there?

I went upstairs and crawled into bed. I had emails and texts waiting for me. The first was a text from Sarah that said that when she got home, her mom had accused her of being overweight during her pregnancy. Sarah had told her it was because of all the wine she had with me. I could just imagine Loretta's response.

The second was from Alex. He suggested that I come to his place for dinner the next night. He would invite Lynn and Carl, and if I wanted to include Marc, I could. He then suggested it would be a way for me to have a visit with Harry. The whole idea sounded wonderful.

There wasn't one word from Nick. Was that a practice of his?

I kept my phone busy until my eyelids couldn't stay open. I wondered if the lights were back on in the brick building. It was all too much.

The morning light was bright. I jumped up to look at the clock. I needed to get my shop open in forty-five minutes. As I got dressed, I remembered Alex's invitation for dinner. I really wanted to go. If I closed at four, I could still get there in time.

As I drank my first cup of coffee, I sent Alex a text and said I would try to make it happen if I could spend the night. It wasn't two minutes before his reply came in. He accused me of being a loose woman and said he'd see me at five. I smiled and decided that the best hostess gift to bring would be wine from the wine country. I had purchased a bottle of River Valley White when Sarah and I were at the Augusta Winery. Lynn loved white wine, so that would work.

I turned my sign to open and put the rocker on the porch. Today I chose two complementary 1930s quilts. I also decided to paint my board, now that I had white paint from Carrie Mae.

I went to the back porch and pried open the paint can with my one and only screwdriver. The paint was thick as I stirred it, but it suited my purposes. I went to the kitchen downstairs and got my old basting brush. Goodness knew when I'd used it last. It turned out to work perfectly for painting the word "QUILTS" vertically on the board. My mission was accomplished, and the board dried quickly as I carried it to the front of the house. I could only imagine what someone like Nick would say about my creativity. I went inside to wash my hands and noticed that two ladies had pulled up in front of the house. They wasted no time telling me that Carrie Mae had sent them to see me.

Chapter 107

One of the two ladies was looking for antique dolls, and the other asked about old linens.

I happily showed the doll lady the two dolls I had purchased from Rosie, and the other had already spotted my stack of linens.

"I want these two," the doll lady decided.

I didn't think she'd even touched them. "You do?" I questioned.

She nodded. She then began to mumble something to her friend about my prices. The items were no doubt a bargain, so I took them to the counter. When I checked on the linen lady, she had several pieces open to look at.

"Do you have any splashers?"

I wasn't sure I'd heard her correctly. "I don't know," I answered, feeling dumb. "What are splashers?"

"Cora, she's new to all this," the doll lady reminded her friend.

"Splashers are embroidered linens with a saying on them, usually in German, Slovak, or Swedish. They were hung behind the washbowl or sink to protect the wallpaper. There are usually signs at the top of each corner of the piece telling where they would be hung from."

"Oh, how interesting," I responded. "I don't recall seeing anything like that."

"Well, you certainly have these displayed nicely," she said. "Everything is very reasonably-priced."

"Now, Cora, she will learn in time," the doll lady again reminded her. "You see, you need to listen to the trends and what folks are buying as you price your things." I nodded, knowing she was correct.

They stayed a while before they paid for their purchases. The linen lady purchased an embroidered laundry bag and a pair of glass candlesticks. They were my only customers that day, but the sales were decent.

I decided to close at three, which gave me some time to pack an overnight bag for my stay with Alex. I was getting excited about my plans for the evening as I drove against the traffic. Before I went to Alex's apartment, I decided to drive down my old street. I was surprised to see a new dry-cleaning store occupying Rosie's antique shop. The "For Sale" sign was still in front of my apartment, and it didn't appear that anyone was living there.

Before I arrived at Alex's apartment, I decided to call Harry to see if he could meet me for lunch the next day. He sounded horrible when he answered and told me he had pneumonia. I felt badly for him, but I also understood why he didn't want visitors just now. He said his cousin was helping him, which made me feel better. When I hung up, I thought of Bertie and how she would have been making him soup for his aliment.

Alex greeted me with open arms when I arrived with my bottle of River Valley White.

"What smells so good?" I inquired as I walked into his kitchen.

"My homemade manicotti. I haven't made this sauce in a long time."

"Oh, Alex, it's so much trouble," I exclaimed, "but you know how much I love your sauce."

"Hey, you're back on The Hill, what can I say?" he teased. "I have bread from Al's and cannoli from Tony's. Lynn is bringing a salad. I thought she'd be here by now."

"The big question is, will she come alone?"

Just then, the doorbell rang, and just like we'd figured, Lynn came in by herself with a salad bowl in her arms. "Greetings, sis!" she said. "My, it smells divine in here! I should have told you earlier that Carl wasn't coming. I thought that maybe he'd change his mind at the last minute."

"So, what's the excuse?" Alex questioned.

"He thinks you all don't like him these days, and he didn't want to spoil a fun time."

"Was he home?" I asked.

"For now, anyway. I think he's starting to feel guilty. That guilt could be about many things. I know there's something brewing at work that's bugging him, but he won't talk about it. I overheard a conversation with the word 'embezzling,' so that can't be good."

"That could explain some of the late hours at work, I suppose," I said, giving him the benefit of the doubt.

"You're being kind, Lily," Lynn sighed.

Chapter 108

Alex began filling our wine glasses. Lynn enjoyed my chosen wine, but Alex claimed it would be a sin not to have red wine with his red-sauced Italian dinner. We all agreed he should save it for another time.

It was a bit too chilly to eat outdoors, so Alex set a lovely table for the three of us in his dining room. He and Lynn had plenty of questions for me. They seemed to get a kick out of my being stood up by someone.

"I hate the idea of dating," I confessed. "I hate second-guessing someone and playing their games. I'm too old for that."

They chuckled.

"Yeah, I understand," agreed Lynn. "I didn't have a good feeling about that guy when I met him. By the way, I almost invited Marc tonight, but I wasn't sure how you'd feel about it."

"He's sweet," I admitted. "He gave me great free advice on my contract. I've told Carrie Mae I'm ready to seal the deal."

"Good for you!" Alex cheered, raising his wine glass. "Here's to Lily Girl's Quilts and Antiques!" We clinked our glasses as I smiled.

While Alex cleared the table and prepared dessert, I shared with Lynn that Sarah had fallen in love with Augusta and had mentioned that she'd like to live there. To my surprise, Lynn didn't think it was a bad idea. I did keep my secret about Sarah's baby's father.

"Drink up, Lily Girl!" Alex said as he refilled my glass of wine. "You don't have to drive home tonight."

"That's a relief!" I said, smiling. "I'll have to leave early to make sure I open on time. I need every sale I can get right now. Lynn, did you give any thought to putting some of your work in the Gallery Augusta?"

"I'm still thinking about it," she said. "I haven't been very productive lately. Carl is always in the back of my mind."

"That's understandable," I said.

We went to Alex's comfy living room to have dessert and more wine. Alex shared with us that he was writing an article on near-death experiences, which generated quite a lively conversation. At twelve thirty, Lynn went home and I settled into Alex's second bedroom, which he used as an office. I was too tired to worry about anything tonight.

Morning came way too soon. I turned over to avoid the sun coming into the room, but the smell of coffee woke me up.

"Come and get it!" Alex said as he knocked at my door. "Tony's bagels are waiting for you."

"Yay!" I called as I quickly got dressed.

"Did you sleep okay?" Alex asked as he poured my coffee.

"Like a rock! Please excuse my appearance, but I should

have left a half-hour ago. Last night was just what I needed. You are a great friend, Alex!"

"Take the leftovers with you," he suggested. "I have everything ready for you."

"You don't have to twist my arm!" I said, giving him a hug.

"Be safe going home."

In no time, I was on my way with a big smile on my face. Today, I would arrange to get a security system installed. I wondered what Carrie Mae would think.

I noticed on the drive that some trees were already changing colors. When I pulled in front of the house, I noticed tiny leaves blowing from the weeping cherry tree. Fall could be wonderful, but it was the doorway to winter, which I dreaded. I glanced over to the doctor's office before I went inside the house. Would this be the day to check it out in the daylight? My cell phone rang. It was Carrie Mae.

"Was The Hill still there for you last night?" she joked.

"Oh, yes! Alex was a great host and served a wonderful Italian dinner."

"It's none of my business, but how come Alex was never the guy in your life?"

I smiled and said, "Alex is like a brother."

"I see. Well, Lily Girl, I think we can close on the house tomorrow, if you're free. My attorney thought he could be here at nine in the morning before the store opens."

"I'm free and ready! I will see you then!"

Chapter 109

I put my purse in the house and then cautiously proceeded to the little brick building. When I finally forced it open again, it wasn't much lighter than when I'd looked inside at night. The open front door was the main source of light.

I once again had to step on broken glass as I moved inside. To the right I could see the medicine bottles, but most of the labels were worn and rotted off. Everything looked broken. A stool with three legs was on its side, and a small white cabinet was turned over with its door open. Nothing appeared to be inside the cabinet. Maybe through the years this had just been a good place to trash or store things. I'd thought folks used a sinkhole years ago for that sort of thing. That's where those things should have been disposed of. How this room was big enough to see patients in was beyond me. I didn't have on gloves, so I didn't want to move things around. Somehow, I felt I was somewhere I didn't belong. As I left and locked the door, I couldn't help but notice how sturdy the structure of the building was. I couldn't tear it down. I also hadn't solved the mystery of the light. For now, that challenge would have to wait. I had a business to run and a house to renovate.

Once inside the yellow house, I was about to sit down and pay bills when my phone rang. It was Loretta, and somehow I knew this was not a social call. "Hey," I answered.

"Are you with a customer?"

"Wish I were. I'm doing the fun part of the business, which is paying bills."

"Any regrets so far?"

"None! In fact, tomorrow I close on the house! I know I'm taking on a lot, but little by little, I'll get there."

"I'm calling about Sarah," Loretta finally admitted. "She told me everything."

"Everything?"

"Yes. Of course, I want to kill her. Before I start my rant, I do want to thank you for having her. She adores you, Lily, and she had a great time. She's a grown woman now, but she does listen to you more than me. It's not worked out here like we'd planned, but I'm not going to lose my daughter over all this."

"I'm glad you see it that way, Loretta," I said with a sigh of relief. "I can't help but be excited for Sarah and her baby. The baby will bring everyone a lot of joy, despite the challenges."

"She couldn't wait to show me the darling crib quilt you gave her. Sarah is a good girl who has made some poor choices."

"How is she feeling?"

"She tires easily, but doesn't want to admit it. Did she tell you she's having a girl?"

"Yes. That's what the Rosenthals do, right?"

She laughed. "My friends here, mostly from work, are having a shower for her this weekend. I wish you and Lynn could come, but I understand. This is Lynn's busiest time of the year. I hope to see her soon. The foliage is really beautiful right now."

"How about I send Sarah a bouquet of flowers since I can't come. I saw an arrangement in an advertisement the other day that had baby accessories on it."

"That would be awesome! She'll love anything coming from you. On another topic, I recently talked to Lynn, and she agreed that Christmas in Green Bay would be fine this year, with the new baby's arrival and all. Do you think you can make it happen?"

"Sure. I wouldn't miss it, you know that. Things die off at that time anyway. I'll get with Lynn about the flight arrangements."

"We have plenty of room in this big old house. It will be fun. Do you think Carl will come? I hate to always ask about him."

"He'd better. Otherwise, what is the point of that marriage? Lynn's really trying hard to keep it all together."

"I can't believe how everything has changed. I love Carl."

"I know. I do, too."

"Now, Sarah also told me about her desire to live in Augusta. I have to admit, I was upset at first, but getting away from the father of this baby is a good idea. I told her I would support her if she waited until the baby was born so that we could help her financially and physically. She agreed to pursue her degree online, so we'll see."

"Well, that is big news," I said.

"Yes, but I'm afraid someone may change her mind."

"Does Jerry know he isn't the father of the baby?"

"Yes. It's complicated, but I'll go into that another time. I need to run. I wanted to make sure you were on board with Christmas."

"I'll be there with bells on," I said, ending the call.

Chapter 110

There had been a lot to digest in that conversation. This situation would be interesting as it evolved.

I went back to paying bills, but looked out the window and saw a man get out of a big pickup truck and come to the door. When he came in, he announced that he was sent by Carrie Mae.

"Well, great; how can I help you?" I asked in a friendly manner.

"I'm Chuck Waller from Kentucky," the man said. "As Carrie Mae may have told you, I come through these parts and buy up quilts. She said you have a sizable inventory with some good prices, so I thought I'd stop and see what you have."

"Oh, sure," I said with excitement. "Most are in the next room. Are you looking for any particular kind?"

"I'll know it when I see it," he said in a cold and direct manner. He was a large, serious kind of guy that clearly wasn't going to be social by any means. I watched him pull about eight quilts from their hangers as he checked the prices and put them aside.

"What parts of the country do most of these come from?"

"The Midwest. I've collected for a long time, so when I opened this shop, I decided to sell some of them."

"I see you have a hankering for red and white!"

"As a collector, I know about most of these. Some of these quilts were with some other inventory, so I don't know their histories."

Mr. Waller was careless as he handled the quilts, which made me uncomfortable. After a while, he said, "I'll take all of these if you can halve the price."

I was shocked, thinking I may have heard him incorrectly. I shook my head and smiled innediately. "I can't do that," I firmly said. "I'm not in the wholesale business, and I happen to know that my prices are very reasonable to begin with."

The look on his face said that he was recalculating.

"Okay, then. I'll take these four red-and-white quilts for your asking price. You're making a mistake not letting me take the others off your hands."

"That's okay. I'll keep the rest."

"Okay, but if you change your mind, I'll swing back around next month. You may need some cash by then." I resented that remark, but let it slide.

The man had cash, and a lot of it. He threw a wad of it on the counter alike it was peanuts. Out the door he went without even a polite goodbye. Well, it was my sale of the day, so I tried to be thankful.

I was shocked to see the next person coming in the door.

It was Korine, the cleaning woman that Rosie had scared off.

"My goodness, Lily, you really did pull this off, didn't you? I love your sign out front."

"Yes, I did, and it's so good to see you again."

"I feel bad I desert you, but this place scared me to death more than once."

I nodded. "I understand. I can still use you if you change your mind. I live here now, so maybe that would make a difference."

"I'll think about it. The place sure looks mighty clean though, if I do say so myself."

"Thanks. I clean when I have no customers. Since I'll be buying the building, I'm having new porches built. That will cause all kinds of dust, I bet."

"I don't think your customers will care. Look at Carrie Mae's shop. She doesn't worry about such things."

"She has so much, I'm sure she wouldn't know where to begin!"

"Well, Lily, I just wanted to say hello. I hope it works out for ya!"

After she left, I closed the shop for the day and heated up some soup. I wanted to keep up my journal, but I was getting so far behind. Each day something unique was happening, and I still had hopes of writing that novel someday.

Chapter 111

It was almost ten when my phone rang. I had been about to jump in the shower. When I saw the call was from Marc, I slipped on my robe and smiled.

"I hope I'm not calling too late," he said nicely.

"Not at all," I responded.

"I'm coming out to Washington for a meeting tomorrow afternoon and wondered if I could catch an early dinner with you."

"Oh, that would be nice! Do you go to Washington often?"

"No, not really. I'm meeting up with another lawyer on a matter we're working on. How's business?"

"Not bad. The good news is that I close on the house tomorrow."

"Well, we'll have something to celebrate! My friend suggested going to Chandler Hill Vineyards. Have you been there?"

"Not for a meal. It sits in a beautiful spot. Do you want me to meet you there?"

"No, I'll pick you up. You can help with directions. I'll make the reservations."

"That's great! It'll be fun to catch up. We're closing on the house before Carrie Mae opens her shop in the morning."

"That's great. Just make sure nothing has changed since you looked at the agreement the last time."

"I will."

"I'll call you when I'm on my way."

I hung up feeling that the timing was perfect to see Marc. He would be fun to celebrate with.

My nightly prayer list was getting longer.

The next morning, I awoke to a beautiful sunrise. It truly was the day the Lord had made. I was up early and took my coffee out to the front steps. I stared once again at the brick house, wondering what its purpose would be.

I arrived at Carrie Mae's ten minutes early. I was nervous when I greeted her. Carrie Mae's lawyer was a crusty old man who could put on the charm when he talked to her. I wondered about their past. We all sat around a small square table with Nippon china teacups, ready for Carrie Mae's famous tea. Before I signed, they both asked if I had any questions. I told them I didn't and then shared what my thoughts were about the brick house and dilapidated barn.

"I must warn you, child, the doctor's building is quite historic and should be saved, or else you'll have the city fathers coming after you."

"I understand."

In silence, I once again went over the contract before I wrote my check. I then signed, along with Carrie Mae, and it was done! I was the owner of 5542 Chestnut. We lifted our teacups and made a toast to the transaction.

I thanked Carrie Mae for everything and told her the quilt man from Kentucky had made an appearance. I admitted that I hadn't budged from my prices, which pleased her.

"This Lily Girl is going to do just fine, don't you think?" Carrie Mae boasted to her attorney.

We shook hands, and I went on my way.

When I got back to my front porch, I felt a strong connection with Rosie.

"See, now! This is all your fault. You'd better help me out!" I said out loud. I proceeded to put out the rocker with a couple of quilts. Alongside it, I placed a small bookshelf that would attract some attention. I felt inspired as the house's new owner, so I hoped it showed. The morning was quiet, and it wasn't until one that I had any customers.

Four women stopped by who had just had lunch at one of the wineries. They giggled continuously, making fun of each and every item I had in the shop. They also told the typical stories about what their grandmothers once had. One woman kept complaining about not liking antiques, and another was anxious to move on. I tried to engage them in conversation so the others could look around, but it was difficult. None of them gave me much respect. I guessed I was just a salesgirl in a creepy old shop with really old things. That was not what I needed to encourage me.

My words of "please come again" fell on deaf ears. Why hadn't Rosie rocked the chair or scared them in some way? This was not the way I'd envisioned Lily Girl's Quilts and Antiques to be. It was time to turn the closed sign. I was done, and very disappointed.

Chapter 112

When I got a text from Marc saying that he was on his way, I was delighted. I took extra care trying to look as nice as I could. I decided on a dress with a light cardigan sweater in case we sat outdoors.

When Marc arrived, he was full of compliments. I had to extend a few to him as well, but then Marc always looked very sharp.

As I gave him directions to the winery, we chatted about my closing. He seemed to sincerely share in my success for the day.

Driving up the hill to the winery was impressive. Judging by all the cars, it appeared to be a popular place for dinner. When we entered the massive dining room, we first stopped by the tasting bar to sample a few wines. We both settled on one of the red wines and ordered some appetizers for our table. The hummus with crackers and celery arrived on a board showcasing the Chandler logo.

When it came to dinner, I realized that Marc was a meat and potatoes guy. I followed his lead in choosing the right steak and complements.

"You should join their wine club dinner," Marc suggested as he was reading about it on the menu. "You said you wanted to learn more about wine, and it would give you an opportunity to meet other folks out here."

"It does sound interesting. I'll check into it, but you may have to join me."

It didn't take long for Marc to start talking about baseball. He encouraged me to attend more games when I could. I loved his enthusiasm for life in general as I listened.

Hours passed before we finally left. It was very dark out, which made me nervous on the curvy roads. Marc seemed to be perfectly at ease with the situation.

"Are you sure you don't mind the drive back home tonight?" I asked with sincerity when we arrived at my place.

"That is a leading question, Lily Girl," he teased. "I'll be fine. I'm so glad you agreed to this. It was a nice way to celebrate your new shop and home."

"It was! I hope you'll let me treat you to dinner next time."

"I can do that."

"Do you want to come in?"

"Considering the hour, I'd best be on my way. Let me give you a hug and kiss. This has been a wonderful evening."

He pulled me close, and his kiss was so endearing that I didn't want to pull away. I wished he really could stay. Suddenly, he pulled back and grinned at me.

"You are trying to make it difficult for me to leave,

Lily Girl," he softly said. "You've become very special to me. I hope you know that."

"That's what I want to hear. Keep that thought."

He walked me to the door, and after a kiss on the forehead, off he went.

I went in the house with a smile on my face. The day had started with my exciting closing and ended with an exciting evening. I hoped Marc would remember to text me when he got home safely.

As I undressed, I pulled down my bedroom blinds and noticed there was once again a light in the brick house! It certainly hadn't been there when Marc and I arrived. There was so much that I didn't understand about this place. It didn't frighten me, but it was frustrating.

I was almost asleep when my phone gave a beep. I smiled, thinking it was Marc arriving home.

I was shocked to see it was a text from Nick. It read:

> Are you still speaking to me? I thought I would text instead of call. I would like to explain my absence at the party. Please!!

I couldn't believe him! What excuse could he possibly have? Why explain a week later?

I reshaped my pillow, and the phone beeped again. It read.

> Please!

I felt guilty. I guessed I should at least let him explain. After all, this guy had given me a gorgeous free sign for my business. I replied back.

Maybe later. Goodnight.

He quickly responded back.

Great! Goodnight.

Why did this perfect evening have to end with thoughts of Nick?

Chapter 113

The next morning, I realized I was now a stockholder in the city of Augusta. I had to make this investment count in many ways. Before I officially opened, I called a few contractors who could come by and give me bids on what needed to be done. I felt excited about getting the security system installed right away.

I got a text from Lynn telling me how much she'd enjoyed Alex's dinner and that she would be going to Green Bay with or without Carl at Christmas. I prayed for Lynn as she figured out how to deal with her marriage. Christmas was always a highlight for our family that brought us closer. That reminded me that I needed to start shopping.

As I thought about opening the shop, I was starting to realize that no one ever seemed to show up until after lunch. Should I have been open at noon instead of ten? The extra time would help as I worked on the house. There would be a lot of painting ahead, or even better, time to write.

Kitty called and asked me to take out a joint ad for the Christmas walk. It sounded expensive, but I was going to have to do more to tell folks that Lily Girl was open for business.

As the day continued with contractors going in and out, I was convinced I was an easy target that could easily being taken advantage of. I had to fake my knowledge on construction as the contractors talked to me as if I were a damsel in distress. The security guy installing my system was creepy enough for me to want to call security. By the end of the day, I suddenly realized I hadn't had one sale. Thank goodness Rosie's gift would sustain me for a while. As I removed my rocking chair from the front porch, Nick drove up and parked.

"So, how did Lily Girl do today?"

"It was busy, but not with customers," I explained. "I was talking to contractors today and got my security system installed."

"Well, that sounds like progress to me! You have a lot to be proud of here. I think we should celebrate. What about tomorrow night? We can make a few stops at some of the wineries, or we can stay here in town and have a bite to eat." I couldn't believe his nerve! He was the last person I wanted to celebrate with.

"I thought you wanted to get together to explain your absence at the party. Did I miss something here?"

He scratched his head and his expression changed. "Okay, I'm sorry," he said in a serious tone. "I had a medical emergency and I completely forgot about the party."

"Like what? Did you become ill? Why couldn't you send a simple text?"

"I'm trying to tell you," he replied sternly. "I've been diagnosed with the Big C."

I couldn't believe what he'd just said. "Oh, Nick, I'm so sorry."

"It's okay, but I'd prefer to keep the news private. I do feel I owe you an explanation. I didn't take the news very well, so I took to drowning it in booze."

"If you don't want to talk about it, I understand. Will you be okay? Can you tell me that much?"

He shrugged his shoulders and smiled. "Hey, I'll deal with it. I don't want anyone feeling sorry for me, so I'll keep it close."

"I understand."

"So, Lily Girl, back to a night out tomorrow evening. The weather has been awesome for sitting outdoors."

"Okay, I give in."

"Wow, a real date, huh?" he said. "I'll see you around six?"

I nodded.

Off he went, and I sat down to digest our conversation. What did it feel like to be told you have cancer? I truly understood now why I hadn't heard from Nick. Giving in to an evening with him would erase my guilt from getting a free sign and cheer him up a bit.

The rest of the day, I kept going over my plans for the yellow house. It kept my mind off of Nick. I also sent texts to Alex, Holly, Sarah, and my sisters, telling them I was now officially the owner of the yellow house and that construction plans were developing. I'd have bet most of them didn't think I would make it this far and were wondering where all my money was coming from. I complained about the complicated security system, but said that I was glad it was there for me. I didn't tell them about my dinner date with

Marc or that I had agreed to going out with Nick. These things would unfold in time, and I didn't want them asking any questions. It was late when I finally turned in. Now if I could just control my dreams.

Chapter 114

I was so happy to see Carrie Mae stop by the next day before she opened her shop. I offered her some tea and told her about my plans.

"You know, those young men of mine can be helpful to you with some of these things," Carrie Mae reminded me. "They could take that barn down in no time."

"Do they have a place to dump all the debris? I'd like to have that space cleared. Who knows what's living in there."

"They seem to. They sure have hauled off a lot of trash for me. You may want to wait until next spring since you have all this other work going on."

"Good idea. You know, I'm still puzzled about the mysterious light in the doctor's house."

"It's still happening?"

"Yes, and if I open the door, it goes out," I explained.

She shook her head and chuckled a bit. "Well, as long as you don't get hurt." Those words were not very comforting.

"On another topic, I agreed to meet with Nick tonight for some wine and maybe dinner. He says it's all he wants as payment for that beautiful sign of mine."

"You still want to go out with him after he stood you up? You'd better be careful about what he thinks is payment in full!"

"I know, I know. He actually did have a pretty good excuse." I left it there to keep his secret.

"He'd better have! I don't know, there's something about that man. Maybe it's the artist in him."

"Well, he didn't charge me a dime, so I'm going out of guilt, for better or worse."

"I'm glad I'm not in the dating world anymore. I'm just too sassy and mean!"

I laughed. As Carrie Mae went on her way, something made me give her a hug for just being her. What would I do without her?

My cash drawer took in a big fifty-nine dollars and sixty-nine cents for the day. That would hardly pay for my daily utilities. The sales were small, but Rosie had always said no sale was too small, because they added up. Oh, I had so many questions I wanted to ask her.

The evening had a chill in the air, so I decided to wear my black jeans with an orange pullover sweater. Halloween was at our doorstep, and I certainly looked like it when I looked in the mirror. I wore my hair down instead of in the easy ponytail which I usually sported during the week. My hair was growing quickly, and with the cooler weather, I liked it.

At six o'clock sharp, Nick drove up to the house in his convertible with the top down. I wondered if I would need a jacket instead of a sweater. Nick did look handsome in his khakis and black sport coat. We looked like we were going on a real date! I told myself to enjoy the moment and not be too critical of him.

"I think the last time I rode in a convertible, I was in high school," I told Nick when he arrived.

"It's such a great evening, I couldn't resist. You really get a better feel for the scenery with the top down."

I thought he would ask my opinion on the matter, but he didn't. "Okay, I'm game. Let's go!"

Off we went. Ironically, Nick wanted to start out by going to Chandler Hill Vineyards, where I'd just had dinner with Marc. The whole time, I was wishing that it was Marc sitting in that driver's seat.

"Good to see you back again!" the waiter said when he saw me.

I nodded and smiled.

"Well, I see you're starting to get around," Nick teased. I smiled, but offered no explanation.

Nick knew exactly what kind of wine he wanted, so he ordered a bottle without getting any input from me. Since I really didn't care, I didn't say anything. After he finished his first glass, he ordered some appetizers. I had told him that if I was going to be drinking wine, I definitely needed food.

Nick was certainly in a chatty mood, but didn't mention one word about his illness. It seemed that in conversations with Nick, it was always about him. He rarely asked me any questions, which I supposed I should be grateful for.

"You should escort me to The Hill in the city one night

for dinner," he insisted. "They have so many fine restaurants I'd like to try."

"Yes, they do! The area is more about food, where here it's all about wine."

As I talked, Nick kept drinking. I couldn't believe he'd finished the entire bottle and was ready to go to the next place, which he announced would be Sugar Creek Winery. How could he drive with all the wine he had consumed? He must have been used to drinking wine like I drink iced tea.

As we continued our drive, I closed my eyes more than once. When I looked over at Nick, he seemed to be enjoying every moment.

The sharp curve up the hill to Sugar Creek Winery was scary. I couldn't imagine what it would be like coming back down. The outdoor activity was booming. Some folks were inside the large house, but Nick preferred we sit outdoors, where the view was spectacular.

"Isn't this the best view you've ever seen?" Nick asked as if he owned it.

"Many of the wineries have great views. I'm partial to Wine Country Gardens. It's so much easier to get in and out, which I appreciate."

"You have a point there." He nodded as he ordered a bottle of wine.

"You've been here before, haven't you?" the cute waitress said to Nick. He was flattered.

"I have! So, what's your name?" he asked in a flirting tone.

"Emily," she answered with a big smile. "Can I get you any appetizers?"

"Yes, please. I would like your sampler platter," I ordered without waiting for Nick to respond.

As she walked away, I watched his eyes follow her. He then excused himself to go to the restroom, but it could have been an excuse to get her phone number. I couldn't have cared less. The night would be over soon and my debt would be paid.

The music from the band was quite good. I thought that if I'd been there by myself, I would have been having a really good time. It seemed all the wineries were having live music these days.

When Nick returned, he refilled our wine glasses. He said he'd stopped to talk to some friends.

"You know a lot of folks out here, don't you?" I asked with interest.

"You will too, just wait!" *Not the same friends*, I assured myself.

"Here's to Lily Girl's success!" Nick said, raising his glass. I smiled and nodded as I put the glass to my lips.

After an hour of listening to Nick's travel stories and watching him finish the bottle, I suggested that we leave. He reluctantly agreed and said that there were many more wineries ahead.

"Are you sure you're okay to drive, Nick?" I asked with concern.

"This is nothing new for me," he said with a snickering tone. "I guess I've built up quite a tolerance level. I like wine and have it with almost every meal, and I know these roads like the back of my hand."

"I can't possibly have another swallow. Do you want some coffee?"

"Nah! Okay, we'll head on if you like."

I was getting nervous, but I also knew I was very green to the social life out here. Nick was a single guy that was out all the time. Tonight was just my turn to spend time with him.

Chapter 115

Nick said his goodbyes to nearly everyone, including the band when he gave them a tip. He put his arm around me and tried to kiss me before we got into the convertible. I somehow avoided it. I was sure my refusal was even more challenging to him.

"Do you want to put the top up?" I asked, thinking how chilly the drive home would be.

"The night air is the best, you'll see. It will sober you up."

Nick didn't have the manners to ask me, of course. He was the one who needed to sober up, not me.

Nick handed me my jacket to put on, and off we went.

"I'd like to have dinner with you sometime soon!" he yelled into the night wind. I just smiled back at him as we somehow made it down the hill to the main road. I could hardly look.

The breeze of the night air wasn't loud enough, so Nick turned on his radio. He seemed to be enjoying something I wasn't aware of. He looked over at me at one point and laughed. I could tell he was enjoying making me squirm as we flew around the corners. As we met traffic, I had to close my eyes a time or two.

"Nick, I wish you would slow down. You're scaring me."

He took my hand and squeezed it, like it would comfort me in some way or show affection. He looked my way and winked as we swerved around the next corner at full speed.

"No! Stop! No!" I shrieked before everything went black.

Cozy up with more quilting mysteries from Ann Hazelwood...

WINE COUNTRY QUILT SERIES

After quitting her boring editing job, aspiring writer Lily Rosenthal isn't sure what to do next. Her two biggest joys in life are collecting antique quilts and frequenting the area's beautiful wine country. The murder of a friend results in Lily acquiring the inventory of a local antique store. Murder, quilts, and vineyards serve as the inspiration as Lily embarks on a journey filled with laughs, loss, and red-and-white quilts.

THE DOOR COUNTY QUILT SERIES

Meet Claire Stewart, a new resident of Door County, Wisconsin. Claire is a watercolor quilt artist and joins a prestigious small quilting club when her best friend moves away. As she grows more comfortable after escaping a bad relationship, new ideas and surprises abound as friendships, quilting, and her love life all change for the better.

Want more? Visit us online at ctpub.com